BLOOD AND MASCARA

COLIN KRAININ

pulplit

New York

Trade Paperback ISBN: 979-8-9899868-0-4

Edited by Catherine Dunn.

Cover design by Boja.

Published by Pulp Lit.

For Joseph M. Krainin and Henry H. Platek

CONTENTS

PART I
DEEP BLUE

1. What Then of the Devil?   3
2. Christ Jesus   6
3. Recalled to Life   13
4. Romance   27
5. Sound and Pain   36
6. A Strange Power   41
7. The Little Fellow   51
8. Losing   57
9. Our Kind of Lies   62
10. The Speech   66
11. The Lodger   71
12. The Machine   84
13. The End of the Party   92
14. Wounds   111
15. Big Bill   120
16. A History of Names   123
17. Deep Blue with a Cherry at the End   133
18. Bronze   139

PART II
THE HAUNTED MEN

19. Antiques   143
20. Absolute Bottom   146
21. Hopeless Discipline   150
22. A Commission   158
23. The Cloakroom   166
24. The Last Lover   170
25. Closed Case   181
26. Presidential Suite Dreams   192
27. A Hole in 6th Street   199
28. The Client   212

29. Red Sage   217
30. Semi-Automatic   230

PART III
SING, GODDESS

31. Wrath   239
32. Upstairs, Downstairs   248
33. Judges and Kings   271
34. A Chorus of Ghosts   283

PART I

DEEP BLUE

I have heard the mermaids singing, each to each
I do not think that they will sing to me.
—T. S. Eliot, *The Love Song of J. Alfred Prufrock*

1

WHAT THEN OF THE DEVIL?

IRIS

I have seen things in the dark which I shall not describe. Visions of my mind's creation.

There is no refuge. Not in cleaning the dishes or watering the plants or closing my eyes and pleading for sleep. The same thoughts run through my dreams as relentlessly as they haunt my waking mind.

And him.

Also, I am thinking of him. I am thinking of Bronze.

I am lying in bed and staring into the darkness of my room. Nothingness. Heavy weight of darkness.

And visions.

Horror and beauty and Bronze.

And when I think of Bronze—I think of him bleeding.

I rise from the bed and move in the darkness, practiced steps avoiding the obstacles of my bed corner and my bench piled with clothes and the wooden legs of my reading chair. I find my window and look out into the night. There is light out there. Iron lampposts shine weak globes of yellow in the black all around. Moisture swirls like dust wherever the light touches.

I do not see him—just shadows and the infinite shades of darkness. Where are you, Bronze?

His thoughts are too much like mine. He might be out on assignment or he might be sleeping, he might be looking at a beautiful woman through his camera lens or his own face in a steamed-up mirror, but wherever he is, whatever he is doing, it comes to him like a transmission with no off switch. He is *there* still.

He is still out there, endlessly looping beneath the trapdoors of his mind.

He is out there bleeding. Slowly walking on a broken sidewalk. The trees arch above him. One foot drags itself forward. Then the other. Awkward. Interminably slow. Dragging, shuffling, limping, whimpering *forward*—the last instinct of a dying animal.

Yes, indeed, in his mind these moments loop. Stumbling down the sidewalk, blood on his face and soaking down his pant legs until his hand reaches out for that door, then back and down the sidewalk again. And again. And again. Bleeding. Bleeding. Bleeding.

Almost gentle, this repetition.

(If God works in mysterious ways, what then of the Devil?)

I do not choose to look further back. Those moments before ... the cruel blade and the nightmare rooms.

I suppose ...

I suppose in the end I must look—unwavering and with total exactness. I must look at it all before the end.

But I prefer these particular nightmares. I prefer him fighting. I prefer him forcing each foot forward when another would have collapsed and died.

How often does he slip back further in time? Back before the sidewalk? Fall back from the sidewalk into hell? How often does he look at those toenails painted turquoise and step forward to see a rainbow of red?

When he dreams of it, does he imagine himself the killer?

I hope not. I hope he spares himself that, at least.

But I know that I would. I would wake in a feverish sweat, stomach bile churning, a cold dread curling my toes and strangling my brain, weeping in relief to remember I was only a failure and not the beast himself.

And if I would, I suppose Bronze must as well.

Yes, I suppose that is how it must be.

2

CHRIST JESUS

MAY 5, 1997

B ronze didn't care much about the story of the dead congressman until he saw the guy's picture and realized he was looking at either the second or the third man he'd seen balling Carolyn Haake two nights before.

Bronze threw the *Post* down and sank back on his busted couch, already defeated at 7:48 a.m. on a Monday.

Today had been the day he was finally going to start meditating.

"Christ."

Bronze was a non-practicing Jew; his father was a non-practicing Jew. Yet, just like his father, "Christ" was the curse that came unbidden to his lips in moments of sharp duress. Why? How had that seeped in? And become so ingrained as to emerge like an alien voice from his unconscious depths?

"Fuck."

That was more like it. He came by "fuck" honestly.

"Jesus."

There he went again. Bronze didn't know what, from a religious standpoint, differentiated the names "Jesus" and "Christ," but he instinctually grasped their distinctive natures as curse words. "Christ" was a burst of anger, "Jesus," resigned pain. The man or god or whatever might have been "Jesus Christ," but Bronze's life had been one long "Christ Jesus."

Bronze looked over at his phone—its loosely curling cord dangled with arrogant ease, like an insult, like a dare.

He knew what he needed to do.

Knew what he needed to do, but the gears connecting mind to brain and brain to body were not yet moving. Lacked some essential element. Low on grease or power source, or maybe the clockmaker just wasn't careful enough when he slotted the pieces of Bronze together.

Again ... Bronze looked over at his phone—decided to take five.

The coffee maker was gurgling out the last spits of his morning joe, and his pack of Chesterfields was looking mighty fine lying there, already cracked open on the gouged-up coffee table.

Bronze rolled himself off his dull green couch and looked down at his indent, which did not undo itself but remained as a permanent fixture. The foams and fabrics and fibers of the cushions, once so youthful and springy, now seemed to have fulfilled en masse the stipulations of a suicide pact.

Bronze poured his coffee and switched to sitting in his favorite and only armchair, which he called the "dog chair," since it had wooden dog heads carved into the ends of its arms. He sipped his coffee. He lit a Chesterfield. He closed his eyes and thought of nothing for a glorious moment as that first drag filled his lungs.

He released the smoke and thought about his furniture.

The dog chair still maintained the dignity of its shape despite not-infrequent encounters with Bronze's posterior. This wasn't a knock against the workmanship of the old couch, but as it was set closer to the ground, Bronze was perhaps to blame for dropping himself—kerplunk—onto it and failing to rotate the cushions or his position with sufficient (or any) regularity.

Bronze looked at his phone.

Would everything break down in here eventually? How long had he been in this apartment? Years now. Long enough that it felt as if everything before it was an illusion, a trick of the mind. Had he really been married once, going to dinner parties where the men wore tweed jackets and brightly colored ties, got sloshed, and made out with the wrong wives in laundry rooms? Had he really been a little boy reading Silver Surfer comic books all day? Had he really lived that year in Japan? Had he really been an English major at NYU, learning the Manhattan neighborhoods by staring out of the bedroom windows of a steady march of solemn women? Divorcees on the Upper East Side; artists in the East Village; on the Upper West Side an Orthodox woman with haunting light green eyes encircled with heavy black eyeliner; in Greenwich Village a young widow with rain perpetually pattering against the windows of her loft; in SoHo a wealthy émigré from Hong Kong with slight hips and a slighter waist who left Bronze's heart in some unmarked alleyway between Houston and Canal.

Or had he always been here? Banging about this basement apartment. Rubbing his shoulders along the walls, bumping his shins, his oils and sweat and essence seeping in everywhere from his mattress to his floorboards, his breath seasoning the air, the drying remnants of the microscopic saliva that flew forth with his speech coating every surface, his dissipated flatulence clinging to the shower curtains and linens and hiding among the cracks in the walls, his very words and even the detritus of his past thoughts transforming the psychic space of the apartment into a Bronze chrysalis—*and what rough beast shall slouch its way forth once the metamorphosis completes?*

He looked at his phone.

Looked at the *Post* lying on the floor, the pages in loose disarray. He had meant to blow by the front page, to find a diverting story on the hyped chess match between Kasparov and Deep Blue, IBM's new chess-playing machine—a way to ease into the day.

He looked at his phone.

Looked at the cold dregs of his coffee.

Looked at his phone.

Looked at his cigarette, burned to the filter now.

Looked at his phone ...

Sighed and dialed the number.

"I need to talk to Roth ... How many Roths you got in Metro PD? ... The bald one ... They're both bald? Jesus. *Mark Roth* ... It's concerning the congressman who got himself murdered ... Yeah, I know they haven't decided that it's murder yet. That's why I'm calling."

WALKING OUT INTO the May sun, Bronze felt like a vampire about to disintegrate. His eyes saw only splotches of white mixed with flashes of green and dull red from the trees and brick townhomes that lined N Street. The skin around his lips and eyes stung in the glare. The cherry blossoms were off the bloom and it was only downhill from here as DC descended into the swamp of summer, empty of fleeing politicians, followed swiftly by the lobbyists that held their bridal trains down the aisle back to wretched Wisconsin or the wastelands of West Texas or to urban decay in St. Louis or whatever nightmarish American province had selected them to hold forth as endlessly speechifying but ultimately impotent robber barons.

Bronze lit a Chesterfield and beat a retreat back to the shade of the stairs that hung over the door of his basement apartment, deciding to take a quick five while he adjusted to the venomous sun.

A feminine voice drifted down from above. "Almost made it out this time. Not even nine o'clock yet."

Iris. The landlady. More than that. Surely Bronze was in love with her by now. But what did that amount to? At this point, the list of women he loved had gotten so long that it had blossomed into a kind of insanity. Each one was just another tired variation on a theme, a ***NEW LIMITED EDITION*** summertime promotional flavor—a get-it-before-it's-gone cocktail concoction, syrupy sweet and full of chemicals, good only for a loose tongue and a dull headache.

But ...

Oh yes—*but*.

But he *does* like the taste of this one. The Iris flavor is slippery subtle with a delicate depth, a love like still waters in an ancient well, dark blues and winter greens, layer after plunging layer of melancholy color ...

Yes, this is what he deserves. A short-distance yearning held back by a dam of shame and unworthiness. A new nuance of pain to experience. A new sum to add to his tally—his ledger of many-flavored loves unmoved by time hanging upon his now-stooping soul, their weight building toward crushing as the years grind on.

Needless to say, Bronze left his feelings unspoken.

She was the landlady and Bronze, the tenant—although if this Carolyn Haake thing blew up in his face and Roger Haake stiffed him on the back half of his commission, he wasn't so sure where the next rent check was going to come from. So what was he then, really?

An occupant.

You could not deny him that.

He took up a bit of space. A bit of space down underground

while the tree-lined street and all that was respectable saw only the elegantly curving stairs to Iris Margaryan's multimillion-dollar townhouse.

Bronze stepped forth gallantly into the unabating sun and the no less penetrating glare of Iris's eyes of deep-faceted blue, locked on unblinkingly with that writer's stare of hers, seeing through Bronze as surely as an MRI machine, teasing out the crooks, cracks, and gullies, finding her way unerringly in to the central point of his character. And once she had him pinned, would he soon populate one of her romance novels? What would he transfigure into? A lascivious paramour? A cuckold husband? A throwaway side character perhaps, maybe a doorman with just a few lines—*to swell a progress, start a scene or two?*

"I do my best work at night," he said.

Iris sat on her steps with one of her thin cigarettes between her fingers. She crooked half a grin at him. "You wouldn't be the first to tell me that." Then the grin began to fade and her eyes softened, became unfocused. "Me too. Wish I was a morning writer, but I suppose our fundamental natures are unmoved by our desires. Pray tell, Bronze, why should *being* and *desire* contradict? Who set that system up?"

So she was in a philosophical mood. Bronze just hoped he could keep up. Iris's mind was so quick, it often seemed she was lapping Bronze before he'd even heard the gun go off.

But he wasn't surprised to hear of her writing predilections. He had long ago associated her, somewhere deep in his unconscious, with the contemplations of nightfall. Dark wavy hair framed those deep blue eyes, and there was something unmistakably of shifting shadows about her, an aura of midnight blue, as if the fates had woven the threads of her life by crescent moon and starlight in the blue–black hours before dawn.

"I'd like to answer that one, but I'm afraid I don't have it in me."

That almost got a full smile out of her. "So, what bee's gotten in your bonnet that you're up and about at this unspeakable hour?"

"Billy Kopes."

Iris pointed to the folded paper next to her on the steps. "The congressman who washed up on the banks of the Potomac?"

"The one and only."

"Jesus."

"That's what I said."

3

RECALLED TO LIFE

MAY 5, 1997

1 150 15th St. NW. The *Post*. The newsroom. Esther McNamara née Klein. Arms akimbo, staring right at Bronze from all the way over there. He hadn't been over the threshold a second before she scented him. The look she gave him made him feel like a little boy in short pants.

Withering.

That was the word. He withered everywhere that mattered. But if he was honest with himself, there was a pinch of redirected blood flow to a place that didn't. And with the warming flow, the shame came on all the stronger. Like his body had been split in two, the thinking part hating the unthinking part.

And vice versa.

Vice fucking versa, growled that deeper part of him that hated every pompous, ponderous thought forever seeping out of his good-for-nothing skull.

After an interminable, unhurried pause to look at Bronze from a safe distance, she started walking toward him. There had been a vague hope that he could avoid her. A barely obscured desire that he wouldn't. He had a couple of hours before Roth could meet. His thinking brain had thought, *Maybe I can sneak in and corner Lonnie. Find out what I need to know from him and get out.* The unthinking part vibrated an earthquake in his stomach, flashed twisted visions of entangled flesh across his mind's eye, pounded a beat that spoke in every way but words of fragmented, scotch-drenched memories. *Esther, Esther, Esther.*

She walked forcefully, no expression on her face at first. Her arms swung; her black skirt lifted precisely two inches with every stride. Within striking distance, she forced a smile onto her face. The smile said, "I'm in control of the situation. The situation is not personal. The situation will be handled on my terms." But undergirding the smile was a taut rigidity. The rigidity said, "I don't know I don't know I don't know I just don't know what I'm supposed to do."

She lifted a hand to shake his and he responded, felt his arm floating up through something thicker than air, like he was moving in a dream.

"To what do we owe the pleasure, Bronze?"

"Esther. It's been ... how are you? How's Chris?"

"Chris is fine. You?"

"Ah. Actually, I'm here on a case."

"I do like your jacket. Very, um, William Hurt, maybe?"

"William Hurt? Oh yeah, it's herringbone. I like him. But he always seems a bit slow in his movies, doesn't he? Like he's going for this aura of sly intelligence—like he's playing at an obvious ruse of stupidity, but you can never put your finger on what is—if anything is, really—behind the ruse. So I'm always wondering, what's the ruse? Is it a ruse?"

"What's the case?"

"You look good too. Do women like that? That kind of William Hurt thing?"

"Your eyes ... they're clearer."

"Billy Kopes."

Pause. Her hard fake smile disappeared into the ether.

"Shit."

"Exactly."

~

THIS WOMAN IS SITTING NEXT to him drinking coffee at the K Street Diner.

She's really there.

There is a feeling of total unreality, like a dream where you step inside your TV screen, the world changes from drab grays to popping primary colors, and you have no idea what role you're supposed to play.

They are seated at the U-shaped counter on blue uphol- stered stools affixed to the ground by single chrome columns that let you spin a little in your seat. A middle-aged man with slicked-back black hair has served them their coffees and left them alone. He's now lounging against the opposite end of the counter, tired eyes pointed at a small hanging television playing CNN on low volume.

They keep showing images of the Potomac, of divers, of police officers in jackets with their badges hanging from lanyards around their necks. They show a smiling campaign photo of Billy Kopes. They do not show his body, blue and bloated, with candy wrappers stuck to it, broken beer bottles lying next to him.

After her first steaming sip of coffee, Esther's eyes darted around the diner as if recording the details for later use in constructing the atmospherics of a story. Then they landed with a steady thud on Bronze's face, not quite looking him in the eye but maybe somewhere halfway up his nose. She held them there for a long beat, then the adversarial parties in her mind seemed to reach a settlement.

As she dropped her gaze and stared straight ahead, she asked, "You get to step 9 yet?"

The question hit him like a squarely landed straight right. No pussyfooting or jabs for Esther.

He nodded slowly. "Yeah."

"Funny." She let that word hang there until the pause bordered on perverse. "I don't remember getting a call or letter."

His mind went quiet. This was normally a welcome, if extremely rare, relief, but there was no pleasure in this sudden silence. Merely dislocation. And fear. He felt as if he were watching himself from a great distance.

And from that distance he saw Esther too and all the things she probably hated about him. All the times he had casually hurt her—Berlin in '89, Riyadh in '91. He had never made his way for a sit-down with her because, well, wouldn't it just hurt more for him to show up, bring back memories she'd buried long ago? Wouldn't the apology really only help him? Wasn't staying away the better thing, the nobler thing? How do you apologize for not being who someone thought you were? How do you apologize for that when you wish with every molecule in your body that you were the person Esther imagined you were the first time she walked fresh-faced into your office, beaming and babbling over all the well-gee-mister-just-amazing crime stories you'd broken? And you'd never write one again now. Not for the *Post*, anyway. Not for any legit paper.

Now that you weren't actively drinking, that was all just some other life anyway. Blurred images in your head. You'd been a lie and she had believed some different, better lie about you. The real you is ... *disappointment*. Disappointment without excuses. There was no way to make amends with Esther. Esther would always be betrayed by the reality of him. Was being betrayed right now.

Maybe he could say the words, though. Maybe that would

mean something. Maybe not in this life but in some alternate dimension, on some other channel God watches more closely.

"Esther ... Esther McNamara ... your new name's got a kind of sing-song quality to it. Es-ther Mc-Na-mar-a. Your old name was sharp. Esther Klein. Esther Klein. Like you could cut someone with it."

She looked like she was about to say something but just shook her head.

"I am sorry, though. You're right. I avoided saying it even though I knew I should. And even now, I would prefer if I could avoid going through the litany. I will someday. I promise. But for now, I hope a wholly inadequate 'I'm sorry' can be something. A start, maybe."

She was looking away. She took a sip of her coffee and slowly set the cup back down on the counter. When she turned back to look at Bronze, the remnants of tears were in her eyes.

"Yeah. It's something. It's something just to see you here breathing. And *speaking*. I thought you were going to die. When they finally fired you—I *knew* you were going to die. I don't mean to be ... I just thought—he's *dead*. It was easier to think of you that way. And now. Here you are. Alive. Really alive. *Recalled to life*. Do you know that line? Dickens. Recalled to life and you never even called to let me know. Years went by, Cal."

She'd slipped into using his given name. Her dark hair was tucked behind her ears. It had been stiffly formal before, but it had come loose somehow. Stray strands were flying all around. Her face was red and puffy and looked young again. She looked like the girl who had walked into his office all those years ago. But without the smile. Without the illusions.

"How's Chris?" he said.

The air went out of the room. Esther's husband was the opposite in every way to Bronze. A sure, steady Irish Catholic to Bronze's wandering Jew. Straw-colored hair to Bronze's almost black. Fierce, penetrating baby-blue eyes to Bronze's dark gray eyes that looked blue or black or green depending on the light or the viewer but always muddled, always looking within. Chris McNamara was a full-faced middleweight round with pale muscles who moved with a bouncing step while Bronze's ranged about, sharp featured, tall framed, and broad shouldered, thin and angled everywhere.

"I love him," she said.

He nodded. Thought through the next step with slow deliberation, as if laying out the logic of some abstruse algebra problem.

"For some time all I could do was *not* drink." Would he ever stop lying? It wasn't ever really the drinking. Not *really*. It was the women. All he could do was *not pursue women*.

Isn't that the real reason you haven't seen Esther?

"Everyone else I knew was moving ahead. Already moving up through the middle management of whatever career they'd picked. Even my protégé ..."

He looked at her with a small, inviting smile—felt sick inside.

An almost-smile replied for a flash across her face.

"... had been promoted past where I'd peaked out. And I was back to square one. The only thing I could think to leverage was my investigative skills, such as they were. Hence the PI business. Thought I could work my way back into society's good graces that way. Far from the normal route, but maybe I could be *interesting* again. Maybe a bit vintage, but ..."

"Vintage has always been your style." A lightness returned to her face. It was a bit blotchy from the wild swings of emotion, but her lips danced tentatively with a smile.

He smiled back. "The problem was that hardly anyone came. Enough cheating spouses to keep the lights on, but no more. So in all the down time, I played around with writing a memoir. I still had some good stories. And I had the big story ..."

He saw the horror on her face at that. No need to explain that he meant Rachel Boyd. That he meant Caleb Keaton and Madam Richelieu's. That he meant June 14th, 1988. That he meant blood and turquoise everywhere.

"So, in the long hours waiting for jobs, I started jotting those stories down. I thought when I'm finished, maybe that would be an explanation. Maybe then I could phone everyone up and not be so ... disappointing."

"I wouldn't have cared about any of that." There were no tears in her eyes anymore. She had regained her balance. She was composed and fully back within her new self.

But he was still lying even now. Still the old Bronze.

"But I did," he said and realized that at least that part was true.

"I'll give you what we got on Kopes. We're sorting it all through ourselves now. Got it all in boxes. We can go back and make copies. You seen Roth yet?"

"My next appointment."

"He know you're coming?"

Bronze sat in stillness for a moment, thinking of the hidden wheels of Roth's brain smoothly ticking away in perfect rhythm behind that protective veil of good-humored, know-nothing masculinity.

"He knows."

～

RECALLED TO LIFE.

Bronze sat in a booth in another diner, this one back in Georgetown on Wisconsin Avenue, drinking another coffee and waiting. There sure was a lot of coffee in PI work—and waiting.

Roth wasn't here to disapprove yet, so Bronze lit up a Chester-field and tried to complete the look by becoming contemplative.

Recalled to life.

Esther had gotten into his head. He supposed he'd have to read Dickens now. He'd been avoiding it. Bronze preferred the Russians. Dostoyevsky and Chekhov, but mostly Tolstoy. The whole paid-by-the-word thing turned him off Dickens. Hemingway was good. Melville too. Iris had been telling him to read some kid named Wallace, but he hadn't cracked the tome she'd gifted him for, as she put it, "the holidays."

If he were honest, these days, for his pleasure, he much preferred Stephen King to anything "literary." What stopped Stephen King's *The Gunslinger* from being literary, he hadn't the foggiest.

Recalled to life.

Had he been? Was that what the consequences of sitting all night in a tree taking pictures of Carolyn Haake's *active social life* amounted to? A second act. The Big Guy wasn't quite done with him yet. A little story for the entr'acte.

How would Melville put it? A celestial program of entertainment that read:

THE SOVIET UNION FALLS.
Bronze cracks the case of the dead congressman.
THE MACHINES RISE AGAINST MAN.

Makes you wonder. Why does the Big Guy pick the characters he does? What made Bronze somehow suited for the little stories and Reagan, Bush, and Gorbachev suited for the monumental?

Classic nobility of soul, whatever that was?

And how many *real* stories did we get?

If this was finally going to be *his* story, would there be any use for him after? Afterwards, would he be some old mechanical toy plugging away uselessly till death? Would God ease his post-script with some gift like the one he gave Job—the modern equivalent of sheep and donkeys and camels and oxen?

What gift could make up for the melancholy of an ending?

Luckily Roth came in before Bronze had to produce an answer to that one.

Roth was wearing a neatly pressed charcoal suit, a button-down light-blue Oxford, and a regimental tie. He dressed well for a cop. Maybe a little too much of the old well-met college man in the four-in-hand tie knot and the button-down collar, but overall, head and shoulders above the vast majority of detectives. Bronze noted that he'd finally stopped fighting his hairline and cropped his hair close. Last time Bronze had seen him, he had cultivated a wild set of curls from a narrow peninsula of hair that was swiftly losing connection with the mainland en route to a hair island.

He was all the way bald now.

Bronze lifted a hand to his friend and snuffed out the Chesterfield in a glass ashtray with the other. Roth walked over and sat down at Bronze's booth, letting out a symphony of sighs and grunts as he slid himself in along the vinyl seat. A waitress with shoulder-length graying red hair and a ruddy complexion started to make her way over to them.

"This place make a good Diet Coke?" Roth asked.

"Best in the city, I hear."

The waitress arrived with an arched eyebrow. Roth gave her a dazzling smile. "I'll have a Diet Coke. And, hmmmmm, you got a tuna melt?"

"Uh huh."

"Can you do that with cheddar cheese and sliced pickle and, oh, French fries, not chips?"

"Uh huh."

"Wonderful. Thank you." That dazzling smile again.

"Alright, darling." Now she was cracking a smile too, her eyes lingering on his masculine face for a moment before she disappeared into the kitchen.

"Sorry I'm eating. This might be my only chance today."

"Got you running around?"

Roth shrugged. "Congressman dead."

"Yep."

"So, what did you see?"

"Said congressman's erect *un*circumcised penis on a collision course with Roger Haake's wife. Got pictures and everything."

"Jesus."

"That's what I said."

Roth slowly shook his head, staring into the middle distance. "Must have been *quite* the lens on that camera."

ROGER HAAKE WAS, by most assessments, one of the most powerful unelected men in DC. He ran his political consultancy out of a sparkling glass office building located on K Street, along with a good measure of DC's assholedom.

While Roth drove them there in his unmarked car, Bronze thought back to his commissioning only three days prior. There had been something strangely off about the whole thing. He ran through the details of his encounter with Haake again.

For a certain kind of man, the only thing that mattered was the moment-to-moment feeling of his personal power.

Bronze's impression of Roger Haake was that he was such a man.

Bronze worked from impressions.

To form a fixed opinion would cloud his judgment. He had been surprised too often to quickly form clever conclusions—to grasp at something more than an impression. He had learned to make allowances for those surprises that appear like silent intruders through an unknown back door.

Bronze lets his mind work in pencil. He sketches and shades. The pencil has an eraser.

Roger Haake sat behind a large wooden desk. The desk was spare—a phone, some neatly stacked pieces of lined paper, an expensive-looking pen, no computer, no picture of his wife.

His posture seemed relaxed. He sat back in his chair—ankle on a knee, elbows up and thrust out to the sides, head resting in a cradle formed by his intertwined fingers.

Bronze sat across from him in a much smaller chair. Bronze was meant to feel like a servant, a lowly hired hand—perhaps a supplicant.

Haake took a long, almost theatrical pause. Bronze was meant to feel the weight of his next words.

"I suspect my wife is having an affair. I want you to follow her and find out with whom she is cheating. I would like photographic evidence ... Do you want to write this down?"

"I work better simply listening. You suspect or you know?"

"I said 'I suspect.'"

"OK. Why do you suspect?"

"A feeling."

"And where does that feeling come from, specifically?"

"A feeling is a feeling. Look, if this is something you can't handle, there are plenty of other directions I can go."

Bronze let this small threat hang in the air a moment. With the man who must feel his power over others to satisfy some great need within, weakness in others only breeds contempt.

"If you choose to contract with me, my methods are ..." Bronze twirled his finger in a gesture of gears spinning while he tried to think of a word other than methodical.

"... methodical. That starts with you. I will need photographs of your wife, and everything and anything you can tell me about her is potentially of use. Since you suspect an affair, particularly relevant would be the assumed timeline of that affair and an intensive look at her behavior within that timeline. Then I will be able to proceed with the greatest amount of efficiency. I understand that in your line of work, choosing carefully the information you reveal is of the utmost importance."

Bronze gave his own theatrical pause.

"The acquisition of information is my line of work. The more you can overcome your natural reluctance, the better the outcome. Any other private investigator you may interview will tell you the same."

In the end Haake was all too happy to tell Bronze everything. Most men are embarrassed on some level. Roger Haake betrayed no embarrassment. Only anger and contempt.

The photos he showed Bronze of Carolyn Haake were typical—some wedding photos, Christmas photos, vacation photos, a trip to Rome, the Caribbean.

However, it was immediately obvious from the photographs that Carolyn Haake herself was anything but typical.

Roth said something, knocking the reverie from Bronze's mind.

"What?"

"I said what were your impressions of Haake?"

"My impression was that he's an asshole."

Roth let out a snort.

Bronze looked out the car window, not really taking in the sights of the city around him. "My impression was that he knew more than he was telling me."

～

THE SUN WAS REACHING its zenith, ready to banish the world's shadows for a brief moment, just as Bronze and Roth approached Haake's office building. Haake met them at the entrance, walking out the door before they could walk in. He was wearing a linen suit, a pressed white shirt, a silk paisley tie, and an ugly scowl.

"Gentlemen, I'm very busy. If you'd like to talk, you'll have to walk with me to my car. You've got maybe a minute and a half." He pointed his scowl fully toward Bronze. "Isn't the point of hiring a private detective that the matter stays, you know, *private*?"

"Murder sort of trumps that one, Rog."

Always playing the good cop, Roth jumped in, his low monotone pitched at its most soothing resonance. "Mr. Haake, we just have a couple of questions. Bronze was right to come to us with this but wrong to call it murder at this point. Billy Kopes is dead, but we don't know why. What we do know is that you hired Bronze to follow your wife, and we know that in pursuing that line of work, he had occasion to encounter Congressman Kopes."

"Yes, yes, and so what?" Haake asked, never slowing down on the way to his car, which, by his trajectory, Bronze had identified as a silver Mercedes sedan.

"So what?" Bronze had just about had enough of this arrogant prick. "You *knew* Carolyn was having an affair with Kopes, so why did you send me out to take pictures? What were you hoping to gain? Why did he go for a last swim? Why—"

Haake made it to his car and turned to face Bronze, thrusting his index finger furiously in his direction. "Listen, you *has-been*, you fucking loser *drunk*, you have no idea what you're stepping in here. You know who I am, so you should know better, but I guess you're too much of a grasping Jew to ... oh, is that it? Are you looking for your fucking money?"

A loud wasp buzzed by Bronze's right ear. Without taking his seething eyes off Haake, he rubbed a hand about the ear, hoping to scare the little fucker off.

Haake suddenly stopped talking. His jaw dropped open in surprise, then his eyes scrunched in confusion, then came an angry working of his almost foaming mouth up and down, up and down. He dropped his head to look down and his hand came to his chest. Bronze let his eyes drop to look there as well, wondering if a bird had shit on that expensive paisley tie as a gesture of cosmic justice.

There was something dark staining the shirt under Haake's fist.

The wasp buzzed by Bronze's ear again. A hole exploded in Haake's clutching hand. His face had turned a bloody maroon; he looked as though he was screaming at the top of his lungs, but only a wet wheeze issued forth.

Before everything changed, Bronze only had time to think of one word.

Jesus.

4

ROMANCE

IRIS

The last time I was in New York, I saw a young woman reading one of my books on the subway. It was *The Red Shutters*, and I wondered if the ambiguity of the cover —the blood-red shutters and the dark, hidden presence lurking and looking into the pure white, almost virginal bedroom— allowed this small boldness. From the cover alone, the book could have easily been a murder mystery and not a lurid piece of erotica, albeit one labeled as Romance and marketed to middle-aged *hausfraus*. The author picture wasn't even of me. It must have been the first edition from some seventeen years prior, when I was deemed too young to grace the covers of my own paperbacks.

Where had she gotten it? Pulled from some hidden corner of an aunt's library? The book hadn't been in print in years. A second-hand bookstore, maybe?

The young woman had straight blond hair framing a serious face. Her legs were crossed and utterly still—no bopping of her foot. She had sensible flats on. Pants. A dark blouse with a small floral pattern. She looked as though she might as well be reading Dostoyevsky.

At first I was stealing glances, but I soon gave up the dissimulation. I stared, unabashed. I watched her eyes, which never left the page. I watched her unmoving mouth—her slow, steady breathing. Was that breathing *too* steady? Artificial? Controlled? And even then, was there an almost imperceptible increase in the pace?

Those eyes—there was an intensity to the focus, was there not? Certainly not passive—they were perhaps even growing ever so slightly larger. Perhaps she couldn't quite believe what she was reading.

Oh, and she was holding herself so, so still. Did she think the slightest movement would shatter the illusion of control? Steal her anonymity? Break the lie she lived by?

I watched her mouth most of all. I watched for a quirking of the upper lip. I watched for a hint of separation between the lips —for a deeply suppressed gasp, perhaps. But more than anything, I imagined her wet pink tongue might emerge—ever so daintily. Unconsciously. As if only to moisten lips that had grown too dry. I waited for that strange organ that carries our most intimate sense to show just the barest hint of itself, to darken the area behind her bottom lip. Maybe it would stay there, perfectly still, a slight pressure against the nerves of her unspectacular lip—medium sized and pink running toward pale, and really of no particular note. But there would be that special feeling there nonetheless, even if that lip was not full to bursting and pulsating red like the lips of Lara, the heroine of the book.

And maybe even ... maybe even she might run that tongue along the back of her bottom lip. And her eyes might close a little. Perhaps it would all become a little much and the lips would become tucked in and press against her teeth and the eyes would close all the way as if she had some important thought, something she had forgotten or realized, but really there was no thought or even emotion, only—*sensation*.

Alas, none of this was to be. The train screeched to a halt at 72nd Street. The young woman stood up and left. Her face had never changed. For a moment I found myself staring at the empty space she had left in her wake, and only after some seconds' delay did I turn my head to follow her steady walk through the sliding doors.

We lurched into motion again. I was destined for the next stop at 96th, but I should have gotten off. I should have followed her. I could have said: "That book you're reading—a friend recommended it. What do you think?" And I started to envision how she would have reacted. Who was this young woman? What can we know about her? Would she have demurred—"Oh, it's silly. A beach read"—and carried on her way?

No. The way she held herself so still—I don't think so.

She would have considered the question. She would have considered protecting herself with a half lie, but she would have taken the time to see my unaffected curiosity. She would have said, "I am only halfway through, but I am *enjoying* it."

Sitting there halfway between 72nd and 96th, my gaze in the middle distance, I smiled just as I would have on the platform of 72nd, the young woman's lips finally moving, finally speaking, finally revealing her secrets.

I LOST THE THREAD of what Mitch was saying as I stared out of his window into Riverside Park.

It had clouded over and there was the feeling of rain in the air. The people in the park could feel it too. I could see them hustle about with their dogs, hoping to induce them into performing their necessaries before the wet arrived. But from safe inside, the clouds gave a solemnity to the bare tree branches reaching up to the heavens, a mournful holiness to their twisted poses that would be bleached away on too clear a day. The rain was going to come, and the rain, for its part, was just as life-giving as the rays of sun. One must always remember this.

Say what you will about Mitch—and I could say a lot—he had a beautiful view. I wondered if he ever found himself looking out at it anymore. And if he did, was he struck by its beauty? Or had it now grown dull and tired? Or was it ever about the beauty for him? Was it simply a gesture toward a fantasy of beauty, an evocation of mood, an attempt to press a trigger buried deep in his psyche? Buried when? His teenage years, perhaps. The original love affair of his life—broken, gone wrong in some tree-lined park somewhere. Yes, he saw the world through this trigger. He imagined the trigger was universal, that it underlay the hearts of all his visitors.

Yes. Yes, I think so. It was not about the beauty of the view at all but what he imagined it provoked in the hearts of his clientele—the implication of success, the power it connoted.

Poor Mitch.

Could beauty ever really be power? If so, it was a strange power. And all this power we were always grasping at, what was it for if not for the attainment of beauty?

Mitch buzzed on and I forced myself to zone back into his monologue.

"... and, Iris, don't get me wrong, we loved *The Long Dark*, loved it, but the sales are the sales. You're on the 25, it's 4th and 15, down by 3—you've got to take the field goal."

Mitch was pathologically incapable of speaking in anything other than sports metaphors. When he first became my literary agent, back when I lived in New York, I spent a handful of nights at Broadway Dive, uncomfortably shifting my bottom on the hard wooden stools and politely waving away come-ons, trying to bone up on football enough to be able to make heads or tails of what Mitch was driving at.

It wasn't all bad. It had led me to dream up one of my more successful male love interests—second string New York Giants quarterback Jake Russell. He debuted as a side character in *Satin Nights*, but I soon managed to eke out a strong-selling trilogy with him as the male lead—*Ungentle Giant*, *The Russell Hustle*, and then the final book after a trade to the other New York football team, *Jet Steam*. All in all, not my best work.

"But, Mitch, I think it's hardly 4th and 15, and I don't think we're down at all. I think we're up and it's maybe 3rd and 8 and we just ran two run plays. The defense is keying in on the half back, he's huffing and puffing in the huddle, and the QB has got a hell of an arm. Time to run a play-action and take a shot down the field."

"Personally I loved *The Long Dark*. I thought it was up there with your best, most aesthetic work. It was a Larry Bird three-pointer, a Pete Sampras first serve, John Elway airing out the ball down field ..."

Mitch must have been getting truly anxious at this point; he'd hit three different sports in a single clause. I understood his position. After a series of money-making romance novels under my primary pseudonym, Loretta Laughlin, I had felt I'd earned the right to go out on a limb a bit and write something different —hence Henry Gordon had had his immaculate birth and made his sci-fi debut with *The Long Dark*. It hadn't totally flopped in my mind, and I still prayed the sales may catch on eventually, maybe someday even reaching cult classic status, but it had been a year and I hadn't even earned out on the scaled-down advance I'd taken to get the deal done. Now I was proposing another year or more away from Loretta and eschewing "genre" altogether to write a pseudonym-less literary novel as plain old Iris Margaryan.

Neither Mitch nor the publisher was seeing dollar signs.

"Iris, I don't say this lightly—you've got one of the best ground games I've ever seen. Loretta's a hard-nosed little half back. First down after first down, pushing the ball down the field. Grinding out touchdown after touchdown. You put her on the sidelines last year. Great. I'm sure she needed the breather. But leave her there too long and she's going to get cold. You're risking injury here. Why throw another Hail Mary? I'm your agent, OK? I'm just saying if I blow it for a franchise player like Loretta, I'm going to be a *free agent* before long."

My eyes drifted to the window once more. It was going to rain. The body just knew it. The sky was pregnant with it. I imagined the people in the park and how soothing the air must feel as they breathed it in. The rain would be lovely. But the feeling of the fleeting preamble of rain, that's what transcended toward something beyond knowing.

My mind began turning a theory nonetheless.

When it comes to theories, I suppose I have always been most attracted to theories of the unknowable.

I CAN'T SAY what possessed me to stay at the Carlyle on the Upper East Side when all my meetings were on the West Side. There was the vague notion of making it over to the Met, but I never did.

I did, however, get up the nerve to sit alone at the counter in the Carlyle's Bemelmans Bar among all the curling colors of the whimsical paintings that decorated the walls—blue balloons and pink rabbits in green three-piece suits and a warm yellow background bathed in soft lamplight, scenes like childhood dreams long forgotten—and seated everywhere, smiling and joking and arching their eyebrows, the cocktail-sipping old money New York City elite.

Perhaps that was why I was here.

Perhaps I was here to convince myself that I had made it, that I could belong in a place like this. That I too could put on the right dress, apply just the right touches of makeup, style my hair in a manner that was not simply functional or *attractive* but luminescent in the bar light.

My first drink was too sweet but wound up being boozy enough to loosen all my joints and start a warmth deep within my abdomen, running pleasantly along my diaphragm with every breath.

One drink was probably enough, but it seemed too short an excursion, too weak an attempt at adventure. My second drink was a champagne cocktail. It was dry and sour and just about right. The fizz lazed about on my lips with each sip. It came in an old coup-style glass with gold around the rim. It struck the right note, the right image.

But time dragged on as I sipped, and my thoughts began to sour along with my drink. A darkness crept in—that was all I was going to get, an *image*. No adventure. If there was going to be a story, it was going to be one I constructed myself while I sat quietly alone.

Eventually a man did come to sit next to me. He ordered scotch neat, which I do not understand. Why order something at an expensive bar that you could easily have at home? But maybe that was the point. He knew what he liked and he was worldly enough that he need not care about making his outings "count" for something beyond the direct sensual pleasure of his selection. Or so he would have us believe.

He was blandly handsome, clean-shaven with salt and pepper hair and a bit too old for me, although he probably did not think so.

I conspicuously kept my focus away from him. From the moment he sat down, he disturbed the pleasant warmth that had blossomed within me. He even cast away the dark thoughts that had emerged, which, though depressive, had a certain depth and a velvety sense of revelatory pleasure in their unfolding. Now I simply had an itch on my skin and muted but undeniable tremors in my abdomen. And my thoughts were the relentless and ever banal *Will he try to talk to me, and if so, what will he intend? Or will he not, and if so, what does that imply? And I feel his presence like a pressure against my side, and why must I always be so frightened? I am not even attracted ...* and on like this, totally ruining any pleasure I might have filed away into my memory of the evening.

In the end, he didn't stay long and he never spoke to me. He was having a drink while he waited for his wife or mistress to arrive, and when she did, he waved to her and left for a table in the back corner.

Now as I drank my champagne cocktail, something concrete filled my mind. I imagined what our conversation might have been like. I imagined what might have been if I had gone with him to his room or he to mine. As I imagined the conversation, I smiled as I tried to think of clever witticisms back and forth. But my imagination of what might happen in the hotel room itself felt stale and devoid of titillation—sterile, almost bordering on clinical.

I was right to insist on my point to Mitch. I still needed time to get back to a place where the erotic felt fresh and fun, thrilling and new. Loretta Laughlin needed to hibernate or to remake herself or perhaps even to build a funeral pyre on which to be reborn, a phoenix from the flames. Or perhaps her time had simply passed. Perhaps she just needed to die.

The fizz had gone out of my drink. It was down to the dregs

anyway. I sat for a few moments longer before taking the last swig.

I might have toyed with the idea of that blandly handsome somewhat-too-old man. But really he was poor material, like trying to start a fire with wet kindling.

I wanted something else entirely—maybe a younger man. A man full of badly timed touches and words that failed to fit just right, whose body lacked all softness—was just sinew tightly wound over protruding bones. Who would start out posturing but find himself led onto my wavelength, who would look at my body as if he were seeing a woman for the first time.

Perhaps the problem wasn't really one kind of man or another. Perhaps I had just picked the wrong setting, the wrong kind of story to tell. Perhaps what I really wanted was to be swept away to the jazz clubs downtown, not sex and its awkward aftermath but sound and sweat, fingers dancing along metal or ivory, melodies bewitching the mind as rhythms spoke directly to legs and arms and guts, winding wispy billows of smoke and foaming beers that overtopped pint glasses, soft lights in the darkness—*mood*.

What I really wanted was romance.

5

SOUND AND PAIN

MAY 5, 1997

Dazed, Bronze turned to look behind him. He saw cars and buildings and sidewalk and most of all the sun glinting off every piece of metal and glass, a million pricks of light filling his vision with a million white dots of blindness.

A sudden pressure slammed into the small of his back. The world turned sideways and, before he even knew he was falling, he hit the sidewalk with a thud, shoulder first, ribs second, the air flying out of him in a sudden *whoop*.

Roth was on top of him, yelling fragments of incoherent sound.

His stream of sight broke, splintered to gunshot images too fast to register. A red star swallows the earth. Jesus bleeds from hands and feet. His mother's eyes smile, crinkling lines radiating out until—turquoise. Foam bubbles eject from a dying mouth. His father's strong hands slowly sew stitches delicate as dewdrops. Thick red paint seeps down a blank canvas. Wasp larvae undulate. Turquoise bleeds from scared brown eyes. Gum.

A dried-out colorless piece of chewing gum stuck in a crack

of concrete filled his vision. He stared at it. The image of the gum lacked all meaning, hung disconnected from all other images. But after a time, he understood that it was gum. That someone had chewed it and spat it out. That it had stuck there, that people had stepped on it. That the sun had shone down upon it, fusing it with the sidewalk. And as this understanding registered, the immediacy of the world returned. Heat from the concrete. A lingering buzz itching at his right ear. A broad, dull pain running down his left shoulder where he'd crashed to the ground. Roth yelled again, "Stay down!"

Roth rolled off him and Bronze felt his weight disappear. Then came the sound of him yelling into the radio: "Shots fired on 19th and K. Civilian down. I need any cars we have in the area ... sniper, likely military."

The reality of the situation suddenly hit. Bronze's heart began to race wildly. The old wound between his hip and groin began to throb and his mind flew back nine years. He saw the knife go in again; he imagined that this time it was a killing blow, that the blade caught an artery, that it pierced further, was brought upward through his belly, that his guts were spilling out onto the pavement, that he was pressing his abdomen against the concrete, trying desperately to keep his intestines inside him, hot blood pooling underneath.

He began to crawl toward the line of parked cars. With every wiggle, he imagined the bullet would come. Would it hit him between the shoulder and neck, an explosion of tendon and skin as the bullet entered his torso the long way, exiting where? Down at his hip, his ass—could a bullet travel from the top of him through his guts and out of his anus? Or might the bullet just hit the top of his head—sudden silence and total black before there was a single moment to contemplate his situation?

He made it to the side of a dark blue SUV and rolled himself underneath. In an instant he left the world of light and there was only shadow and the acrid smell of hot metal. He twisted his body, trying to find Roth, caught sight of his shoes and legs behind him. Roth was crouched and pressing himself against the back of the SUV Bronze was underneath. He could hear him continuing to yell into his radio.

Bronze looked past Roth and saw the crumpled body of Roger Haake one car back, legs splayed awkwardly, sun beating down mercilessly on him.

Sirens now roared up ahead. Screeching of tires. Screams in the air. Blasts of static shouting through Roth's radio.

Bronze saw Roth's face drop to look under the car.

"You good? You hit?"

Bronze brought his hand to his buzzing right ear, felt at it. Rolled onto his back and felt randomly about his body. Nothing.

"Not hit."

The act of speaking brought his brain back into action. He started to assess.

"That was a fucking assassin!"

Roth nodded. Eyes wide. Scared. Crouching as low as he could against the back of the SUV.

Gunfire rang out somewhere ahead.

Thump thump thump thump thump.

Seemingly endless pounding. Bronze imagined smoke rising from the ends of pistols. Clips being emptied. With all those rounds in the air, surely at least one bullet must have taken the assassin.

Screams over Roth's radio. "Officer down! Officer down! Fuck! For the love of Christ! Gallagher took one in the chest. Oh god ... he's ... oh ... oh no ..."

IT WAS BY LUCK the cops had come upon the assassin when they did. Luck they had been the exact distance away that they had been when the call had gone out. Had they gotten there sooner, he might still have been set up in his hastily assembled position in the men's room on the third floor of 1940 K Street, a vulgar, faceless building of glass and gray metal. Seeing them pull up in his general direction, lights and sirens blaring, he may have decided it was safest to simply execute them from his perch with shots through their windshields. If they had gotten there any later, he would have been smoothly in the wind and on to the next target.

As it turned out, they interrupted him in the act of fleeing out the door into a blind alley, pinned him down with suppressive gunfire, and forced him to improvise.

He put one in the cop from the first car who kept popping up on his haunches whenever he fired a round, head waving about, giraffe-like, with his jerking movements. One good shot in him was enough to distract his partner, who went to administer aid. There was no clean shot on the cops from the second car so he lit the car itself up, shattering the glass, blowing out the tires, puncturing its metallic skin. Then he ran, knowing it would take these far-overmatched men minutes before they looked up from their hiding places to search for him.

When they did, he was gone.

After running only a block in the open, he slipped down another alley, changed to an unhurried walk, and broke the rifle down as he went in sure, crisp movements. When he popped out a street over, the rifle was in pieces, carried in a briefcase as nondescript as any other carried by thousands of other suit-wearing men of business in downtown DC.

When police cars flew past him, he didn't flinch at the zooming sirens or the red and blue lights cast over him. Danger hardly registered. What could these lackadaisically trained constables compare to the relentless violence that had followed him from his very first steps?

These men were trained to direct traffic, to hassle bums loitering too close to places of business, to stand menacingly in place.

He was trained in metal that falls from the sky on cloudless spring days, of gas that smells of sweet apples, making first the birds fall from their nests, then the children scream as their skin blisters away and their mothers spew green liquid, some men dropping in place, never to move again, while others die slowly, bleeding out from a broken femur after falling as they flee in black terror, their eyes burned to blindness—the once-bright world turned everywhere to sound and pain, to screams and convulsive laughter, to endless chemical night.

Yes, he was trained in all that man was capable of.

6

A STRANGE POWER

MAY 5, 1997

Carolyn Haake came to her deep red door wrapped tightly in a silk robe decorated with birds of paradise in a field of cream. Half the tension in Bronze's body let go for a moment and he swayed forward, both hands going to his knees.

He had been sure he'd find her dead. Murdered in some awful manner.

"Yes? Yes? Why are you repeatedly buzzing my door? We don't take sales calls. I don't talk to strange men"—the barest flicker of brightness came to her eyes—"even when they are tall, dark, and sweating profusely."

He hadn't realized how fast he had been racing, how tensely he'd been holding his body until he tried to speak and almost couldn't get the words out.

"Carolyn. You don't know me, but I know you. You must have seen the news; you know Billy Kopes is dead, right? Can we go inside? It's not ..."

A quick emotion ran across her face too fast for Bronze to guess at it. "I don't see what that has to do—"

"You're having an affair with Billy Kopes."

This time her emotion was easier to read—anger. All earlier playfulness was gone. "What is this?"

"It's not safe."

"What isn't?"

"Haake's dead ... I mean, Miss, I'm sorry ... your husband's dead."

"What? What are you talking about?"

Her eyelids had now flared wide, the whites of her eyes luridly sharp under heavy mascara. Fear had banished anything else she might have felt at the news. She was stepping backward away from the door, starting to close it on him. The fear meant she knew something. The fear meant she might agree to do what was necessary. The fear might save her life. But it also might mean she'd slam the door on him and sign her death warrant.

Bronze had maybe two seconds to say the right thing.

"Sasha Lin."

She looked as if he had pointed a gun at her. "Who's that?"

"Natalya Drozdov."

All the color had drained from her face. Her body was still standing there, but it looked as if her mind had fled to some far-off planet. She spoke in a monotone. "What do you want from me?"

"I'm trying to save your life."

CAROLYN PACKED AND BRONZE THOUGHT. He wouldn't leave anything to chance.

Roth's hands had been covered in blood as he applied pressure to the sucking chest wound of Patrolman Peter Gallagher. The rest of the responding Metro PD were desperately chasing the ghost that had rained precision death down upon K Street.

Roth had tossed Bronze his keys and Bronze had lead-footed it to the place the ghost was most probably heading. If he wanted Roger Haake dead for his connection to Billy Kopes, for something he knew, it seemed a fair bet that his cuckolding wife was next on the list. Even if she didn't know whatever Roger Haake had known, she might know, and *might* was dangerous enough.

And it had to be Bronze.

They couldn't just send over a random patrol car. The assassin had been waiting for them on K Street. When they'd left the Georgetown Diner, Roth had phoned in their destination back to Central—maybe it was a bad coincidence, but compromise within the Metro PD couldn't be ruled out.

Bronze watched Carolyn throw articles of clothing into a canvas bag, open a safe and grab her jewels, some cash, and, with shaking hands, an unmarked videotape. Bronze figured any pleading or encouragement or invectives he might fling at her to speed up would only increase her nerves and perversely slow her down.

He felt as if he was sitting in a building wired for imminent implosion.

His hands trembled uncontrollably as he watched her moving far too slowly.

He banished that unseen man from his thoughts. The man who was even now making his inexorable way to Haake's Georgetown mansion.

Bronze breathed in and out with as much control as he could muster, tried to master his breath and himself as he had been trained to do in a distant country in a distant past that felt like someone else's life. He focused his wild thoughts on something concrete. He focused on planning the next steps.

He couldn't just take Roth's car. Although unmarked, it was a police car and, besides, whoever was after Carolyn had probably seen it. The same went for Carolyn Haake's red BMW two-seater. He had to hope that the killer would be waylaid while avoiding the police. Had to hope he had time to drive to Bruce Schwarz's antique store and beg him for his car so that he could help Carolyn flee the city. Then Bruce would have to drive Roth's car to a neutral location, maybe back to the Georgetown Diner.

Bruce would be a sitting duck. He'd have to ditch the car and walk somewhere safe. For the length of that journey, Bronze would be asking Bruce to take his life into his hands for a woman he'd never met.

For Bronze, Bruce would do it without hesitation, but could he really ask? Bruce was Bronze's oldest friend; they'd grown up together from the age of seven. Did Bronze even *want* to ask him?

And afterwards, where could Bruce go that was safe—some place sufficiently far from the antique shop but where Bronze could check in on him?

Carolyn was almost ready. Her face was flushed and there were tears in her heavily made-up eyes from the tension. For half a second, old echoes of Esther Klein—Esther McNamara—flashed across her face.

There was no choice.

And there was no time to warn Iris.

BRONZE DROVE PAST the Beltway and felt the worst of his anxiety begin to ease from searing psychosis to merely redlined nerve burnout. Carolyn looked out the window and spoke without turning to him. "How did you know those names?"

"Your husband."

"He hired you to follow me."

It was a statement, not a question, but Bronze answered anyway. "Yep."

"And you saw me with Billy."

"And the others."

"What you must think of me ..."

He turned his eyes from the road. Her full lips were fixed together in a line. Her dark eyes stared off a million miles away.

"Hell, I don't think much one way or another."

She glanced in his direction, then quickly away. "Not the usual male reaction."

"I don't have much of a leg to stand on myself when it comes to living up to the ideals of courtly Victorian chastity."

The corners of her lips turned upwards in the first slight smile he'd seen grace her face.

"Besides, if I've learned one thing—and it's probably the only thing I've learned with any confidence—is that Hamlet was right. There's more in heaven and earth than I could ever imagine."

She looked at Bronze, then looked away out the window. Time passed in silence.

"About Billy ..." Her voice creaked. "All I know is that Roger knew about him and me."

Bronze nodded. He wasn't going to pry just yet. The woman had been through enough. Besides, with the violence of the day, he wasn't sure if he even wanted to know anything more. Knowing might mean two bullets in his heart.

"Did he know about the other guys?" He couldn't *not* ask that.

She looked down and spoke to him while seeming to study her feet. "I assume so. I generally assume that Roger knows everything ... *everything*."

The trees along the highway were already heavy with leaves. They streaked by on either side in a continuous blur of green.

The highway boiled in the sun, little mirages of false water emerging on the horizon, then disappearing into seared pavement as Bruce's tan Volvo labored along.

Carolyn looked up. "What kind of name is Bronze? A middle name?"

"Nickname. My middle name's Ezekiel, if you can believe someone would do that to their own son."

He stole a quick glance over at her. He had just about calmed down enough at this point to be able to take her in. To feel the force of her sitting there next to him.

He had seen a lot of her since his commissioning. Trailed her for two days almost continuously.

For some reason he was fixated on her mascara. She hadn't been ready for the day when he'd come to her door. But she already had heavy mascara on. There was something to it beyond mere makeup.

She wore it like a badge or perhaps a battle scar.

Women like her always accumulated these pseudo-scars. A prominent tattoo. An odd hairdo. Too many earrings. A style of clothes out of sync with their beauty.

What was it? Armor, maybe. Was the mascara there to protect those eyes of manifold browns, of complex chromatic geometries?

That wasn't quite right. Hiding them was closer to it. The mascara was a glamour of falseness that hid her away. Turned her into a kind of actor. It was too painful to move in the world as herself without pretense.

The mascara was a mask.

Bronze understood masks. Maybe too well. Was he hunting for one? Was he seeing one where none existed?

"On the dotted line I'm Calvin Goldberg. People called me Cal until the '76 Olympics. After I got the bronze, well, someone thought Bronze Goldberg sounded funny."

"You got the bronze in the Olympics?" She turned to him, eyes flicking and dancing about his body, weighing the breadth of his shoulders, the angle of his posture, the length of his legs. "What sport?"

"Judo."

"Judo? '76? You must have been a kid."

"Nineteen."

Carolyn was silent a moment, her shining dark eyes now searching his face, appraising the lines and angles she saw there.

"What happened?"

He smiled. What else could you do when you thought back on a distant pain that never quite disappeared?

"Shattered my arm. Blew out my knee too. I had to use crutches for the medal ceremony. All in the same match—Nakatani—hell of a fighter and a son of a bitch. He would have taken gold again in '80 if it weren't for the boycott."

"So I'm in good hands, then. You still do judo, I assume? You one of those guys with hands registered as lethal weapons?"

"Nakatani—'76—was the last time. And judo isn't much against a gun." Bronze's voice softened, took on a distance as if he was speaking to no one in particular. "Or a knife."

TWO HOURS OUT OF DC, Bronze pulled into a Shell station, filled Bruce Schwarz's car up, and used the pay phone to finally call Iris while Carolyn hunted for Snickers bars and potato chips in the convenience store.

He didn't chat with Iris long. Bruce was safe and lying low at her house. For now, it appeared they had made a clean getaway. Too soon to really tell—whoever was after them, whoever had put two assassin's bullets into Roger Haake's heart, had barely seemed human. Was in the wind with no leads. The whole eastern seaboard was fraught.

Iris asked if there was any more she could do. He thought it best to distract her overpowered mind from falling into worried rumination, so he suggested she go into his apartment and take a quick look at the back articles he'd gotten from the *Post* on Billy Kopes to look for any connections between him and go-to political consultant/high-powered attorney Roger Haake. Any connections beyond Haake's wife, that is.

Before he hung up, he said he would call from the road home the next day.

Bronze took his change from the pay phone and went to stand at the window of the little convenience store, finally able to fully breathe for the first time in hours. He caught sight of Carolyn paying for the snacks and some cans of diet soda that would have to do as their late lunch. The teenage clerk fumbled with his cash register, stole half glances at Carolyn and immediately cranked his head away again.

Bronze watched Carolyn through the glass—really watched her, much as he had done on Saturday night. He watched her move. He watched her mouth as she spoke. He saw the places her flesh was exposed and imagined the places it was hidden. He took a breath and looked truly. The looking was like a meditation ... and yet ...

And yet the sight of her engulfed him in an unbidden longing that poured into the cracks of his heart, that filled his chest to brimming, that streamed over him, drowned him, undid him. The longing came not from Bronze himself but from some automatic trigger, some mechanism at the edges of psychic space far beyond conscious control—a primordial failsafe that need not bother explain itself to the waking mind.

Bronze watched her and drowned. Watched her and ruminated on beauty.

A beautiful man is in possession of privilege, a gift to be used or discarded on a whim. A beautiful woman is in possession of a terrible power—a *strange* power. It lives in the chaos of unknown hearts, their reactions combustible, unpredictable. One man may fall to his knees proclaiming undying loyalty. Another may become enraged. Another may shrink away, lose control of his tongue. Another may endlessly harangue.

A beautiful woman may do anything on this earth except fully contain the effects of her beauty. It is an explosion, a runaway chain reaction—unrestrained physics, chemical combustions overtopping beakers, exponential viral mathematics, infectious mass insanity.

Carolyn Haake turned from the counter and walked toward Bronze. Since he had first seen her picture in Haake's office, the image of her had hardly left his mind, even in the moments he wasn't haunting her steps from a distance. He'd watched her delicate fingers holding teacups from the corners of cafés, seen eyelashes heavy with mascara fluttering as she looked into a store mirror, seen her elegantly emerging from taxi cabs—first the fine architecture that formed the tops of her feet, then the sharp line and rounded curve of her calf muscle, the swell of her thighs at the knees, the twin lines of her swooping quadriceps flashing as those legs hinged her from seated to standing—seen her double framed by the circle of his binoculars and the rectangle of light that shone from bedroom windows, seen the dark of her areolas, the points of her nipples upon arousal.

Jesus.

How would an old noir detective put it?

She had hair like a Chopin nocturne. She had breasts like the Spanish armada. She had an ass like opium dreams in the soft ancient bed of a duchess.

Christ.

Her eyebrows were shaped into thick dark lines. Depending

on the angle and the light, her high cheekbones might appear softened by full cheeks that gave her the guise of innocence yearning for initiation, or alternatively sharpened into a knowing look that promised the mysteries of seraphim and siren if you intoned just the right words in just the right rhythm and melody.

There was electricity in her eyes behind all that mascara. There was liquid fire in the swaying of her hips.

She sure as hell was a beautiful woman.

7

THE LITTLE FELLOW

MAY 5, 1997

I t was three hours of silently sitting on a criminally non-ergonomic blue plastic seat attached to a pale orange wall in the George Washington University Hospital waiting room, surrounded by uniformed Metro PD murmuring dark rumors and intermingling like pigeons jockeying about a discarded hot dog bun, before Mark Roth learned that Peter Gallagher would survive his gunshot wound. It took another hour and a half to track down his car abandoned at the Georgetown Diner. It was evening by the time Roth left the city limits. He was about a quarter mile from home when he brought his car to a sudden stop.

In his headlights, starkly still on the black pavement, was a ball of red–orange. Roth turned in his seat to look out the back window—there was no one coming from behind. He flicked his emergency blinkers on, got out, and walked into the illumination of his own headlights.

Drawing closer, he looked down at the red–orange ball, which had resolved itself into a puff of feathers, a snub of a beak, a crest of red, a black face, and black eyes. Usually the eyes of a cardinal would be dancing about, looking inquisitive and slyly jocular. But this fellow just stared mournfully at Roth, just breathing, just waiting for whatever would come.

Roth supposed he had been stunned—had flown into the window of a car and fallen, unable to gather himself together enough to fly to safety. He hoped it wasn't worse. He hoped that the hollow bones of the bird's neck or back had not broken.

Roth looked up at the trees lining the road, but it was too dark to see among the branches. Did the little fellow have a woman up there? Was there a duller, fawn-colored cardinal fretting about the leaves and limbs terrified and unable to help? Or was the little fellow a loner? Maybe he had lost his mate one way or another.

Cardinals mated like people. Some were married and stayed together year after year. Some divorced between seasons. Some had affairs. Sometimes, when one cardinal died, the other in the pairing would move on to a new mate. And sometimes they could not move on. Sometimes, before nesting, cardinal pairs sing together. Sometimes the male feeds the female beak to beak.

Roth stooped down. The little fellow did not move or shrink away. He slowly brought his large, strong hands out in front of him, ever so slowly cupping them underneath the little bird. He straightened up and raised the bird to his face. The cardinal was warm and panting. Was the bird scared of him? Did he still smell of blood?

He walked with the bird to the forested side of the road, went beyond the beginning of the tree line, and found a depression in the ground. He gently placed the little fellow there. If his woman was watching, she'd find him easily. But he wouldn't be hit by a car and he wouldn't be so easy for a predator to spot. If he was just stunned, he might have time to recover in the little hollow. Otherwise his woman could come say her goodbyes.

Roth got back in his car and drove the rest of the way home.

Angus was waiting for him there. He sat, eyes and ears and snout pointed at the front door, body rigid with anticipation. Roth dropped to the floor and pet the wheaten-colored Cairn terrier from the back of his head to the base of his tail until he flopped over onto his side, then Roth rubbed his belly until the ache in his knees became too much for him to endure.

Angus wanted to go out right away, but Roth couldn't stand to be in his bloody clothes a moment longer. He stripped in the vestibule. His shoes were clean, by some miracle, but his charcoal gray suit was stained at the wrists and thighs and right lapel, while his shirt and tie were even further gone. Angus followed him impatiently as he went about stowing his shoes, finding a clear plastic bag for his suit, and then tossing into the garbage everything else he had on before heading to the shower.

Angus was now quite perturbed—he believed firmly in routine and punctuality. As Roth showered and removed the crusted blood from his skin and black curling body hair, Angus waited on the cold bathroom tiles, producing a low *harrumph* in the back of his throat. When Roth finally exited, dried himself, and threw on some clothes, Angus waited again by the front door, now turning his stare toward his limp leash hanging from the coat rack.

Roth could feel Angus's relief as he finally got him leashed up, then the small golden dog bolted outside, forcing Roth to elevate his walking pace to a near jog. At the very first tree, usually passed over for more exotic fare, Angus lifted his right leg to pee. It was always the right leg, and, as always, he looked back at Roth while he did it.

Roth acknowledged the accomplishment. "Good boy. Good man," he said.

Roth thought about returning to the cardinal, but he worried about Angus's hardwired instincts so close to the wounded bird. So he led them in the opposite direction, Angus walking quite precisely on the thin, slightly elevated stone ledge that separated Roth's street from the grass of his neighbors' front lawns. This peculiar pattern of walking almost always indicated a movement was imminent. Roth tried to keep the leash loose and relaxed in his hands so as not to ruin the aligning of the stars. When the moment came, Angus now looked away from Roth, off into the distance, as if contemplating some great mystery.

When they returned home, Angus sat patiently as Roth removed his collar. He raised a paw when asked, took his treat with gentle dignity, and retired to his corner of the couch for his traditional pre-sleep rest and contemplation.

With Angus settled, a stillness fell about the house. There was nothing left that needed to be done. There were noises—the movements of the trees outside, the settling of the walls, a sparrow calling in the distance. The kind of noises you only hear in otherwise oppressive silence.

Roth stood in his stockinged feet for a time. Then he sat in his armchair. Then he checked that his living room windows were closed in case it might rain in the night. Then he sat again.

The refrigerator hummed intrusively. It sounded more labored than usual—on its last legs, perhaps.

He got up with a grunting sigh, went into the kitchen, and stood before the unquiet refrigerator for several beats, not quite sure what he intended. Then, slowly, a devilish idea came to him.

He took out a jar of half-solid hot fudge sauce and dished it into a ramekin. From the freezer he took out three cartons of ice cream—chocolate, vanilla, and strawberry. He put the ramekin of hot fudge into the microwave and waited for it to turn warm and liquid while the ice cream softened. He dished out one scoop of each ice cream flavor, the hot fudge, and a heaping topping of Reddi-Wip into a bowl. He sat at his round kitchen table. Angus trotted over to join him, flopping down on his side beneath his chair, paws outstretched and crossed over one another.

Roth ate the sundae with his dog beneath him and was briefly happy for the first time since lunch.

When he had finished the ice cream, Angus followed him into the bedroom and curled up in his plush dog bed at the foot of Roth's tightly made four-poster bed and watched Roth through the open bathroom door while he brushed his teeth and put in his daily battery of glaucoma eyedrops. By the time Roth slipped between his sheets and turned off the light, Angus was already snoring lightly.

Roth lay in the darkness with his eyes open for a time. When he closed them, faces swam across his mind's eye. Roger Haake's was the newest and clearest. But some of the old standbys that had faded around the edges, those jungle scenes of horror, were still the worst. Well, it was between those and what he had found at Madam Richelieu's.

Bronze.

He thought of Bronze out there on the road trying to save Haake's wife. What would become of them? What were they up against? Could he have done more to help? What forces were at play? Kopes and then Haake so soon after ...

He thought of the little cardinal he had left out there in the woods. His sad black eyes, his acceptance of his fate.

A sudden flash of fear dug talons into his chest. Roth jerked up in bed, heart pounding—no thought, his body acting without consulting his mind.

He was being unreasonable.

He carefully laid himself back down again, but despite his best efforts, he was back to sitting within seconds. Then, without having made a single conscious decision, he was out of bed, clothes thrown on again, back out into the night.

He walked the quarter mile back to the spot, to the small depression at the start of the woods.

Roth stood as still and as silent as he could manage in the dark next to the empty hollow, hearing his own breath like a wheezing metronome, smelling sharp pine and the sweet decay of fallen beech and ash. The little cardinal was gone. But there was no way to know whether he had recovered himself and flown into the trees and was now safe among the branches—perhaps not ready to sing again but safe—or whether some final tragedy had befallen him.

There was no way to know, but there was hope, and despite it all, Roth was the kind to hope.

8

LOSING

MAY 5, 1997

After the Shell station, they switched to have Carolyn drive for a few hours so that Bronze could take a break. His nerves were blown out. His brain was past exhaustion and spinning empty masochistic thoughts that went nowhere he wanted to be. He was trying to calm himself, focus on something else until some deeper, more compassionate part of his mind managed to finally hit the circuit breaker and short out the cracked funhouse logic that looped and looped without end.

He had the *Post* open across his legs and finally read past the Billy Kopes headline on the front page to the story he had originally intended to check out this morning, a lifetime ago.

The chess match to end all chess matches. Man vs. Machine.

The machines had struck a blow. Deep Blue had won game two.

It was all tied 1–1. After Kasparov had taken the first game, Deep Blue had stunned the world champion—some said the greatest chess player to ever live—with a crushing defeat.

Kasparov was saying it was a cheat. That some rival grandmaster was behind the transistors and electrodes working the gears and levers, using Deep Blue like the world's fastest calculator. IBM was saying it was the brilliance of the machine. Others argued it was actually a bug in the code, an error doomed to lose if the human quality of the mistake hadn't unnerved Kasparov to distraction.

Bronze wanted to know for himself. Wanted to be able to know, but all he knew was that he wouldn't be able to come to an informed opinion. He played chess when he could, mostly with Bruce Schwarz in his antique shop surrounded by the soft yellow light of a hundred ancient lamps, but he was a middling player. And whether Deep Blue's move was brilliance or error or cheat—he'd just have to listen to wiser men make arguments he didn't fully grasp.

The day's events crowded relentlessly back into his mind. The sudden shocks and shifts. The fear. The blood. Haake's face turning crimson–maroon.

The day had been unusual but somehow appropriately in sync with the life that had come before. He was always Sisyphus dusting himself off, slowly climbing an accelerating slope, then thrown to the bottom again with some sudden new unimaginable cataclysm—lying prostrate on the ground wondering if he had the strength to lift his head up once more.

Bronze was a middling chess player.

He looked over at Carolyn, who was focused on the road ahead, biting down a little on her full bottom lip, right forefinger drumming rapidly on the steering wheel, unconscious of her beauty roiling the very air.

He looked away. Fiddled with his lighter and pack of Chesterfields, but not quite moving to light one.

This whole thing was already spiraling out of control— Kopes dead, Haake dead, an assassin on the loose, he and

Carolyn fleeing with no clear plan—he was going to lose again. He knew it.

If Bronze knew one thing, it was losing. He could feel it coming on like a dog feels an electrical storm. It shivered his bones; his stomach hollowed out, his heart listing and slowly sinking like a floundering ship.

How many times had he lost? Lost and lost again.

Had he really been *recalled to life* just to lose once more?

Bronze was a middling chess player *at best*.

And life itself was a chess game.

One played against a vastly superior opponent.

At first, somewhere in the distant past, there had been vague notions of winning, of glory and pleasure. But as move piles on top of move, the opponent's skill becomes apparent. There is then a period of fierce concentration, of trying to think one's way out of the traps that are laid, layer upon layer, seen only well after the fact, too late—the mind-shattering complexity, the infinite subtlety, the unspeakable depth. And though the face of the opponent is empty space, nullity—you begin to realize what you are up against.

Winning disappears.

You realize that winning was always an illusion. You begin to see shades in the blackness of losing—there are better and worse ways to lose. You see now that the once-shining illusion of winning was always shallow. Tinny. Clichéd. There is grace in losing, you think. Especially a grace in knowing you will lose. At least there is truth. Certainty. A plan to wrap yourself in like a warm blanket on a rainy evening.

You're not like those others—those others who still think they might win. So you play with a rogue's smile on your face. You ... you will be the one to get the wink, the head nod, the curling lip from that hidden master controlling the pieces. He will see the flair in the way you play the hand you're dealt. Maybe he will even offer *his hand* to shake as he tightens his grip, crushing all your backward pawns and hanging pieces to death ... but ... but in time ... finally you start to see the last bit.

He's seen these moves before. They amuse him no more than any other.

Now you move just to move. Move because there are legal moves left to make. There's no hand to shake yours. No ear to hear your offer of resignation. You're endlessly tired. There's no option to pass. Your only option is which of several moves. Decide—which of these several moves? All lead to checkmate.

There's one way life isn't like chess, Bronze thought.

When finally you've made the last pathetic shirking of your king and the checkmate comes. There is no end even there. The game continues. Forever, perhaps. You can't wipe the pieces off the table and start again. You just hang there in checkmate. Not even breathing. Maybe the atoms that make you up vibrate a little, but not you. Your fixed eyes look out over the board. Sometimes you imagine taking back a move you made years ago. Maybe there's still amusement left; you play a new game, this one entirely in your head. You do it all differently. Until you see that you still end up the same. Your opponent's skill is inexhaustible—deep, deep blue without end. A different checkmate, but checkmate nonetheless. You are still, and though your eyes stare, they no longer see the board.

You are blind, insensate, unmoving. You are everywhere covered in dirt.

Bronze looked out the window as the green and brown American countryside raced by. He stole another glance over at Carolyn.

He thought about beauty and mascara.

He thought about blood leaking onto the pavement.

He thought about blood dripping down walls and soaking mattresses.

He thought about dirt and ash.

He thought about losing.

9

OUR KIND OF LIES

MAY 5, 1997

J ust across the border in Ohio, they ate dinner in a diner with no name—just a huge sign jutting upward from the front of the roof reading "DINER" in tall electric purple letters, like something out of a 1970s fever dream.

They sat silently in a booth upholstered in bright red vinyl while the sole waitress leaned on the counter, twirled her dirty yellow hair in one hand, and watched *Touched by an Angel* on a small TV that hung from the ceiling.

He ate a burger. She ate a grilled cheese with sliced tomato.

"I'm going to be sick."

"Sick?"

"Eating all this kind of food."

"Oh. It's good for you. It's good to eat road food every once in a while. Helps you absorb the essence of the country. Puts a pinch of the real America in your bloodstream."

She almost smiled. "Perhaps you're right. I used to eat out on the road all the time when I was young. Maybe I was more of a real American back then. Shifting from place to place. Dreaming these dreams that would catch me up one day, and then ... then I'd live my real life. It was all going to happen just down the road a little, right there, right there around the corner."

She took a deep breath, let it out slowly. "You ever read that book *The Degenerate Arts* by, um ..."

"Benjamin Rendall. Yeah. Yeah, of course. A modern classic. Or so they say."

She was nodding slightly, trying to fix his eyes with hers, but there was something there that was too hard for him to look at directly. She continued, "I always liked that part where he says something like—I'm going to butcher it—he says that America can't be understood from any fixed place. That America is on the move. It's in the churn of the road. The main character is talking about his time living in Texas and in New Brunswick, NJ and all these different places, and then he says that those places in and of themselves aren't America at all. That you can learn about a particular city or state living there, plopped down on your couch, eating at the restaurants, getting your hair cut, going to the grocery store, but that's not America. What America is really —and I think I remember this part more or less exactly— 'America is that feeling flying west on the highway, when New Brunswick and Texas fade to background and you hear the low thumping beat of a continent and the melody of America's undying sirens singing saccharine lies that here or there you might be born again.'"

Carolyn smiled briefly, proud to have remembered the quote. But it was only seconds before her eyes cast downward and Bronze couldn't see their color anymore, just the heavy black of her mascara, and he felt a sadness for her that would crush him if he let it.

"I like those kinds of lies," he said.

She didn't look up. "Me too," she said.

∼

THEY PRETENDED TO be married when they checked into the motel a couple miles outside of Athens, Ohio. They got a room with two queens. Bronze lay on top of the tightly made bed that creaked and reared as he laid himself down, springs jangling overenthusiastically with the slightest movement.

Carolyn was taking a never-ending shower. The door was open a crack and steam seeped out into the room.

A dirty ceiling fan weakly whirred its way in a lazy circle, swirling the steam into a slow chaos of undulating motion.

It was impossible not to think of her in there—the water running over the curves of her body, raining down her face, eyes shut tight, pointed up to the shower head as if in prayer ...

Click.

The shower switched off. After the long sound of the running water, the new silence was startling, a hollow void filling the hotel room until the squeaking of Carolyn's feet banished it once more.

She threw open the door, steam racing out with her. She stood before Bronze wrapped in a cheap white hotel towel. Somewhere within, he wanted to look away, *wanted to want to*, but his eyes never wavered from her.

She looked right back at him.

The mascara was gone.

The moment stretched on and on, his eyes stuck immovably on Carolyn's dripping black hair, the enigma of her cheekbones and soft lips, the line where her towel pressed against her breasts.

His ego found itself severed from its place of primacy—a silent coup d'état within. And, set adrift, his conscious thoughts curdled, turned loose and lazy. He thought about the substantial weight of a good whisky tumbler in your hand and the way it felt when you first sat down at a dark wooden bar and the barman tossed you a napkin, the possibilities infinitely vast.

Vague notions of Deep Blue drifted in, his transistors spinning out endless 1s and 0s, floating by weightless as clouds. Contemplations of hard marble chess pieces jerking around the black and white board, their movements preordained by arbitrary laws of physics.

Then a frenzy of images.

Bronze hidden in a small square of black shade as the sun burned the world around him. Esther the size of a giant, looming over Bronze, arms akimbo, staring furiously downwards. Blood pouring out of Roger Haake and turning the sidewalk into a red river; blood dripping down the arm of Bronze's judogi in '76—most of all, blood in '88 seeping down dingy walls, saturating mattresses, blood in blackened room after blackened room that followed one after another like a maze he would never leave.

He imagined Iris standing somewhere in the room watching him and Carolyn, deep blue eyes never flinching, seeing all that was visible and all that was not.

The part of Bronze that called itself *I* might think of any number of things. Ponder and ponder and ponder, finding an end only in death. But Bronze—the *real* Bronze—did not think at all, did not bother with rebuttals or reimagine past catastrophes. The real Bronze was infinitely sharp and perfectly singular. The real Bronze lived in the image of Carolyn, in the sound of her breath, in the citrus smell of the shampoo in her hair and the sweet skim of soap on her skin, in the touch of his own skin against his clothes, in the heat rising from his groin, in the weight pressing in all directions upon his heart.

They were both perfectly still. Neither looked away.

Bronze moved first.

10

THE SPEECH

MAY 4, 1997

The assassin met the man in the blue chalk-stripe suit at the Rivoli Bar in the Ritz-Carlton, London. Just on the edge of Mayfair. A straight shot to Buckingham Palace or the Wellington arch or 10 Downing Street. The Rivoli Bar was supposed to look like the inside of a jewelry box. It was all golds and browns and old sagging British couples.

The assassin wore a dark navy suit, a white shirt, and a maroon tie. The man in the blue chalk-stripe suit wore a light pink shirt and a cornflower blue tie adorned with tiny white pinwheels. It made you wonder, why would a man dress like this when ordering up murder?

The assassin liked the Rivoli Bar. Or at least he liked that it was effective for his purposes. It was a known place but often quiet, especially now on a Sunday afternoon. Most importantly, there were plenty of good corners to give the speech.

The man in the navy chalk-stripe suit and candy-colored shirt and tie combination beat around the bush for about the usual amount of time. He sweat about the usual amount. He tried to the usual degree to hide his anxiety under a show of hearty masculine world-weariness.

The assassin nodded at the appropriate places. He listened silently. He drank seltzer water with lime. The man in the blue chalk-stripe suit had made a show of imbibing a long quaff of his reddish specialty cocktail garnished with burnt orange peel. But as he circled the question at hand, as he sweat more and more and the pink shirt darkened at the armpits, cold drops falling from hot skin onto starched cotton, the assassin noticed that he left the alcohol-laden beverage alone, moisture condensing on the glass as the once near-freezing liquid turned lukewarm.

The man asked the question.

The only one that mattered.

The assassin made the speech.

He said (body perfectly still, back against the chair in an elegant, relaxed posture, voice even and without emotion): "You have managed to contact me, so you must know something of me and my reputation. But before you proceed, you must understand the context in which I am typically hired. I give people, be they private interests or governments, an option they would not otherwise have.

"Say, for instance, you are a government. Say you are at war in some poverty-stricken country. Or not at war. But there is this man there. He is making plans to come to your country and blow up a school, a hospital, a concert for teenage girls. You want to get this man, but you are faced with a terrible choice.

"He is camped out on the top two floors of a building somewhere. Every man on those two floors is a terrorist. But their wives are there too. And there are three floors below those floors. Innocent people. And, in fact, that part is strategic. Done to complicate your calculus. So let us say there are fifty people in this building—the main villain you care about and around a dozen of his accomplices. Maybe six or seven wives that you would prefer not to kill, but ... they know who they are in bed with.

"Then there are thirty other people. Men just going about their lives trying to eke out a living in the hellscape in which they were born. Their wives. Their children. Innocent people. But you have got an obligation. To your own people. Your own innocent people. So you think, should I send a plane over, drop a bomb on the building, almost surely kill the guy, prevent the horrors of a terrorist attack? And more than the attack itself, the knock-on effects that will follow. The fear. The heightened security. Economic decline.

"And in dropping the bomb, you kill about thirty innocent people with high probability. The left in your country protests outside government buildings with placards and sing-song chants. You answer difficult questions. But they do not understand the consequences of not acting. Do not want to understand. Not really.

"Or you do not drop the bomb. Spare those people over there but take the risk that you will somehow be able to pick apart the threads of this monster's conspiracy some other way.

"It is a tough choice. I am certainly glad I do not have to face choices like that.

"I do not make choices. I receive a contract. That is it. All choice is gone once it is in effect. That is the deal I have made with the universe. Or it with me.

"I am simply there to be a third way. A somewhat more pleasant alternative in an otherwise unthinkable predicament.

"Take the previous scenario. You contract with me: I go to the building—alone. I go to the building and I kill the target. Now it is chaos in there. I do not know which men are innocent and which are accomplices. I do not know which women are just trying to survive another day and which have AK-47s under their garments. Which children are running for their lives and which are running toward me strapped with explosives.

"They have all got to die. Everyone I see. The contract cannot have any contingency.

"Remember the other option—bombs do not have contingencies in their contracts.

"You hire me—I come, I go. The terrorist will be dead. As will all his men that do not break and run. Most of the wives. And it is critical that you understand this part. The vast majority of the innocent people as well. You are in that building. You are in my way. You die.

"But think about it. Let us say I get a clean sweep. I get the guy, I get all the men, I get the wives, and out of necessity, I kill twenty out of thirty innocent men, women, and children. Sounds horrible. But really it is ten lives saved. Ten lives the bomb would have taken.

"The visual is worse. If you were to watch the bombing play out on a screen, well—that little boom, a gray dust cloud in the air, no blood or guts ... that looks a lot better than seeing me walk from room to room, shooting sobbing women and eight-year-old girls in the head.

"This is not a hypothetical. These are things I have done and will do again. But hard as it is to stomach visually, it is the humane thing to do. It is why I have the reputation that led you here. I am an option. And, often, I am the one thinking men choose.

"So walk away right now, as you say—no harm, no foul. Otherwise write the names down. Write the location down. Tell me the time frame. Make the payment. That is it."

The man in the blue chalk-stripe suit had gone silent the usual way they went silent. He signaled to the waiter.

"I need a pen and something to write on. Anything will do. A cocktail napkin even."

The waiter hustled off and the man in the blue chalk-stripe suit looked at the assassin. There must have been some hidden iron in the man after all, because he did not blink or look away from the assassin's eyes.

"There's a bit of mess to clean up. The time frame will be quite tight."

11

THE LODGER

IRIS

I hadn't been in the basement apartment in years. The once-familiar space was strangely transfigured. It felt like a violation to come in here. Like seeing your father naked on the operating table. The very air was altered—thickened.

Bruce and I didn't turn enough lights on, as if leaving the rooms in relative darkness was a sign of respect for the absent Bronze.

I could not help my eyes. They roamed about the walls, the furniture, especially the bookshelves. Bruce pointed to the boxes in the corner of the living room. "Guess we can start on these."

"Uh huh." My mouth replied on autopilot as I drifted over to the bookshelves and ran my hand along the spines. Old paperbacks mostly. Bronze had seemingly every Hemingway novel, a good number of Stephen King, a copy of *The Long Dark* that I'd given him, a whole little Loretta Laughlin section too, although they were annoyingly pressed up against several of Henry Baldur's hyper-formulaic *Jack Winters* spy novels; then there was Ben Rendall, my one-time writing instructor, represented with his best book—*The Degenerate Arts*—some Vonnegut, some Tolstoy, and ... just lying there naked to the air, pushed to one corner without adornment, the bronze medal. *How could he be so careless with it?*

I began to reach for it but stopped. Shook my head. *Remember your purpose here.* I left the bronze medal where it was and walked over to Bruce and the boxes. "I'll start on this end. You want to take the other?"

"Sure."

But as I walked over to the last of the boxes, I saw a distinctive box at a remove from the others—it was jammed in the corner just before the door to the bedroom.

The box had the same general appearance as the others, like it too had come from the *Post*, but it was much older, dented and graying.

There were secrets of a different kind in there.

If I tugged on one loose thread of Bronze, how long before he fully unspooled before me? Could I ever untangle him? Could I ever see more than layer after layer after endless layer of skin and surface?

IT WAS HARD to remember a time before Bronze. He had only lived below me for about three years now, but the memories from those years seemed to occupy the greater portion of my mind. And it wasn't even until my fortieth birthday party, probably eight months or so into his lease on my basement apartment, before I interacted with him beyond the surface or transactional level. But I did wonder about him. How could I not? Down below me all the time, buried in the dirt below my feet, catching glimpses of each other by the stairs up to my door or down to his.

So when I really met him for the first time at my party, he already seemed to have a level of inevitability about him. An air.

Even as a mere charcoal sketch, he occupied significant space in my mind before he filled out into three dimensions of color.

What I remember most about him from the birthday party was the way he moved. I would say catlike, but that image just vaguely waves in the right direction. Wolflike is probably closer. But not the jogging "wolf pack on the run" motion—a lone wolf cut off from his pack. Hunting. Downwind of his prey. Stalking, muscles loose and agile, body moving with the appearance of lazy competence, a dose of taut, rigid power but plenty of lithe agility too, not some aging football player's stiffness. Still, the tautness was coiled, ready to spring—a knowing trade-off toward brutal quickness and away from either the pure power of the strongman or the flexible suppleness of the marathon runner.

I had already known he was handsome, but he was the kind of man you could know was handsome just from seeing the back of his neck or his hands. Other body parts would likely do as well. His calves, probably. Maybe even his ears. Every piece of him sent the same message.

His physicality communicated completeness, the parts and the whole seamlessly integrated. He did not betray the turmoil of his interior or any sense of unfinished becoming. He might have a boyish grin or boyish pursuits, but from the way he placed his feet to the way his hands moved through the air, to the very smile or lack of a smile he chose to use, he knew exactly who he was. Or that was my impression.

And I remember he brought a gift—a bottle of chilled champagne. A few guests had brought wine, but I made sure to try his. It was bone dry and quite good. I helped him put it on ice when he first came in. There was a moment when I was pouring the ice into the silver bucket I have for display and never use when the backs of our hands touched. He didn't turn to me or make a joke of it. But I did notice a small private smile flash across his face, as if perhaps the jolt of electricity that had shot through me as I was so suddenly and unexpectedly brought into contact with this walking mystery had had its own echo in him.

He chatted a short time with me but not too long, knowing that I was the hostess and required to go about like some grand butterfly. (Exhausting to the extreme for an introverted writer like myself; after the party I collapsed onto my bed fast asleep without taking my clothes off or opening the covers. When I awoke in the middle of the night to pee, I was completely disoriented and almost fell off onto the floor.) But I caught snippets of him moving about with those sure, wolflike movements, listening and nodding at Mrs. Fournier and now at Jack Rolling, the Hansons, and the Edelsteins.

I never saw Bronze drink a drop of his delicious champagne; only later did I understand the full significance of this. He carried a glass of ice and clear liquid about with him, which I saw him refill in the kitchen sink. Early in the evening, long before Mrs. Fournier became intoxicated and made an incoherent speech about the death of letter writing, Bronze had made his excuses to me and thanked me for a lovely evening. He looked me straight in the eyes while he spoke and just about shattered my social butterfly exterior. There was no good reason why he should have had such an effect on me, yet it was undeniable. And being a natural ruminator, I bandied the image of his eyes on mine back and forth from one lobe of my brain to the other, fruitlessly attempting to understand the meaning beneath the surface.

After the party we started running into each other more. A real friendship, which for adults was always so tenuous in the beginning, having to be built up from weak embers that might blow out with the slightest miscue, began to catch into a more or less consistent fire. Both of our professions allowed a certain latitude in our working hours. And the deal was mostly sealed when we ran into each other each heading alone to a matinee at the Georgetown Cinema on the Potomac. We both happened to be going to see *The Bridges of Madison County* and there seemed nothing to be done but to sit next to each other.

I turned absolutely scarlet when we first saw Meryl Streep naked, looking at herself in the mirror. I instinctually turned to him—he wasn't going to take his eyes off the screen for a moment, yet I could tell he could feel my eyes upon him by the little quirk of his lips. By way of answering my look, he just popped another round of Sno-Caps into his mouth and chewed through an enormous, now truly wolflike grin.

This was the start of an irregular tradition. Every couple of weeks or so, on a Thursday afternoon, we'd go to the movies together. Sometimes there would be nothing good playing at the theater and one of us would pick something out from Blockbuster and we would watch from separate ends of my couch with Diet Cokes or pink lemonades and a big bowl of popcorn between us.

On one of those Blockbuster nights—I think it might have been during Kieslowski's *Blue*—he let it slip about the memoir he was working on. I carefully but firmly offered my services as first reader and sounding board. Little did I know the horrors I would find within those chapters as they slowly trickled like tree sap against the flow of gravity from his underground rooms encased in dirt and hard concrete up into the safe light of my reading lamp.

FOR A TIME, what was now Bronze's apartment had been my writing studio. After my financially ruinous divorce from George, my accountant had recommended returning it to its original purpose as an income-generating basement apartment.

The idea scandalized me at first. I was an adult; what would it be like to share a portion of my living space with a stranger? With an eye toward my profession, the word *lodger* entered into my mind. *But t'wasn't the almighty that lifted her nightie, it was Roger the Lodger, by god.*

I kept writing down in the basement for a while after George left. It had always had a sense of silence, of true seclusion. I used to phone Sam, my old college boyfriend, from down there where George wouldn't hear before I realized he didn't give a hoot who I called. Sam used to laugh and say, "It's your Fortress of Solitude." I didn't know what he meant, which led to one of Sam's classically overelaborate monologues about the mythology of Superman.

With George in the house, energy seemed to focus in the basement, but with him gone it became diffuse throughout all the halls and rooms. Always elusive. Sometimes seeming to constellate midway up the second flight of stairs, only to rush away to new climes.

Now there was silence everywhere.

I could write anywhere, go to bed whenever I wanted, eat as I pleased. Before, I had always complained to George of his constantly going to bed late—as if he was purposefully sabotaging my work, banging around in the bathroom, turning lights on and off, just generally *rummaging*. With George gone, I found myself staying up until two in the morning. Sometimes I would just crash at eight thirty p.m. and sleep until seven the next morning. I'd wake at three a.m. and spend an hour writing down a dream to later weave into a novel.

Before I had needed a tabernacle of silence. Now, if anything, what was wanted was a focused place of noise. There was silence everywhere, only punctuated by the creaking of floorboards that haunted my steps.

I began to write in the solarium at the top of my row house, which had always been intended as my office but had for some reason seemed poison to creativity when I was under the occupation of George. Now the light cascading down on me seemed to elevate, whereas before it had only blinded. I began to think of the basement apartment as a place of darkness, a place of occlusion.

I had written cheap romances in the basement. In the solarium, I would write something *more*.

Then Bronze had come. After the conversation with my accountant, I had been toying with the idea of placing a vacancy ad in the paper for a few months, not sure if I would ever actually do it, when I had gotten a call from the Katzes, who had heard about my intentions from Ben Rendall. Joan Katz had practically bellowed on the phone, "Iris, for heaven's sakes! Don't put an ad in the paper—who knows what kind of crazy you'll wind up with? We've got the perfect candidate here. Cal Goldberg, a true mensch if there's ever been one. Everyone calls him Bronze, hell if I know why. A bit down on his luck, but you know what, Iris, I am very optimistic about him, very ... very optimistic."

THE WRITING WAS NOT GOING WELL. Neither Loretta Laughlin nor Henry Gordon was easily banished from the mind. In particular, Loretta played upon my insecurities. "Write a romance at the same time as *the masterpiece*," she whispered. And I had given in to that fear, intending to spend half a day on what I was so far calling *White Light* and half a day on whatever Loretta pushed for. But soon I'd find myself losing a whole week to her. Knowing that I was avoiding the hard task with an easier one, I resolved to banish her altogether, only to find untoward elements of eroticism building within *White Light* itself.

I was flailing about, writing random desultory brainstorms, desperately trying to pierce into some deeper portion of my brain that had seemed so readily available when I was young, but now layer upon layer of complication had built, clogging my access with the plaque of a billion thoughts. My energy was dispersed and incoherent. I had siphoned my strength into a thousand characters that now refused to enter deep freeze and defiantly milled about my brain like they owned the place.

So I would hide beneath my bed like a child searching for something within, I'd enter the solarium at midnight to stare at the moon, I'd do breathing exercises, listen to guided meditation tapes, sit halfway down a flight of stairs imaging all the places in between things, and most of all I would gaze down upon the floorboards, through them ... More and more, in the agitation of my unconscious blockages, the concept of Bronze came to dominate my mind.

This morning ...

I felt Bronze prowling beneath the floorboards.

I stood in stocking feet and imagined that his motion did truly vibrate up and through my body. I walked slowly along the floor, not lifting my feet but feeling the wood slide under the pads of my feet.

Bronze was down there. I could almost picture his physicality. The dark brown, almost black hair. The lean musculature. The broad shoulders. His actions were blurred, though. His movements, in my mind's eye, were like the swirl of shadow and the afterburn of direct sun.

I lay down upon the floor. He seemed to pulse upward like a steady heartbeat, rubbing his essence along his wall. Why was he moving so steadily? Why did he carry a shadow wherever he went? Was that a stumble? Was he drinking again? Or perhaps his basement apartment was full of case files?

Something snapped to attention within me. I realized the

absurdity of lying on the wooden floor, sat up, paused for a breath, and slowly stood. I cut myself loose from the unseen umbilical cord tethering me to Bronze below the floor. I let him wander down there alone, unseen and unknown. I went into the kitchen and turned the coffee maker on.

I leaned back on the counter and watched it drip—petulant and slow at first, and then with a raging, shouting speed. I thought of lying on the floor feeling for Bronze. How it was almost easy to fall into a dream there on the ground with the townhouse stretching above and my tenant rubbing against the walls below.

How easy it was to dream—random vibrations and singing neurons. And when we latch on to one ... when we see visions in so much meaningless undulation of memory and fear and hope, are we walking the path our unconscious has opened for us? Leading us into that deepest underground river, that swiftly running stream that turns nothing into something? Opening our eyes to a cascade of synchronicity, of infinite meaning and eternally recurring revelation? Or are we walking a kind of insanity, seeing form where there is only randomness? Schizophrenic illusions. And maybe it's both. Maybe it starts with an illusion, a grain of nonsense, then the great pattern maker works on it and smooths it over and smooths it over until the nonsense is covered in layers of perfect milky pearl that would never have come but for the insanity at its core.

And yes, I could dream. I could dream of Bronze and almost hesitate to walk down there and bring clarity to him. For in the dream, among the moving shadows and the circle of burning light wherever you turned, you could almost let him be. Let him forever remain unformed and unchallenged, just a nameless struggle that would never be revealed or resolved. And he could remain there, pure in the mind's eye, hanging just below the floorboards, reaching upwards for something ... anything.

And that might have been enough for some people.

Not for me. I felt Bronze down there in that buried basement of my mind. I had to see more. Had to see clearly through the admixture of light and dark. Maybe I'd drop my hook through the cracks in the floor and pull out the mystery from a faceless sea. And in the unforgiving air, I might kill the fish if I were not careful in my handling. And perhaps it was wiser to let be what would be.

But that was not in my nature. No, I must have my theory, always another theory of the unknowable.

BRUCE'S ARRIVAL HAD dispelled the usual haunting meshes of the afternoon—the bottomless dread that comes when the writing doesn't. I greeted him warmly, as I would any distraction that emerges at such a time. But Bruce's face was ashen at the door, asking to come in and promising explanations of a dire sort.

I had previously met Bruce Schwarz on two occasions. The first was on a brilliant spring day about a year ago when meandering around the outskirts of Georgetown. I had come upon Bronze emerging from a Starbucks followed by a shorter man, his face dominated by sad drooping eyes. Though I later learned Bruce and Bronze were almost exactly the same age, the difference in height and Bruce's natural congeniality made him seem like a younger brother. We chatted a pleasant minute or two and that was about it.

Sometime later I had mentioned in passing wanting to buy a lamp and Bronze had suggested I try Bruce's antique shop. I went, if I am being honest, mostly to pump Bruce for information on Bronze. I was not disappointed in that regard, Bruce having been Bronze's best childhood friend and full of stories.

I also wound up with a lovely art nouveau lamp.

Bruce had impeccable taste.

I WAS ABLE to resist the old box in Bronze's bedroom for the length of time it took me to go through two of the new ones reading about the details of Billy Kopes's congressional campaigns, the impossible wealth of his old Virginia family, his sponsorship of a bill expanding Buy American provisions for defense contracts in the late '80s, his positions on abortion and tobacco and taxes, and speculation about a senate run in '98.

I tried to look casual, stretching a bit as I raised myself from my reading position on the armchair. Bruce looked over from the couch, shook his head, and tut-tutted as I made my way to the edge of the bedroom and the old box hiding there. But he watched me with undisguised interest as I lifted the top off the box.

"You think this is one of the ones we're supposed to look through?" I called, both of us knowing I was creating a convenient excuse.

When I saw what was in there, I almost immediately shut it again.

It was the raw, unvarnished material of Bronze's memoir. It was all his old clippings and research on Caleb Keaton—on Rachel Boyd and all the other girls.

Some of the papers were just cut-out *Post* articles, the bylines mostly reading Calvin Goldberg. Some were Bronze's notes, but there were also police reports, interview transcripts, even a forensic psych profile of Keaton.

Close to the top was a Xerox of a letter Keaton must have sent to the *Post*—a letter they had, of course, never published. It was dated May 29, 1988—after Rachel Boyd but before the massacre.

I read it and wished I hadn't.

Free yourselves, Brothers! I awoke from mud, same as you. And like you, no sooner did I eject from mother's toothless sucking maw than did I have my mind twisted to the whims of Cabal and Coven. But though I am meat as you are meat, I have seen through the scheme layered schemes. Through pilgrimages of soul fire and icy descents to the blackest heart of this unseen empire I have seen TRUTH. No, this is not my singular privilege. It is an obligation for all good men! We must sever the unsleeping channels to our skulls that pulsate the sex sedatives, the corrosive alchemy by which we become our own slavers.

Brothers! Look within your whimpering hearts. You know this to be true. These rutting-moaning-mindless submissives about you serve this slave state in their hallucinogenic ignorance; they possess no claim to the natural rights of free man. And only free men can lay claim to life, so though it may falsely tug at our softened hearts, we must be willing to sacrifice all manners of smiling and crying and hip-swinging meat to the ultimate ends, for liberation, for the final freedom that is to come.

The Coven's in Washington. It sits its haunches straight down upon our illusory seat of government. They were in Paris until their orgies went too far. They've learned a greater subtlety since then. They were in London till decadence toppled those white powdered clowns. If only they'd listened to the Ripper as I plead you listen to me, they might have ended things then and there. Instead the decrepit British passed it to us in the war like some virulent strain of VD.

Do not believe the television, the radio—my God, do not believe the papers. The movies—useful tools to work the levers of your subconscious. There's nothing in their grotesque music. Look for the undeniable. Look for my actions and words and you shall know how to follow. I shall extirpate those that I can. Witch and beta witch

submissive alike. Maybe I shall find a path all the way to the
warlock Cabal itself—but likely that shall be your work. As I baptize
by the blade, you shall baptize with fire …

I stopped reading. It went on and on and on like this. I knew where these thoughts ended. I did not need to dig through the box to know Bronze had the pictures of the massacre buried away somewhere near the bottom.

When I looked up from the paper, Bruce was standing next to me. He must have seen my shaking hands and watering eyes.

I dropped the paper and fell into Bruce's arms. He held me and patted my back. His arms felt strong and warm, holding me there.

"Oh, honey," he said. "It's OK. It's OK."

It was my first physically intimate moment in half a decade.

12

THE MACHINE

MAY 6, 1997

Mark Roth waited and hurt.

His hands, wrists, and elbows hurt from fiercely applying pressure to Peter Gallagher's wound. His right shoulder hurt from where he'd slammed it into Bronze trying to get him down to the ground and out of sight of the shooter.

His eyes hurt from his glaucoma drops. His knees hurt—the right one from lack of cartilage, the left one from the lingering effects of a torn ACL, both old football injuries. Whenever he was on the move too much, as he was today, his lower back hurt from a herniated disc that threatened to worsen to the point of necessitating surgery. When he worked at his desk too long, he re-irritated a pinched nerve in his neck that shot electric pulses of searing fire down his left shoulder to his left pinkie and ring finger. He'd taken a gunshot wound in the same shoulder in '88. It throbbed whenever it rained. As did the shrapnel wound in his right ankle and calf, acquired ninety-eight days into his tour in Vietnam and good enough to keep him out of the jungle for the rest of the war. Wearing shorts on vacation, he'd tell kids at the beach or pool that were bold enough to ask that he'd been bitten by an alligator and to stay the hell out of northern Florida.

Roth sat on an uncomfortable bench with a view of the Lincoln Memorial, attempting to block his proximity to the Vietnam War Memorial from his mind. If he got too close, his compulsion would take over and he'd have to visit the names there, and that was good for at least an hour-long spiral into guilt and depression and horrific visions that he simply couldn't afford today.

Instead he thought of Lincoln sitting in the white marble building in front of him. Tourists funneled in and out. Lincoln sat and watched. All day like that, no matter the weather. Sitting and watching and disappointed in what he saw.

397.

That's what he saw.

397 murders last year—more than a murder a day in a city of under 600,000. Per capita, that was six times New York City's number. There'd been over 800,000 people living in DC once. The bad old crack cocaine days were finally starting to fade, but those people weren't ever coming back. Maybe new ones would come eventually, but Roth would be long since retired by then.

397 and how many solved? A little more than half, perhaps? And of those solved, how many were caught basically bloody-handed? Roth thanked god for all the cop TV shows and detective novels and murder mystery movies. Kept the public thinking they couldn't get away with murder. When it was more like a flip of a coin.

Roth caught sight of a gray pinstripe suit approaching on his right periphery. He didn't bother to look over, even as it closed the distance and stood almost directly above him for a moment, sighed, and sat down on the bench.

Roth spoke without turning. "I thought you FBI boys weren't

supposed to wear pinstripes, just navy suits and white shirts and red foulard ties."

Roth finally looked over at Special Agent Leo Rossetti, who beamed back at him with that full head of perfectly slicked-back black hair and those kind brown eyes under heavy eyebrows.

"Why you always got to bust my balls, Roth? You know I love you, right?"

"It's the hair."

"I knew it. And completely uncalled for, by the way. My father's balder than you. Both grandfathers too. I assumed my whole life I had till maybe twenty-five with this hair, but I can't help a miracle. Isn't it enough that I had to live in fear of it? And I'll tell you what, thinking it was coming wasn't all a bad thing. Made me appreciate my youth in a way you don't see these days —not with this generation, at least."

Roth was nodding. Rossetti always had a way of getting him on his wavelength. And Roth was glad of it. He would much rather be on Rossetti's wavelength than the Roth equivalent.

"They're all so goddamned sullen. What do they have to be sullen about?"

"Prosperity! That's the problem. It breeds contempt. When there aren't big hulking problems to rebel against, the youth go after the little ones, and that'll just drive you bananas in the end. We had Jim Crow and Vietnam, they have ... I don't know ..." Rossetti pointed at two angry-looking teenagers, both with boxer shorts hanging out of their loose jeans. "A lack of effective belting?"

They were both smiling now. It was a shame they had work to do.

"So, what have you got for me?" Roth asked.

"What have I got? I'm the FBI. You tell me what *you* got, then maybe, after, in due course of time, I tell you what I got. Capiche?"

"OK, well, what I've got's not good."

Roth took a deep breath and brought out his notepad for reference.

"So, as you know, Kopes, dead, banks of the Potomac, Sunday morning. You boys come in and take the body for an autopsy. We start hunting down timeline and location. We were able to place him at a Republican Party fundraising event for dinner on Saturday night, then his driver took him home at about nine thirty p.m. And that was it. Billy Kopes lives at 30th and N, so that's less than a ten-minute walk to the Potomac right around the Georgetown Waterfront Park. We figured maybe he went for an evening stroll, had a heart attack, and fell in. Maybe he got jumped by some kids, had a heart attack, and fell in. He's a young guy, but the rumor was that he wasn't exactly as averse to cocaine as his stance on the war on drugs would have you believe, so maybe a heart attack isn't out of the question. The body was pretty beat up when we found it, but there was no gunshot wound, no knife wound. We figured it could have happened as he bopped around along the bottom of the river.

"Then Bronze Goldberg comes to me and places Carolyn Haake at Kopes's house around ten to eleven p.m., engaged in vigorous extramarital activity. After, Bronze follows her to James Howell's Foggy Bottom apartment for more of the same, with time-stamped photos and everything, so she's pretty much out the window as a suspect but supplies more than a modicum of motive. Yesterday we followed up with Howell. He's a big swinging-dick lobbyist for the defense industry, and after some equivocation he copped to the affair but denied any further knowledge of malfeasance. Meanwhile about 300 people place Roger Haake at said Republican fundraiser through at least midnight.

"We also met with one Zachary Jackson, a young law professor at Georgetown who moonlights as a political operative for the Democrats. Bronze had photographed Jackson with Carolyn Haake earlier in the evening, and when questioned by us, Jackson became quite agitated upon learning of Carolyn's affair with Billy Kopes. He claims to have spent the night home alone. We did track down a Chinese delivery guy that can place Jackson at his home at around eight p.m.—apparently he's a regular and likes sesame chicken—but no other alibi for after that.

"He's certainly got a motive, but I don't like Jackson for this. He makes a comfortable living, and though passionately involved in Democratic Party politics, I don't see sufficient money or connections. The events of Monday morning, Roger Haake's murder in broad daylight by what appeared to be a highly trained assassin, seem to point in a different direction."

Rossetti's face had gone entirely slack as he concentrated on what Roth was saying. "What about Carolyn Haake?"

"Given her affair with Kopes and the implications of Roger Haake's assassination, Bronze and I agreed that Carolyn Haake was in immediate and grave danger. There was little time and, given that the assassin seemed to know in advance that we were meeting Roger Haake, concerns about potential compromise in the PD and, uh, other involved agencies. So we arranged for her immediate departure under less-than-ideal circumstances.

"Our fears that the assassin may have been targeting her next have been at least partially confirmed, as upon obtaining a warrant and searching Haake's home, we found subtle but fairly clear evidence of a break-in, but no workable forensics.

"And that's where the thing stands on our end. Once we'd communicated our initial timeline to the FBI team, they took over forensics at Kopes's house as well as the autopsy.

"Now we're trying to work our way further back on the Kopes timeline and digging into Carolyn and Roger Haake. We've got absolutely zero on the assassin who took Haake out."

Rossetti was nodding. There was something unusual in the look of his eyes. Fear, maybe?

"That's where I might be able to help you out. I'm not directly on the FBI team handling the Kopes case; I don't work the purely domestic stuff."

Roth shifted in his seat in a futile attempt to get into a comfortable position. The pinched nerve in his neck had started firing down his arm. In all these long years, Rossetti had never quite told him in black-and-white terms what exact role he really occupied at the FBI.

"That's why your call was such a pleasant surprise, Leo."

Rossetti's lips lifted in a mechanical imitation of a smile. "Not so pleasant, I'm afraid. This assassin you have been unfortunate enough to encounter ... we believe we know who he is. Well, roughly at least. The MO and forensics on the bullets used in the K Street shootout indicate it may be a particularly disagreeable individual I have the ill fortune of knowing, albeit only by reputation.

"We do not know his real name. We don't know what country he's from. He's professionally known by a veritable slew of names, nicknames, and code names but most commonly the Merkuj or the Seytan—the Assassin or the Devil. I once heard a British counterpart call him the Automatic Assassin. But in the States, in particular circles within the CIA, he is primarily known as the Machine, or that's at least the code name used when *we* apparently hired him to, and I quote, 'supplement' NATO airstrikes against the Bosnian Serb Army during the recent Yugoslavian unpleasantness. But he's also known to do swift business with Russian oligarchs, Saudi princes, African warlords, that kind of clientele, in addition to the occasional sovereign nation. He seems to work alone, to have absolutely no regard for ideology, and to be brutally efficient. Despite the movies, the world's a cold place for an international assassin for hire—life spans tend to be cut rather short, but the Machine seems to have maintained robust health, with the big boy players like the CIA and the recently rebranded KGB perhaps finding him more useful than not.

"Though it seems he may have gone too far this time. If the Haake and Kopes killings are indeed connected, the Machine's involvement in multiple assassinations on American soil is perhaps biting the hand that feeds you a little too aggressively, even for a favorite pet."

Rossetti paused, jaw rhythmically clenching and unclenching.

"There's something more. Something you alluded to that has gotten under my skin as well. There hasn't been a federally elected official murdered since Congressman Allard Lowenstein in 1980. And the killer was just some guy who'd gone schizo and stood there at the scene of the crime waiting calmly for the police to come arrest him. Before that, Congressman Leo Ryan at Jonestown. Before that, the Kennedys. And not a one of them in DC.

"Now we've got a congressman dead, Haake dead—maybe the hottest shit unelected power broker of the moment—here, *in DC*, and the killer is a trained *foreign* assassin with a history of working with the CIA. If this is allowed to go on, if this *Machine* has been hired by the Russians or the Iranians or the North Koreans or whoever, if he succeeds in another high-level assassination ... I worry. I worry about our international reputation, about cooler heads failing to prevail, about escalation ... I make my living worrying. But right now, I'm worrying about the worst thing, about that thing inside all the others, about that thing that sends you turning and turning in circles. I'm worrying about who on my side might not really be—about who I can trust."

Roth massaged the palm of his left hand with the thumb and

forefinger of his right hand. "You're about to say, 'But I can trust you.'"

"But I can trust you," Rossetti said.

Roth looked away from his old friend and back toward Lincoln. "My friend, this is well above my pay grade."

Silence reigned for several beats. Eventually Roth's eyes drifted back over to Rossetti, who was staring into the distance somewhere to the right of Lincoln's marble house, just about in the direction of that unseen wall full of names that used to be boys. Rossetti was silent for a few more moments, then he shook his head and turned back to Roth, big black eyebrows drawn down in a look of sympathetic commiseration.

"My friend, you know as well as me, it's the worst paid that do all the real work ... all the worst work too."

13

THE END OF THE PARTY

MAY 6, 1997

C *ome with me*, she said.

They had left the motel that morning and driven to the Cincinnati bus station, a low, flat, colorless building at the corner of Gilbert Avenue and E. Court Street.

Why Cincinnati and not Columbus? Why Ohio and not Kentucky?

There was no reason. They had to go one way or another. Left or right, north or south—direction had no meaning. They just went.

Come with me, she said.

Fluorescent white light flickered down from a ceiling that was somehow both too high and too low. It seemed to push down on you at the same time as it left you floating disembodied in space. The floor was made of copper-colored squares, dirty and hard on the feet. The walls were off white, harshly cast in glare and shadow from the lights above. The place was almost empty, so the stanchions meant to set off various waiting lines had the feeling of random obstacles arranged to confound the mind.

Come with me.

He told her to buy a bus ticket. Don't even tell him where she's going. Don't tell *anyone*. They made sure she had enough cash to last for a time without the use of a credit card or bank. She could pawn some of her jewelry if need be. She'd run out before long, but there was nothing to be done about that. The longer she lasted off the grid, the less chance they'd come after her. The longer he would have to solve the case and set her free again.

He wrote his phone number on the back of an old receipt. When he handed her the paper, she took his hand and not the number.

Come with me, she said.

And he almost had.

He could never forget that—he had almost gone with her.

Or maybe that was an illusion. A trick of the mind. A delusion of choice.

Still, that sense of choice made it all so much more painful later. Later, lying in bed at night, when the knife of the memory would stab into his gut, it would twist and turn, opening the wound ever wider; it would oscillate back and forth with the endlessly reverberating thought:

She said, "Come with me." And what if I had?

THE FIRST GAS station he stopped at was a smear of concrete and peeling paint dropped at random in flat grasslands. The sky was enormous above, half blue with veins of thin white clouds and spots of black birds visible at great distances, the other half sharply defined in a jagged sheet of gray–black cloud that sucked away at the wet heat to the west, with a dry, cold wind kicking up grit and dust.

Bronze stood with the gas pump handle in his hand looking out over the unbroken country and up at the cracked sky.

He felt like a solitary animal bracing himself, feeling in his bones the dark portents of air and sky. The animal in him knew he should go to ground, look for a hollow or any low place he might hide.

Instead he was running. Running right back to the swamp, to the east, into the gray–black that sheathed the land in a bone-weary dread.

The tank full and the attendant paid, Bronze got back into Bruce's old tan car.

He drove into the black–gray sky. Soon the blue was gone entirely and there was only the monotonous sheet of dark cloud. The air outside the car had turned harsh, whipping about like daggers, ready for frenzy.

Then the sky itself began to crackle and seethe.

Ahead Bronze saw a great billowing structure of black cloud. Red and white lightning arced from a black tower to a black bulging tendril and back with rhythmic regularity like some unfathomable war between titan and god.

Bronze drove toward the great black cloud and the searing flashes of light that seemed to dance along ahead, always the same distance in front of him, leading him on.

He lit a Chesterfield and cracked his window, and now he could feel the ominous air prying its hands into the open slit while the cigarette smoke lashed about grotesquely.

He finished the cigarette quickly and without satisfaction, tossed it onto the pavement, and rolled the window back up. There was nothing left to do but think and so many things he did not want to think about.

He did his best to block Carolyn from his mind, but that just opened the door to Esther.

Esther. The way she had looked yesterday with her hair

tucked back over her ears. The way she had looked in the old back then with her hair cut short, especially during the war.

The differences and the sameness.

Those last days of the war, it had seemed like a beginning. He would say it was really the beginning of the end, but the truth was less and more than that. Less dramatic and more depressing. It had been, like everything else, he supposed, just another bump in an unremarkable road that went nowhere special.

Like the road he was on now, almost empty but for his weak yellow lights in what should have still been daytime.

Bronze stared at the black line of the pavement ahead, his body driving without need of conscious input, and he walked in a dream of the past, the younger Bronze knowing nothing of the broken ghost that watched him.

Riyadh, Saudi Arabia: February 28, 1991

By the time Bronze regained consciousness, Bush was on TV ending the war. The sun penetrated the thick hotel curtains, casting heavy shadows and pools of light across the room so that Bronze figured it was late afternoon already. A sinking realization came that he was still dressed in his navy suit and a now-yellowing white dress shirt. Bronze boggled at Bush, whose image seemed to swirl and shimmer unpleasantly. He momentarily tried to process the implications but thought better of trying to get a grasp on anything so biblical at a time like this. *Just let it roll by. Sense will come in time.*

More pressing was the freezing sweat that soaked through his shirt and underwear and right on through his suit. The air conditioning in his room felt military grade. Like they'd hooked it up to a nuclear reactor.

But the one thing that topped it all was the need for water.

He felt like he had tried to swallow the whole shithole desert. Maybe he had, for all he remembered of the last few days.

Reflexively, he groaned as he rolled himself off the bed, his vision a blurred tunnel pointed shakily at the bathroom door and the salvation of the faucet beyond.

He slammed through the door, half with his shoulder, half with his face, the pain of the impact registering somewhere deep in his brain's queue. He fumbled with the faucet knob, bending his head full into the sink once the lukewarm water began to flow. He sucked it down. Relief one second, then almost immediately the sickness surged up from his stomach and he lurched over to the toilet, spraying his inner contents all over the toilet seat and down the sides, maybe thirty percent getting into the actual bowl.

After the heaves subsided from voluminous projectiles to wet pockets of bile to dry spasms of thick spit, Bronze collapsed away from the toilet to lie with his back against the bathtub, slick streaks of pale yellow and pink dribbling from his lips down his neck and onto the collar of his shirt.

It was in this moment that Bronze finally realized that Esther was present. Yelling at him.

She stood on the bathroom threshold, backlit, arms akimbo, a stream of noise ejecting out of her at him.

Bronze waved his arms in front of him. "Esther, Esther, goddamn it. Hold on, just hold on."

"What?"

"I gotta ..."

Bronze paused as the world started to spin anew, but he gallantly kept his composure. Gripped the solid edges of the porcelain bathtub for support and merely burped a big gulp of air.

"I gotta know one thing."

"Yes? And what is that, pray tell?"

"Did we screw last night?"

"No, we didn't fucking screw!"

Bronze couldn't make her face out clearly, but he imagined the pretty features distorted into a dark, ugly rage. A clear thought passed through his brain—he had done that.

That was what he did.

He took pretty things and turned them ugly.

Esther turned and started to storm off.

"Esther! Esther, please! I'm sorry. I'm a jerk. I know."

Some noise from outside the bathroom. Then a female figure reappeared on the threshold. Her movements seemed unnaturally slow and there was a calm to her presence now. She reached in and flicked the bathroom light on. The harsh neon blinded Bronze for a moment, but as his eyes half adjusted, her face appeared out of the light like an angel descending from heaven. Her face was slack and calm. No expression. There was something in the look, though, and he was sure as shit the angel had not come to lead him to heaven.

She came to pass judgment.

"When I was in journalism school, I had cutouts of your articles pinned to the walls of my dorm room. The Cortez Murders. The Greengate Robbery. The Richelieu Massacre. At first, to come to know you was to hate you. But if I'm being frank with myself, for a long time I cultivated that hate to cover how I really felt.

"The truth of the situation.

"Because really ... I pity you. Like a bum I walk by on the street and think of throwing a dollar to. You aren't worthy of hate. You are just a tube for booze. That's it. A simple theorem but perfectly accurate. Every action you take is just a mechanism to keep the tube in business.

"I came up here to throw you a dollar, to make myself feel good in pointless magnanimity. To ignore that it's just another

dollar thrown down that gullet of yours. Do you want the dollar
or not?"

Bronze nodded and the world turned into a temporary tilt-a-
whirl. He heard Esther's words clearly, but he wasn't ready to
parse them in his forebrain. They registered somewhere in the
deep, though. Later he'd be able to pick them over like a scab.
But now he just nodded. Knowing that if he didn't, he would be
fired. And if he was fired, his life would be over. And he cried a
little as he nodded. But why he cried wasn't clear. It might have
only been the sour reek burning his eyes. Or he might have been
crying for himself. Or for some vague vision of who he might
have been.

"Good. That's good. You've got"—she checked her watch—
"forty-seven minutes to get yourself together and get to the press
room."

"Why? The war's over, isn't it? Bushy-boy just said so."

"Because there's been a murder out at the base."

Bronze's eyes narrowed. A touch of a fox's cunning came into
them.

"There we go." Esther smiled without the barest hint of joy.
"Old Cal's still kicking in there somewhere, Bronze."

THE RAIN HAD STARTED.

Big heavy drops smacked against the windshield in a staccato rhythm, then the air opened up and it flooded viciously
down. The first minute or so, Bronze's heart raced and his eyes
strained ahead into the yellow cylinders of streaking water and
slick black pavement awash with rivulets of cold rain.

For a minute or two he wondered if he would have to pull
over to the side of the road and hang there until the rain slowed,
always in danger of an out-of-control truck smashing his car into

a crumpled cage of deranged metal while his soft flesh was torn and twisted by the congress of machines operating with inhuman force and speed.

He kept going and the rain turned less dire but no less all-encompassing. His heart began to settle. Now it was the rhythm of his wipers slapping away the water that unburdened his waking mind into a hypnotic reverie.

He thought again of those old days at the *Post* with Esther.

He could remember viscerally his constant fear of being fired. Of being found out. Then he remembered when the ax had actually fallen.

Washington, DC: August 18, 1992

Bill Cunningham was disgusted. Bronze could see it painted all over his face. He didn't care in the least. Bill was a piece-of-shit journalist promoted until his incompetence no longer mattered. The unearned arrogance of the Management. Just because you played golf with the right people and laughed at all the right times about old shenanigans at all the right schools, that didn't qualify you to sit in final judgment of a real reporter.

He wondered if ol' Bill Cunnigham could smell the beer on him. Would be bullshit if he got fired over that. It was just beer. Cunningham didn't know what real drinking was. He thought he looked sophisticated at corporate parties sipping on his one gin and tonic for the night. He had no idea what a complete joke he was.

Cunningham continued looking at Bronze from across his desk for a long while without saying a word. Bronze thought, *Go ahead and say your piece, you fuck. I've got a half-decade's worth of shit I'd like to say to you in turn. You think you know the first thing about investigative journalism sitting behind that desk writing your anodyne editorials. I'd like to see you last a day in my shoes.*

Cunningham finally seemed on the verge of speaking, then closed his mouth, got up, and walked around to the other side of his huge wooden desk layered with stacks and stacks of papers. He took the other chair next to Bronze that faced the empty spot where the big boss man usually sat.

When he sat down, his shoulders collapsed downward and his head hung. Bronze watched him rub his hands together, back and forth, back and forth interminably.

He looked up. "Bronze."

"Yeah."

A sigh. Pause. The silence perched in the air anxiously, waiting to fall to earth. Bronze realized he was so angry, he wasn't even looking at Cunningham's face but staring daggers at his midsection. *I can at least stare the fucker down.* He raised his chin.

That was when he realized Bill Cunningham was quietly crying.

"Cal." His voice cracked. "You know ... you know you can't work here anymore, don't you?"

The crying was catching. But Bronze held it down.

"Yeah," he said. Clamped down even tighter on the sadness and self-pity that welled like a geyser. Added, "I want you to know ... I appreciated the opportunity, Bill."

"I hope you can get help, Cal. We all know what you went through with Keaton. I just ... I can't help you here anymore, but if you get sober ... come see me. I'll do what I can."

But Bronze had never brought himself to ask for that help. And Bill had had a stroke in '95 and was living in an assisted care facility last Bronze had heard. Even then, Bronze hadn't ever gone to see him. An ice-cold blackness filled his stomach as he remembered that last detail. Made him want to jump out of his skin.

In Bronze's memory the narrative sequence of being fired

was completely fragmented. From drink or self-protecting repression, he didn't care to guess. But burned in detail was walking out the door of the *Post* building for the last time. He had all of his things from his desk in a box. There weren't any cabs nearby, for some reason. Cosmic punishment, probably.

His box was too heavy to carry more than a few feet at a time. Too many books. The DC summer heat was sweltering. So, sweating alcohol freely out of every pore, he walked down the sidewalk, stopping every few paces to set his burden down. Heave ho a few paces, then collapse. Arms torn with rubbing from the cardboard. Shirt fully sweat through. Heave ho, collapse. Heave ho, collapse.

The memory went on and on.

He must have eventually made it to the Metro, but in his broken recollection there was no end to it. The memory cut off with him somewhere on the sidewalk, people watching and whispering as he tried to bear his burden and failed over and over again.

But even that wasn't the end of the party. He didn't hit the bottom for another ten months.

And, as unbidden images of last night's motel room flashed across his mind, of Carolyn's face and the way her eyes unlocked and laid bare the open wound within as she pleaded with him *come with me* in that awful bus station, Bronze remembered that last hour when he was fully and finally revealed.

New York, NY: April 4, 1993

She was easy pickings. Begging for it, really. She was even wearing plaid knee-high socks, which Bronze figured was entrapment in any sane penal code.

He still had his looks, though a bit more ragged than in the old days. He still had his stories. He still had that reporter's boldness. When her friends said they were going to another bar and she said she'd meet them later, he knew he had her.

Wasn't this always the root of the thing? Didn't it always come back to women? (It's not the apple, it's Eve! And she all the time blaming the lunacy of a talking snake.)

It had always been there. Long before any would believe. At five he'd snuck downstairs when his parents were fast asleep to leaf through a picture book of Renaissance paintings and Greek statues, his eyes, bigger than saucers, staring at the curves of the goddesses' breasts and buttocks. Later they'd had an encyclopedia set and he'd learned their names and stories. Aphrodite and Hera and Athena. Elaborate fantasies followed. He would sit on a high throne where the goddesses worshiped him, indulged him in whatever fantasy he concocted. This was all before the age of thirteen, all before the hormones started. And when they did, it was like they short-circuited his brain.

He remembered the first time he'd made it for real. He was sixteen. He was working as a lifeguard at a small beach down at the Jersey Shore. The lifeguards threw a party on the beach. Everyone was drinking booze except him. He couldn't do that to his teetotaler father. He had promised him again and again he wouldn't touch the stuff. At least until he was of age. His father thought he'd make an excellent lawyer someday. Maybe even a doctor. And while a gentile might make it any which way, a Jew had only one path: Overwhelm them to the point they could not find a single excuse to say no.

Karen Bianchi was probably nineteen. Certainly a college girl, not one of the high schoolers. But summer break and lifeguarding intermixed the two social classes. He had heard her telling jokes about him. That night he saw her around the bonfire on the beach laughing and looking his way, while he drank soda pop with his best friend Bruce Schwarz who would soon come out as gay (but not to Bronze), flee to Greenwich

Village at seventeen, and later open up his own antique store in Georgetown, where Bronze would find him again one day.

Karen had sauntered over. She was wearing khaki shorts and a polka-dotted top that was little more than a bathing suit with frills. She was drinking from a sudsy beer can and smiling this big, impossibly wide smile that showed every molar. The polka-dotted top was stretched to capacity, and the tanned cleavage moved and beckoned like all the mysteries of the universe in one.

She told little Cal Goldberg that she had something to show him in her car. She put her arm around him as she walked him to her green steel Ford, Bruce Schwarz looking desperately forlorn as they left him standing there alone.

She had a huge nose and her breasts and butt were disproportionate to her body. She didn't look anything like Aphrodite. Confounding at the time, but when Bronze thought back on her now, he realized that she was an incredible beauty. Just not the beauty he was ready for or had expected. Nonetheless, when she took her top off in the back of her car, Cal came in his underwear and the stuff seeped all the way through his shorts. She laughed and laughed and eventually kissed him on the mouth and it felt nothing like he'd imagined it would, the tongue large, hot, and invasive. She put his hand on her breasts and they felt so strange, better and worse than he had imagined they would. Her nipples sharpened to points and he worried that if he was too firm, he might break them off and so he oh so gently touched her there.

She pulled his shorts off. And she took hers off in turn. She told him that when he felt it coming, to pull his thing out. Which he did right the first time. But the second time he left it in too long and her eyes rolled back before they both panicked.

Later, in New York, as he walked the young girl from the bar back to the building she'd indicated, he remembered somewhere back in his dead drunk skull the shame he'd felt as he'd stood under the shower in his parents' house for forty minutes until the heat went out of the water and he just let the ice cold streaks stream down his body and shivered and fell into bed promising God that he wouldn't do a thing like that again for as long as he lived and how he'd cried and thanked the God of his people when Karen had called a week later and told him she had gotten her period. That maybe they could meet after work, and little Cal Goldberg had told her that his dad needed him to work the rest of the summer in his tailoring shop and that he couldn't work as a lifeguard anymore.

Bronze remembered the catch in Karen's voice. How she hadn't understood in the least. He still felt sorry remembering it. He remembered how a year later he had broken his promise to God. How after that it had gotten easier and easier. Until blond Ellen had come along to make an honest man of him. And if not her, then the deadening drink would. And then after the divorce, the drink and the sex had gone together hand in glove. A never-ending party. A party that just this moment was adjourning to an Upper East Side apartment building with a girl hardly older than Karen Bianchi had been back then. But this girl was a slip of thing with a tiny button nose and skinny, smooth legs above the knee-high socks disappearing into her pleated skirt.

The apartment belonged to her grandmother. She was pushing ninety and fast asleep in her bedroom, but they could have a drink on the couch, the girl said. The whole place was decorated in flower motifs. Even the couch was upholstered with a floral design. The place certainly looked and smelled like someone's grandmother, right down to the silver tray on which she had her liquors in her own glass bottles with glass stoppers on top. A classy old school touch, hiding away the brands. The girl asked if he wanted bourbon or scotch. He said scotch and bring the bottle.

She brought the bottle, two heavy tumblers, and a silver bucket full of ice. She sipped on hers and he drained his in one swig. Poured another and took it a little more slowly with this one as he told her a tale from the '80s about hunting down the story on a killing that was really a cover for something else—for a massive embezzlement at a private bank. The story was full of gold bars and gun-toting tough guys and cocaine in yachts parked on the shores of the Cayman Islands. It was one of Bronze's better yarns.

He finished the second drink and after he poured the third, he stopped to kiss the girl lightly on her painted lips. When he did, she immediately cleaved her body to his, unconsciously pressing her pelvis against his torso in long slow thrusts. He began to fumble with the buttons on her blouse.

Suddenly she stopped and pushed herself away from him. She put a finger up and smiled, then disappeared into the other room. He drank down his drink while he waited. When she came back she held a small glass mirror with lines of white powder. She had a rolled-up $100 bill and a coquettish smile on her face. She did her line first and handed the bill over to Bronze.

He waved it away. He had always had an aversion to the stuff, even when deeply drunk. Seemed dirty somehow. He wished she wouldn't do it either, but he was too far gone to say anything. And past caring what was clean and unclean.

She made an exaggerated pout, then poured him another glass of scotch, took a sip, and handed it over. He silently saluted her as he took it from her, then she turned away again and did the line that had been meant for him.

He drank slow sips and waited patiently for her to finish. When she turned back there was a look of such pure calm in her eyes that it made him wonder what he was missing.

The world went wobbly as he put down his drink and kissed

her and removed her blouse in slow motion. The feeling was like he was on a boat shifting about in rolling seas and there was absolutely nothing to worry about. He remembered smiling like he'd never known what living really was before and seeing her smile back at him the same way.

Everything was OK. Everything was A-OK.

When he woke up, he realized he had never gotten past opening the buttons of her blouse. The blouse was still tucked into her skirt and her white bra was still on. Her face was blue. Her chest had gone cold. Her grandmother was walking in circles in her pale, faded nightie, hands clenched to her head and bleating out a wordless high whine that must have been as close to a scream as she could muster. Bronze looked at the coffee table and the powder and the tipped-over bottle of scotch that had leaked its contents all over the Persian rug.

"9-1-1," he yelled.

The old woman seemed to snap out of it. She boggled at Bronze a moment and went over to her ancient rotary phone, her old, shaking hands excruciatingly slow.

Bronze couldn't find a pulse or hear any breathing. He started on the CPR. He still remembered a bit from his life-guarding days three lifetimes ago. As he thrust down on the girl's chest in rhythm, he thought of that other girl from Madam Richelieu's, the one with the turquoise toenails, but it was too much for him and, like an angel, Karen Bianchi swept back into his mind and he could almost feel her holding him in her arms while he continued the chest compressions. He cried to think of her, and how he wished she could truly come and lead him away to some place in the past where the last twenty years had never happened.

By some miracle, mere minutes before the paramedics arrived, there was a huge sucking sound from the girl and she stumbled back to the land of the living and cried out little whimpers of pain.

He went with her to the hospital. It was like he was floating outside his body sitting in the waiting room still drunk and full of misery. It turned out the girl and the grandmother were from an old New York family. Old Upper East Side New York money. No one thought it worth their time to press charges over the drugs.

When the doctor came out and told Bronze the girl would live, he also told him that in the process of performing CPR, Bronze had cracked her breastbone and broken two ribs.

BRONZE DRANK ALL day after that. He remembered that he had slept at Penn Station that night. He hadn't deserved to go back to his shitty little hotel room. The next morning he'd caught the 5:25 a.m. Amtrak back to DC. He showed up at an old college friend's house whom he hadn't seen in years. John, a successful tax attorney now, had always been a nice strait-laced guy and his wife was quiet and sweet. They had put Bronze up with fresh linens and neatly folded towels.

That night he went to his first AA meeting. It wasn't the last drink he'd taken. He'd relapsed a few times in that first month. But eventually it had stuck.

Or had stuck for now, at least.

He was low on gas again and he needed to bite the bullet and call Iris. He had hoped he could wait out the downpour, but though nowhere near as violent, it still poured down steadily as he pulled into a town and gas station made totally anonymous in the heavy rain.

He filled the car. And he remembered.

He thought about how he would have done it all differently if he could have gone back. He thought he'd start with that night with Karen at the party on the beach. He would have done things differently. If only he could have been her friend and not so afraid all the time, maybe it would all have been different and better from there on out.

He left the car sitting by the pump and ran into one of two empty phone booths set against the side of the station convenience store. Inside the booth, rain thundered above and washed down the glass sides.

Iris picked up on the second ring.

Yes, she had found something—or Bruce had, really.

"It's something to do with Kopes's planned senate run in '98. Crawford, the senior senator from Virginia, is up for reelection, and the *Post* says the rumor is Kopes plans to take him on—that Kopes is probably a shoo-in to win, with his family money and the power his father wields down there. Anyways, apparently Crawford wasn't willing to politely step down and hired Roger Haake to make use of his skill with the dark arts of political intrigue and shift the calculus of the race."

Fucking DC, Bronze thought. *Who gives a shit who is senator and who isn't?*

"Thanks to you and Bruce, Iris. I should be back in a few hours. Don't wait up."

"I wouldn't dream of it, Bronze."

BY THE TIME he parked Bruce's car a few blocks away from his basement apartment, the rain had stalled to a drizzle. All the lights were off in Iris's house. Bronze felt like a thief in the night, stealing his way back into his own apartment.

He walked in without flipping the lights on; the light from the street in the window seemed enough. He'd almost forgotten the boxes that littered the living room and just avoided tripping over one. Nothing to be done about them for now.

He took off his shoes and fell onto the green upholstered dog chair. He lit a Chesterfield. The last of the day—the last of what felt like one very long day going all the way back to Monday morning.

He dragged long and deep at the Chesterfield, then balanced it on the edge of his ashtray. The ashtray was dark jade carved into the shape of a dragon lying in a circle. He had purchased it on a judo trip through mainland China. That was after eight months in the best dojos in Japan. (He had a real wakizashi sword somewhere in the bedroom closet in case he was ever asked to prove it ... or commit seppuku.) There was a little slot in the back of the dragon's head to put your lit cigarette in so it looked like there was smoke coming out of the dragon's nose, but he didn't bother with the effect now.

He would just sit here a while, let himself have this little time before dragging himself into the bathroom to go through the whole pre-bed rigmarole. He closed his eyes for just a moment. He thought of Esther again—she had forgiven him finally, and he smiled to think of it. He needn't worry any more over all the ways he had failed her. Out there somewhere, Karen sat in a warm living room full of family, drinking cocoa and thinking fondly of him. A dark-haired girl, skin glowing with turquoise, tiptoed on bare feet and whispered in his ear that she was safe and free. She turned into Carolyn, who now brushed full, soft lips against his ear and said *Come with me.* And he did. And a heavenly warmth crawled up his body and tickled at his skin. A ghostly Iris sat there on the couch steadily watching over him, protecting him as the streaking rain and road played endlessly against the back of his eyelids, burned by long hours into his retinas.

Hours later, in the black of night, he suddenly woke from a

dream of brutal murder and booze. He was soaked in blood and vomit. Whisky filled his rotting body and twisted his mind.

In the dream he had been drinking again. Drinking on the job hunting a killer. He was so ashamed—he had broken his final covenant with the universe—so ashamed he wanted to die. And when he awoke, exhausted but sober in his chair, the relief was so strong, he cried a little in the pitch blackness that covered him.

He thought about all the tears no one had seen him cry.

Then he got up and stumbled over a box in the dark, banged his knee on the doorframe to his room, hadn't even the energy to yell in pain, then flopped on top of his bed, finally granted for a few hours the dreamless black nothingness he craved.

14

WOUNDS

IRIS

Bronze had returned in the night, unseen and unheard.

And now, as I futzed about my cupboards looking for store-bought cookies to put on a plate, Bronze sat on the other side of the green striated marble of my kitchen counter drinking coffee. He took his coffee black. Most of the time. Sometimes when you offered cream or milk, he would shrug and say "Sure." Bronze was a "most of the time" kind of guy. You couldn't quite pin him down on anything. He preferred chocolate desserts to ones made with fruit. Most of the time. He preferred brunettes to blondes. Dramas to comedies. Steak to sushi. Autumn to spring. Asses to breasts. Moonlight to sunshine. Leonard Cohen to Lou Reed. Lou Reed to the Beatles. Novels to television. Heartache to numbness. Most of the time.

How do I create a character from *most of the time*? It would be criminal not to squeeze at least part of a novel out of Bronze's adventures. And really there was no choice. Every day as I sat down to write, he made his presence known, coming through my words unbidden. But a character must *desire* and do so simply and coherently. And behind that desire they must be wounded with one big stab of a wound. The wound gives depth;

it explains. We know the wound and the desire in one breath. But does a real person have *the* wound? Or maybe more death by a thousand cuts. A thousand wounds remembered and a thousand more forgotten. And if I measured each to each, would I ever find the wound to end all wounds?

What wounds lay in the files in front of Bronze? On the kitchen counter, he had my selection of the Billy Kopes files from the *Post* boxes laid out in front of him while he sipped and frowned. Or sipped and glowered. Every once in a while, he went so far as to sip and brood.

The day after Bronze's return to DC, after his mad flight westward with Carolyn Haake, Roth had reached out to him about continuing to consult on the Billy Kopes and Roger Haake cases. I was now immersed in the details of the Kopes family circle and made an argument for myself as a kind of temporary Watson to Bronze's Holmes.

He tried to put me off, saying he shouldn't have gotten me involved in the first place. I had entered my appeal with a more or less dignified: *I need the writing inspiration. You would be doing me a favor.* He didn't put up much fuss before he sighed and relented, especially when he realized how thoroughly Bruce Schwarz and I had gone through the *Post* files while he was away with Carolyn. I like to think that he also might not have been completely appalled at the prospect of spending some additional time with me.

I had meticulously organized the selection of files in front of Bronze—one pile on Billy himself and other smaller piles dedicated to the major players twisting about the days close to the end of Billy's life. To Bronze's left were Billy's father William, his brother Fred, and Billy's chief of staff, Harold Peterson. To Bronze's right were Roger Haake, Carolyn Haake, and Senator Alexander Crawford. Next to Carolyn were her other lovers—a medium-sized pile on James Howell and a thin pile on Zachary

Jackson. Hidden without any documentation and lurking like a nightmare behind all of the piles was the assassin who had shot Roger Haake and then completely disappeared into the sun-drenched DC afternoon.

Bronze pointed to the file on William Kopes. "So the father runs the company, then?"

I shook my head. I had become far more of an expert in the last few days on Kopes Industries and the various doings of the Kopes family than I would ever have dreamed possible. "He used to run it. William Kopes was CEO and Chairman of the Board for a large portion of company history. And that history, I have come to learn, is long and complex. The company was founded by William's grandfather, Ansgar Kopes, in 1874. It was originally called the Kopes Corporation and primarily made precision tools, using former slaves as cheap labor in a factory outside of Richmond, Virginia. As time went on, the company developed into making ever more sophisticated industrial machines. By World War II they had massive contracts with the US government, making the machines that made the engines of war. As of today, the company has grown to be measured amongst America's largest privately held corporations—the district Billy Kopes represented, it seems like the whole county has ties to Kopes Industries."

I had finally found a half-eaten package of what was probably slightly stale chocolate chip cookies and laid them down on the counter along with my own coffee, a light tan after an ample portion of half and half. I took a seat on the stool next to Bronze and leaned over the files while my recent studies of the Kopes family history swirled in my head.

"Ansgar Kopes was a colorful but murky character. He built the palatial Kopes family seat over the course of a decade from about 1880 to 1890. That's where Billy and Fred grew up and where William still resides. In 1877, Ansgar married a seventeen-year-old girl named Genevieve Pelit, William Kopes's grand-mother. Ansgar was thirty-five. Rumors have persisted to this day of illegitimate children with young women that worked for him. He held a firm grip on the company until his late eighties. His son, William's father, took over as CEO when the old man turned ninety, but Ansgar didn't relinquish the chairmanship until dying in his sleep at the ripe age of ninety-six.

"For all the color of William's grandfather, William's father, Ansgar Jr., lived a lonely, sad life. His wife, Rachel, died young by presumed suicide, drowned in a pond on the family estate. They had had three kids. The daughter, Aster, died in infancy. The older son, Ansgar Kopes III, was killed in a botched kidnapping-for-ransom attempt in his early twenties. And so Ansgar Jr. was left only with his horses and his drinking and a strained rela-tionship with William, who was apparently his grandfather reborn and shared not a single trait with his father. The first two comforts would wind up being Ansgar Jr.'s undoing. In 1944, a drunken Ansgar fell off his horse. The horse then—accidently or not, who can know the mind of a horse?—stepped on his abdomen and pulverized his spleen. It took him four days of agony to die.

"William—all of twenty, who had been effectively running the business in his father's stead for three years at this point, ever since Rachel's drowning and his father's subsequent surrender to drink—now became head of the business in name as well as fact."

Bronze was staring mournfully at the file on William Kopes. "That's a lot of violent death in one family ... When did William give up control? Who runs the company now?"

I took a sip of my coffee and a breath.

"William ran Kopes Industries until 1989, when he abruptly stepped down to leave Billy's older brother, Fred, in charge. Unlike Billy, Fred has spent his career like his father and great-grandfather before him—thoroughly focused on Kopes Industries." I pointed to the file on Fred, then to the one on Harold Peterson. "Though there's really no separating Billy Kopes from the family business. Billy's chief of staff, Harold Peterson, had been a long-time Kopes Industries employee before becoming Billy's head gofer. Billy's biggest legislative achievement, the Buy American Security Act of '88, transparently benefited Kopes Industries. And"—I arched an eyebrow in Bronze's direction, proud to share my most obscure discovery—"it's the Buy American Security Act where Roger Haake first makes his appearance."

I now pointed to the other side of Bronze, the Haake side. "Carolyn Haake's affair with Billy and Roger Haake's work for Senator Crawford, Billy's likely opponent in the upcoming senate race, are the obvious connections between Roger Haake and Billy Kopes. But there's one more. The Buy American Security Act of 1988 is the other, earliest point of intersection I can find.

"Haake was working for the Kopes family as a political consultant at the time. He and Harold Peterson were the main workhorses whipping up votes for the bill to pass. This was a major victory for Kopes Industries; at the time, they were suffering under increasing pressure from cheaper competitors in Asia and higher-end manufacturers in West Germany. The Kopes position was being squeezed on either side of the value equation. Apparently the pressure was so acute that the very survival of the company was at stake. William himself even condescended to come up to DC and was personally involved in greasing the wheels of the legislation. Notably, this was William Kopes's last major move before retiring. After '89, he seems to have vanished off the face of the earth. Or at least vanished from the papers. When he is mentioned, it's only in passing as part of the background for some article about Billy or Fred."

Bronze took a bite of a hard chocolate chip cookie and nodded thoughtfully at that minor mystery. I imagined what he was thinking. Given the nature of men and power, and especially with the frequent comparison of William to his long-serving grandfather, it seemed strange for William to have ceded power in his early to mid sixties.

I continued. "This is where we start to see another surprising intersection. After the fall of the Soviet Union, the Buy American Security Act of '88 would turn into a critical bulwark for the entire defense industry as the United States disinvested in defense and former Eastern Bloc countries started hawking cheap Soviet arms across the world." I pointed to the file on James Howell. "Howell made his name as a lobbyist for the defense industry and was a chief rival of Roger Haake. He lobbied to keep the Buy American Security Act firmly in place and worked to expand its provisions over the past nine years or so."

Bronze was now dipping the cookie into his coffee, probably in an effort to soften the staleness. "Perhaps that's it, then? James Howell and Roger Haake in some kind of deadly competition? Billy winds up caught in the middle?" He shook his head. "Or maybe an arms dealing gang from the Eastern Bloc? Some foreign competitor hires this assassin to kill Billy Kopes and Roger Haake for their participation in the Buy American Security Act? Perhaps Howell is next on the list?"

That didn't fit my sense of story built up over too many novels. It didn't seem personal enough. "If anything, I would have thought Haake would have been after Howell for having an affair with his wife. And neither theory addresses the question of why now? The legislation is long since enacted. Who knows, maybe the murder was meant to be a message against future defense industry protection? But this seems too direct and risky a move. The last thing a former Soviet arms dealer needs is the US government taking a focused look at them."

Bronze was silent a moment, musing while he chewed his cookie dipped in coffee. "Anything on Zachary Jackson? What about Harold Peterson? Anything more on him? Maybe the butler did it, so to speak."

I shook my head. "Nothing on Jackson. I would need more raw information. I don't think your old colleague, Esther, thought to look into him, not knowing his, um, connection to Carolyn Haake and therefore Billy. As far as Peterson goes, the most I have is a whispering in the gossip pages amongst Billy's former lower-level aides, always anonymous, that Peterson was the iron fist in Billy's velvet glove.

"Billy was a walking scandal ready to happen—rumors of affairs all over town, but no one seemed to want to call him on it. Former aides talk about griping over their car loan within earshot of Billy, only to find out the next week that he'd quietly paid it off for them—stories like that. Who knows, maybe the stories were planted in the press by Peterson to further his boss's ambitions. But the storyteller in me senses a sincerity to it. Despite his faults, I imagine there was a sweetness to Billy absent from William or Fred."

Bronze was smirking a bit, but there was no humor in his eyes. "Sounds like more than a few women were sweet on Billy. I imagine some of those payoffs were young women."

I felt myself blushing and grabbed my own cookie to chew on to buy time. "You might be right. But shouldn't we look for some virtue in the dead?"

The smirk dropped from Bronze's face and he looked up from rifling through the files to catch me squarely in the eyes. I took a sudden in-breath and felt a flush of adrenaline in my blood and guts to be so nakedly appraised, my heart already racing from too much coffee and talking.

"Always," he said. Then he twitched his head to the side slightly as if shaking off the repugnance of some unwanted thought. "Well, almost always."

I dropped my gaze back to my coffee. He shifted in his seat. Looked behind him at the living room, at the couch where we had now watched several movies together.

He sighed, then slapped his thighs to punctuate a change in conversational direction. "After everything over the last few days, I'm burned out, Iris. I think you were right on the phone. The Roger Haake working for Senator Crawford angle is still a good one for now. And Howell is worth the follow-up. We need to understand exactly why someone would want to kill both Billy Kopes *and* Roger Haake."

"I'm sorry, Bronze, I shouldn't be pushing ... You've been through so much, you must be ... I can't imagine."

He was looking at my TV now. "I don't suppose ... well, we probably shouldn't." He shrugged with a tired, boyish grin on his face that failed to hide some turbulence beneath the surface. "You've got your writing, and I need to get back on the horn with Roth again. I appreciate it, Iris. I really do."

"Were you thinking of a movie? You're probably right ... I really should try to write."

"Yeah." He smiled, any inner disturbance better hidden this time. "Rain check, then?"

"Soon. Yes. Let's pick something out soon."

I helped him gather up the files and walked him to the door. There was a moment as he passed my threshold—he looked at me once more and seemed to focus his gaze on my lips while nodding goodbye and without the slightest warning, adrenaline was flying through me again with such force, I thought I might lose my balance. Wildly, I almost leaned out to kiss him farewell, unconsciously, like a wistful old lover might.

Before I knew it, he was already turning and walking away. I hadn't actually done it. *Had I?* For a moment I couldn't be sure.

But I soon shook away my doubt. I knew I could never do such a sudden, foolish thing. Absolutely never.

Who exactly am I reassuring? Was I getting at some lie within me?

All these people in the files, all these *suspects*. Did they live their days full of half-understood lies? Or were they perfectly explicit in their deceit?

As I shut the door behind Bronze, I thought about *most of the time*. I thought about people and suspects and characters and lies.

More than even the desire or the wound, *the lie* might be the crux of the matter.

The main character in a story must believe in a lie. The big lie that will come undone in the end. What lies did Bronze believe? What about Carolyn Haake and the whole cast surrounding Billy Kopes? On what paths did their lies set them? Which lies had led to murder? What about my own lies, the ones I kept well and truly hidden from myself—where were they leading me?

I pressed my ear against my front door and listened to the light thump of Bronze's graceful footsteps walking down my stairs, then down his own stairs, and finally the creaking of the door leading into the basement apartment below.

In a story, the lie must finally succumb to the truth. Truth sets you free.

But does it really? Most of the time ... maybe. Living out a real story, not one in my head for perhaps the first time in my life, I wasn't so sure.

What about the truth of death? Of randomness? Of victimhood? Of duty? Of violence? Of love unreturned? Are there not many truths that chain, that bind in boxes, that lead one by the hand into a lonely room full of dead hours in which to wither?

15

BIG BILL

MAY 7, 1997

The calls hadn't stopped since Billy had been plucked from the Potomac like a dead trout. Fred Kopes had to suffer through them all, thick hands massaging at his temples, feet up on the enormous desk in his temporary office at the Hay-Adams Hotel in DC. Weepy women and men speaking in hushed tones. Oh, everyone loved Billy.

Billy, Billy, Billy.

So handsome. So whip smart. So talented. So caring. Always a kind word, the right word at just the right time.

The country had lost its next bright shining star—part politician, part movie star, part royal heir. Like a Republican Jack Kennedy.

At least Jack Kennedy could make a speech between his affairs and gallivanting. What had Billy done except the Buy American Security Act in '88? And Harold Peterson, Big Bill, and Roger Haake had made that one happen. While the grunt work was done, Billy had been in Vegas pursuing an affair with a Lido de Paris showgirl, showing up only to introduce the legislation on the House floor, cast his vote, and take the credit.

But, strange as it was, everyone really did seem to love Billy. Far be it from Fred to explain the phenomenon.

Even Dad had gone into virtual seclusion at the big house in Virginia. William Kopes himself. Big Bill. (But never Big Bill to his face. Only Mr. Kopes, William to a select few, but most often *Sir*.) Who knew Big Bill cared so much for his son that he would spend days hardly seeing anyone save Peterson?

Would he have cared nearly so much if it had been Fred?

Fred, who worked his fingers to the bone running *the company* and making the money by which they all lived? Fred, who daily dealt with all the headaches coming from new competition out of the former Soviet Bloc? Fred, who was even now cleaning up the messes Billy had left behind?

The phone rang again. Fred sighed. Reminded himself that these were the people he would need if the plan was to work. The people with enough connections and power and wealth. The people who could grease the path.

He picked up. "Fred Kopes. Speaking?"

"It's Peterson."

Fred relaxed back into his chair. "Thank god. If I have to comfort another kerchief-clutching old bat or sundowning ex-mayor whimpering out their condolences, I don't know what I'll do. Well, Peterson? At least tell me Big Bill's on board?"

"Fred, I've got you on speaker here."

Fuck. Fred quickly lurched into an upright sitting position, his heart pounding in his chest. *Peterson is such a little prick.*

"Frederick," Big Bill's voice growled at him.

Slick sweat suddenly made the phone slippery in his hand. "Hi, Dad."

Just a harsh hum of static came back from the other end.

"So ... what do you think?" Fred asked into the static.

"You really think you've got the chops for this? I'm not going to back you if you're just going to shit the bed."

Fred's face flushed. He counted two breaths and held the quavering rage out of his voice. "I do."

"Fine. *See* that you do. I'm sending Peterson back up to DC. He'll put together a meet and greet for next week. You can announce then."

They hung up. The black handset glistened with streaks of moisture. He wiped his wet hand on his pant leg.

And just like that, Fred was going to be a senator.

16

A HISTORY OF NAMES

July 3, 1984

Natalya Drozdov stands naked on butcher paper, her yellow sundress, white bra, green shoes, and tiny purple purse scattered around her like random blotches of paint.

Her father calls her Natasha and named her after Countess Natalya Rostova from Tolstoy's *War and Peace*.

Red blood trickles down her left thigh and mixes there with black dirt.

The nurse has blue gloves on. Her hair is a wavy dark blond, pulled back tightly in a bun. She is carrying sheets of paper to individually wrap the discarded clothes.

A second-year female resident with short-cropped black hair and a storm of angry red blood vessels in her bug eyes is preparing the colposcope.

Half of Natasha's body is sharp pain. The other half is numb. Later the numb parts hurt worse.

She doesn't think of him. She thinks of how close she was to the bar. How she saw the light ahead and heard the murmuring of conversation as the patrons spilled out into the street and the hot July night. When she called out to them, there was no catch in the sound to acknowledge her. Just murmurs punctuated with laughter and good cheer.

She was on hard concrete and the light of the bar was ahead of her and filled with murmuring as she thought she would suffocate or explode or tear apart down low in the dark of the alley, watched over by overfull tin cans of garbage.

The light ahead of her ... She could almost imagine silhouettes in relaxed disposition, laughing, smiling, holding beers, cocktails, hips swaying a little to the music and murmuring and murmuring and murmuring ...

Later a detective with a bad comb-over of oily brown hair and a red bulbous nose just shook his head when she looked through a binder of Polaroids without a hint of recognition.

The hospital sends her a bill when she doesn't press charges. She catches it in the mail before her father sees it, and she pays it with the money he'd scraped together for her birthday the week before.

September 30, 1987

"Nah, no script—the only important thing is when I ask if you've got a boyfriend, say 'yes' ... *Do* you have a boyfriend?"

"Yeah."

"He know you're here? I don't want some tattooed teenager sticking me with a knife in the parking lot, you know what I'm saying?"

"No. He doesn't."

"I'm going to go ahead and suggest breaking up with him soon as you can, OK? For right now, it'll be good for the scene—you know, *use it*, as the real actors say—but it's better if you don't have one. If you need a boyfriend, get one that'll understand the biz. Don't have to be an actor, easier that way, I think the lighting guy's single ... Vinny!"

"Yah, boss?"

"You single?"

"What my old lady don't know won't hurt, I don't think."

"Fuck you, Vinny, I'm trying to help ... ah ... I'm sorry, little lady, what's the name again?"

"Sasha Sweet."

"I'm trying to help Miss Sweet-thing out. You really got an old lady?"

"Nah, nah, just fuckin' around. I'm free on Thursday if you're interested, Sasha ... I know a great Dairy Queen over on the Boulevard ... It's the best, you know ... not one of them dirty ones, well *managed* ... I just love a good Dairy Queen. What about you, Sweet-heart?"

"By the way, darlin' ... Sasha Sweet? I don't know about that. You're Asian, right?"

" ... "

"Right?"

"Part Filipino."

"So, Asian, though ... I mean, I ain't never seen an Asian as, ah ... huh, well, I guess you been eatin' good in the ole US of A, gettin' all your vitamins and whatnot."

"What's being Asian got to do with my name?"

"Well, you see, it's not so polite, the biz, you know. The customers go in the store, the tapes are labeled and classified. Part of that will be your age. If you're eighteen through, I don't know, twenty-four depending on the girl, we put you in the teen section. How old are you again?"

"Nineteen."

"You see, that's just perfect—bang, you're in the teen section. Now the teen section gets subdivided. See, you could also be in the Asian section, but this particular film, being a teen first-

timer film, will be in the teen section, but since you're Asian, it
lets us cross-list it as Teen First-Timer *slash* Asian. Doubles the
potential eyeballs. But people are going to be confused as to who
you are and what your brand is if you don't have something
Asian in your name. Sasha Sweet sounds like either a Russian
runaway or maybe a southern blond belle a bit down on her
luck, you know what I'm saying? Can we maybe throw a Lin in
there? Would that work for you?"

"Lin's a Chinese name. I'm part Filipino."

"That ain't gonna matter so much. What's your real last
name again?"

"Do I have to say?"

"Got to write the check out to someone, darlin'."

"Drozdov."

"Russian?"

"..."

"OK, so your mama's Mrs. Drozdov née what, sugar?"

"Karingal."

"OK, let's stick with Lin if ain't too much trouble all around,
OK?"

"Sasha Lin?"

"Sounds like money to me, darlin'."

December 31, 1989

She'd taken the bus from LA to Vegas. She remembers dirty
sand on the bus floor, that the last passenger in her seat must
have spilled Sprite down the armrest, and that the whole thing
smelled of sooty, stale air and diesel fuel.

Some of the passengers loaded the bus with heavy luggage.
Some heads hung heavy against the dusty windows. Some were
just plain heavy themselves, wearing, according to the dictates
of gender, loose Hawaiian shirts or floral printed muumuus.

But she was traveling light. Only a canvas bag, a black eye, and dark sunglasses.

That was two years ago. She had checked in that night at the Star Spangled Motel, the recommendation of a garrulous busybody on the bus with skin like old leather.

The motel required she give a name at the front desk. The night manager at the hotel had a scar starting in his hairline and running right across a dead glass eye on the way to his jaw. *If you pay cash, any name will do, darling.*

She found a dash of sardonic amusement in writing down "Carole Lin." Maybe the next place she would be Sue Zanne. After that, maybe Abbie Gail.

But when she tried using Carole Lin as her name at an interview for a waitressing job at Caesar's Palace, her name tag had come back with "Carolyn" on it and she didn't have the energy to complain.

Now, two years later, she was working as a blackjack dealer at the newly opened Mirage.

Tonight she was heavily made up—thick black mascara, eyeliner, and dark purple lipstick, wearing a low-cut black dress that flashed a black lace bra. Gareth, the floor manager, had been sufficiently pleased with her appearance to prominently display her at a centrally located $100 minimum bet table. A constant stream of male heads turned to look at her as they strolled by, like drivers slowing down to view some horrible car accident.

At first her only customer was a dour middle-aged bald man wearing rectangular frameless glasses and dressed in a tight black V-neck T-shirt. He was playing five different hands at a time, losing badly, and hardly tipping.

Eventually a man in his late thirties or early forties sat down, dressed in a charcoal gray suit and a French cuffed white shirt but no tie.

"I am not someone who enjoys or wants company while I gamble," said the bald man in a put-on tony accent.

"Fascinating," said the man in the charcoal suit, not even bothering to look over at the bald man. He threw twenty hundred-dollar bills on the table. "Chips," he said, looking squarely at "Carolyn."

The bald man snorted in dismissive frustration. But before he could say anything else, a woman with long blond curls and a bright print dress came up and laid her arms across his shoulders. The woman made a bubbly speech, which the bald man punctuated with increasingly resigned "nos" and then finally an "OK, fine." The woman skittered off, while the bald man collected his remaining chips.

He looked at Carolyn and the charcoal suit man once more before departing, shrugged his shoulders, and said without a hint of amusement, "She's not very smart, but she's a wonderful lover."

By way of reply, the charcoal suit man merely twisted his cruel, thin lips into a sneer.

The bald man now gone, charcoal suit man put down his first $100 bet, split aces, busted one hand, and made 18 with the other. Carolyn had a ten of hearts showing and flipped over the jack of spades. In one smooth practiced motion she took the man's money.

He slid over a $300 tip.

She gave him the full-wattage smile she'd perfected over the last two years. "Thank you."

"I'm Roger Haake," he said.

January 1, 1991

When Roger kissed her on the stroke of midnight, she dared to think she might never have to worry about money again. The diamond ring he'd put on her finger an hour ago glittered alongside her one inheritance, a tennis bracelet of alternating diamonds and blue sapphires. It seemed to Carolyn that the stones had been borne across continents and millennia with the singular destiny of eventually joining together there upon her wrist and hand.

Earlier, all the eyes in the ballroom had turned to her as she had strolled down the grand stairs in a daring green velvet dress with a slit all the way down the front.

And for the first time, the looks had felt ... right and proper.

And she had smiled a million dazzling watts right back in all their faces.

Carolyn never fooled herself into thinking Roger loved her.

She fooled herself into thinking he needed her. And that there were limits to what he knew.

March 15, 1993

She packed her bags, mascara running down her cheeks. He waited for her in the living room.

"Before you leave," he said, "there's a short film I'd like to show you."

Her stomach dropped within maybe three frames.

Her tears dried. There was no sadness. Only hate.

He made her watch the whole thing. Even the part where she had suddenly gotten hiccups and you could make out the lighting guy cackling and the director cursing before an awkward cut and jump in time.

He put the tape in the safe. It was the only copy remaining, he'd made sure of it. He said she could do what she wanted most of the time, but she couldn't leave and she couldn't disobey.

It took eighteen months to guess the right combination. But still she didn't dare leave.

Because it wasn't just the tape. It was everything behind it. The power it took to acquire the only copy. The maniacal will. The cruelty. The promise it implied—that he would break her one way or another.

May 9, 1997

The day after she got to Austin, Carolyn took up running. In the mornings, before the night crew had gotten off, she would come out the elevator jogging through the lobby of the Sheraton, smell the stale beer on 6th Street burning off in the morning sun, run along the Colorado River, then turn up Congress Avenue, fly past bleary-eyed businessmen and bums sleeping in bus stops, all the way to the pink granite State Capitol building before circling it and turning round.

She walked around town wearing dark sunglasses, T-shirts, shorts, and sneakers. She had Band-Aids on under her socks. She ate breakfast tacos and went to bed early.

She kept to herself.

She felt like she was becoming herself again.

Becoming what she might have been.

Something more than a survivor. But still ...

She thought about Mexico and what she would do for money when she got there. Should she stop there or go further, to Colombia or Brazil or all the way to Argentina, to the very tip of the continent, maybe? *Imagine that.*

She still had the tennis bracelet her father had given her before he died, the one she had pawned and bought back in '87 when she'd moved to Los Angeles. She wasn't going to pawn it again.

Roger was dead. Billy was dead. Bronze had left her.

She could call Zach or James.

One loved her and one didn't.

She called the one that didn't.

He said "yes" without hesitation. He asked her where to wire the cash. She told him. They got disconnected before she could say goodbye.

THE ASSASSIN HATED TAKING CHANCES. He couldn't be one hundred percent sure which man she would call. But logic dictated James Howell. Zachary Jackson hadn't known about the other men. Howell did. Jackson might have illusions about her, might be willing to die to protect her. Howell wouldn't.

She would feel guilty calling Jackson. Less so calling Howell.

And Howell had plenty of money. He had given her expensive gifts before.

If she was stupid enough to try, she would find her accounts frozen.

The assassin held the phone to Howell's ear until he heard him repeat the word "Austin" and hung up before the man might decide to be brave and warn her.

Relief washed over the assassin. Howell stunk of shit and piss, having been tied to a chair in his living room now for going on forty-eight hours.

If there was one thing that got to him about his job, it was the smells men made.

Howell was whimpering that he untie him.

The assassin looked around the room, searching for any trace he might have left behind, seemed about to head to the door, then, as if remembering an almost-forgotten pair of keys, turned to the tied-up man and pointed the long silencer at the end of his pistol toward Howell's head.

Howell squealed and jerked his head back and forth with

furious desperation, face flushing a frantic red, neck muscles straining to the point of tearing.

His arm poised stiffly in the air, the assassin waited the fourteen seconds it took for Howell to exhaust himself.

1

2

3

4

5

6

7

8

9

10

11

12

13

14

Howell stopped moving and looked at him with watery, resigned eyes. Like a rabbit in a snare. Like a bloody deer panting on the side of the road. Like a dog as the euthanizing needle goes in.

The assassin fired.

Retrieved the bullet from a black–red stain on the white shag carpet.

Left the awful stench behind.

17

DEEP BLUE WITH A CHERRY AT THE END

MAY 11, 1997

In their first match in 1996, Garry Kasparov decisively defeated the IBM chess-playing machine Deep Blue. The 1997 rematch against a more powerful version of Deep Blue seemed destined for the same outcome, with Kasparov easily winning the opening game and the IBM team defensively claiming a "bug" in the system. In game two, Deep Blue, playing with the white pieces, shocked Kasparov and the chess world at large by winning the game on the strength of a critical move that seemed impossible for a mere machine to make. The next three games resulted in draws, Kasparov, shaken and off his game, missing several chances to put Deep Blue away.

On May 11, 1997, exhausted and harried, Kasparov attempted a dubious opening to throw Deep Blue out of its comfort zone. He lost in fewer than twenty moves.

Game. Set. Match.

A machine had beaten the world chess champion for the first time. And not any world chess champion, but *Kasparov*— the man widely considered to be the best chess player of all time.

It was on the front page of the *Post*.

Bronze did not care.

He hung up the call from the Austin Police Department. They had found his phone number among Carolyn Haake's effects, written on an old receipt from a diner in Ohio.

Bronze dressed quietly, then walked to the nearest bar.

4 YEARS 31 DAYS 23 HOURS 57 MINUTES 6 SECONDS.

He had overestimated how long it would take for the waiter to retrieve his scotch. The bar was busy, but he should have known that the bartenders were nowhere near capacity; most of the booths in the back, where he sat staring at the small tumbler of scotch, were empty of occupants. It was still dinnertime for most people. Here, there were only those preparing for a long night of fun and those who'd eaten their early dinners alone and were looking for the hope of socialization before home and the TV.

And there was Bronze.

There was no ice melting. The scotch was neat. He could wait a little until the time came.

4 years 32 days 0 hours 0 minutes 0 seconds.

He didn't know the precise time, of course. He had made a record of it to the minute in his mind, repeated it to himself over and over again, but that level of precision was a convenience. Only a small lie in the scheme of things. There was something within that needed to record the time precisely even if precision was impossible.

But, all in all, he really couldn't be off by more than five minutes. He'd wait it out, just to be sure.

Bronze looked at the scotch and did not look away, even when laughter burst out from the bar area. It was the glorious, uplifting laughter of a woman with a deep voice who wasn't faking it at all.

4 years 32 days 0 hours 6 minutes 17 seconds.

He was ninety percent sure one minute or so ago, but now he was ninety-five percent sure. A couple of minutes more and he'd be at a hundred percent. Best to wait until then. Best to get to a hundred percent sure.

For the record.

4 years 32 days 0 hours 9 minutes 30 seconds.

He was sure. But his hand didn't move to the drink. (Carolyn's hand would never move again.)

4 years 32 days 0 hours 11 minutes 4 seconds.

He could perfectly imagine what it tasted like. (He could perfectly imagine her eyes softly closed.)

4 years 32 days 0 hours 11 minutes 31 seconds.

Might as well make it to the end of the minute—for the record. (There was no record.)

4 years 32 days 0 hours 12 minutes 0 seconds.

If he could make it twelve extra minutes, he could make it fifteen. There were a few things in his favor. The crowd was picking up, so the waiter was busy. But it wasn't so busy that they would be needing his booth anytime soon.

And clearly the waiter was afraid of him.

This pleased Bronze.

Bronze was always so afraid and spent so much of his energy hiding it—when he was the cause of fear, there was a certain malignant thrill. (And shame. Always fear or shame fear or shame fear or shame fear or shame fear or shame ...)

Bronze wasn't afraid right now. Bronze wasn't ashamed. Bronze wasn't anything.

Bronze knew it was over already. It had been predetermined for the first anyway. There was nothing to be done.

4 years 32 days 0 hours 14 minutes 25 seconds.

The waiter had gotten up the courage to ask if everything was all right and blown the whole timing.

Bronze didn't even turn to look at him. "Yes, everything's fine. I'll have another."

"Is there something wrong with that one? Is it the wrong kind?"

"No. I just want two. Just like this one. Another one, please. Another one just like this one."

The waiter nodded and backed away.

4 years 32 days 0 hours 15 minutes 58 seconds.

The second one arrived. Bronze arranged them neatly next to each other. The minute was almost up.

4 years 32 days 0 hours 17 minutes 0 seconds.

He was going to do it eventually. Even if he got up now and walked out, he was absolutely one hundred percent without a doubt in his soul he was going to do it.

Seventeen extra minutes wasn't bad. Thirty-two extra days wasn't bad. Four years wasn't bad. Four years wasn't five years, but he wasn't anywhere close to making that. That was beyond the pale.

They'd make note of it in his final tally. Four years, thirty-two days, seventeen minutes. Good show. White knuckles to prove it. Good show.

Of course it wouldn't balance the scales.

Not even a little bit.

(There was no one watching the scales.)

(There were no scales.)

4 years 32 days 0 hours 17 minutes 45 seconds.

Fine. Fine. It was ridiculous to try to make it to twenty minutes. He'd made it to eighteen.

That would have to be enough.

(There was never enough. There was no enough. There was nothing.)

(She may as well have never been.)

4 years 32 days 0 hours 18 minutes 0 seconds.

One sip.

4 years 32 days 0 hours 18 minutes 30 seconds.

He might not even count it if he didn't have another. No one would count one sip, would they?

The fire, though ... a burning hollow in his throat, his eyes, his guts. (It was a feeling at least, wasn't it? That and the drama of pretending contempt at your own weakness. Pretending you weren't relieved to have finally given up.)

Bronze had his second sip.

It felt almost casual.

Come with me.

4 years 32 days 0 hours 19 minutes 14 seconds.

One drink down. It had been quite a ride, hadn't it? It was OK, though; it would be OK. Just a couple. Then·A-OK. Maybe he would find he was even in control of it after all this time. It didn't absolutely have to be like before. It was all a mind game anyways. The mind was infinitely pliable. It didn't need to conform to just this one way of looking at things—a rigid frame that trapped you, sent you spinning in ever-accelerating circles until ... *boom*.

4 years 32 days 0 hours 20 minutes 20 seconds.

With the second drink down to its last dregs, he waved the waiter down and ordered a Manhattan. If he was going to drink, why not make it a bit fun?

He smiled at the waiter while he ordered and the waiter smiled back. Wasn't this better after all?

Past the waiter he saw the girls at the bar talking and giggling. He thought he could pick out the one that had laughed with that deep voice earlier.

4 years 32 days 0 hours 25 minutes 19 seconds.

The Manhattan arrived. He sipped and watched the bar.

After the scotch it tasted so soft and elegant.

There was a bright red cherry at the bottom. He could just

imagine how it would burst in his mouth with sweetness, with its saturation of booze.

Bronze caught one of the girls looking over at him. He gave her back his best go at a rogue's grin.

WHEN BRONZE GOT to the cherry, he didn't check his watch. He just stood up and started his saunter toward the bar.

He thought about his next order.

He thought about which girl.

There were many things he did not think of.

He bit down on the cherry.

It was just as sweet as he had imagined.

18

BRONZE
IRIS

It is May 11, 1997—Kasparov has lost to Deep Blue and Calvin "Bronze" Goldberg is drunk.

He was a drunk, he was sober, and now he's drunk again. He would tell you straight off that the drinking is a cover. Whether he is drunk or not papers over the real issue. He can be just as distracted from the real issue by obsessing over sobriety as he is by blasting it from his mind with scotch.

Bronze is aware of this. He is aware of the real underlying issue—which is, of course, women. Bronze is obsessed with women. And having them or not, fucking them or not, talking to them or not, looking at them or not, losing them or not—he fears—is all he was ever built to do or contemplate or imagine or enjoy or be terrorized by. He can put it any way he wants, frame it in whatever manner he or you or I might please, but there's no escaping this fact.

He is crushed by women.

He is a moth to a flame. He is a male mantis. He is any collection of atoms too close to a black hole.

He is fear and desire and shame.

He is giving up.

Bronze is a spasm, a pleasurable contraction of fine musculature, involuntary but inducible through hand, mouth, vagina, or anus.

Bronze fears and fears and fears.

He's had all his chances now. It's best to drink until there are no more hangovers—until there is nothing.

When I think of Bronze, I think of him bleeding.

PART II

THE HAUNTED MEN

The life of a creature is in the blood, and I have given it to you to make atonement for yourselves on the altar; it is the blood that makes atonement for one's life.

—Leviticus 17:11

ANTIQUES
JUNE 14, 1988

Bronze stumbled through the door, smearing blood on the rickety glass doorknob.

The blood ran freely from his nose down his white shirt and pooled warmly in his underwear from a wound he dare not think about.

His shirt was torn and half untucked. At the knees, his suit pants were black with dirt and shredded, as was the skin of the knees beneath. The sweat pouring into his eyes obscured his vision, as did the sudden transition from the bright streets to the dim lighting of the shop.

"Sir? Sir, we ask that you not be actively bleeding in the store."

Bronze's eyes began to shake off their occlusion and take in his refuge.

It was an antique shop—Tiffany lamps and highboys and blue–white china and knickknacks and a million precious little things and a precisely groomed little man behind the counter.

Bronze raised a bloody hand as if to excuse himself, then felt himself falling. It seemed to happen so slowly, almost gently, like he was already lying in bed and just drifting within his mind toward the warm embrace of sleep.

The crashing, shattering noise that followed was far away, like the distant sounds of the street in a penthouse apartment.

"Not the rose medallion!"

Someone was screaming somewhere way down there on those distant streets, just sound without meaning. It needn't concern Bronze anymore.

BEFORE BRONZE OPENED HIS EYES, the first thing that came to him was the ache of bruises, the sting of minor cuts all over, and black nausea from the sickeningly painful wound between his hip and groin—all the pain joined together in a chorus, singing sharp discordant notes to return him to consciousness.

But almost immediately upon waking, consciousness took a half step back, like a quickly withdrawn hand from a burning stovetop. Besides, beyond the pain, cradling him all around was a womblike warmth.

The antique shop had been an illusion. He had truly fallen into a soft cloud of bedding and morphine. The pain at his hip disassociated, almost stopped screeching away as he felt the comforting embrace that wrapped him up ever so tightly. The pain was there, but it was only happening to his body, to this piece of meat with which he had only a loose association.

Bronze opened his eyes. He saw the slight, perfectly coiffed cashier looming over him. And next to him was someone else— a worried face with drooping eyes and deepening wrinkles and three days' growth of black stubble. It was a face he knew from another life.

It was little Bruce Schwarz grown up and grown old. But that was impossible.

"Bruce! He's awake."

"I can see that, Lawrence. Cal? Cal, can you hear me? Do you recognize me?"

"Schwarzy?" Bronze said, feeling loopy and dazed. *Of all the antique shops in all the towns in all the world ...* He opened his mouth to grimace or smile but instantly regretted it as he felt the cuts on his lip and inside his mouth tear open, sending metallic blood down his throat. He coughed and sat up, coughing and coughing while old Bruce Schwarz rubbed and patted him on the back.

Bronze reached out and firmly grasped Bruce's upper arm, as if to prove he was real.

"What's it been, Bruce—fifteen years almost?"

"Cal, do you know where you are? You're in the hospital. Lawrence and I drove you here after you collapsed."

Then, suddenly, it started coming back to him—the pain and the memories. His eyes went wild in his head, searching about the room, frantic and frightened. And though he knew it couldn't be—the whole room, the walls, the curtains, the beeping medical machines, the fluorescent ceiling lights, Bruce's very skin—everything everywhere was bathed in turquoise.

"Bruce, Bruce, we can't wait ... we have to stop him!"

Images flashed. Memories of turquoise. He saw her again —*the girl through the second door, lying on the mattress, naked, her feet perfectly still. Her toenails ...*

Turquoise everywhere.

"Miss," he whispered through grinding teeth. "Miss! You've got to get out of here."

Then he stepped further into the room and looked down upon her —seeing her fully for the first time.

Now it was Bronze who screamed.

20

ABSOLUTE BOTTOM

MAY 12, 1997

B ronze returned to consciousness and saw Bruce Schwarz's sad drooping eyes looking down upon him. The pain in his esophagus and stomach was vicious and immediate.

He was glad of the pain. It distracted him from thinking.

"Is the girl still here?" he asked.

"You mean the assistant secretary of the Labor Department?"

"Huh?"

"The woman, Janet De Luca, who was here when I first arrived and left several minutes ago in her wrinkled charcoal skirt suit is the assistant secretary for administration and management at the United States Department of Labor. Or at least that's what it says on the business card she left."

Bruce had been fiddling with the card in his hand and now held it up in front of Bronze's face.

"Jesus. This fucking town ..." Bronze rolled himself over into a sitting position, resting his head in his hands and his elbows on his knees, the springs of the couch groaning and aching like arthritic joints.

"So, what brings you here, Bruce?"

"Iris called."

"Ah." Incoherent flashes of knocking on Iris's door at two a.m. flashed through Bronze's memory. That was a lot to process. Too much.

Bronze decided to back away from the psychic issues for the moment and attempted to focus on objectively assessing his physical situation.

His mouth was barren of moisture; his gums felt scraped and bruised and bloodied like he'd brushed them with a hacksaw. A pulsing throb cascaded rhythmically through his skull, not yet quite bursting into the searing pain that was to come. He was still half drunk and had that to thank for keeping the head pain at a level such that he might manage to converse with Bruce. All four of his limbs merely ached. But his stomach was filled with some vile admixture that ought to be vomited up. And he could feel the impulse of his body toward purging, but it was too weak to actually produce an expulsion. He would have to sit with the feeling of being on the cusp of vomiting until his body simply absorbed the poison fully.

He had broken his final covenant with the universe. He was a drunk again. But before the horror and shame of that came, he remembered the greater horror ...

Carolyn. Dead.

The universe had broken its end of the bargain first—no more drinking and no more dead girls.

So the universe could go fuck itself.

Carolyn. Her eyes softly closing as he lightly kissed her upper lip ...

What was the point? What possible reason could there be? What was power or money next to Carolyn? Didn't they see that Carolyn *was* the point? That beauty and soul were the point? The ends beyond all of that mundanity? How could they be against her? Against a woman with soft skin and hair and lips and black mascara and such sad eyes?

For Bronze, to say a woman like Carolyn was beautiful was in fact nonsensical. For a man like Bronze, a woman cannot really be beautiful. Instead, beauty *is* a woman. The definition of terms flows in the other direction. And when a man accepts that notion, it follows immediately that the thing about women, the thing that haunts him, that he can never quite put his finger on is, in fact, *awe*.

That was the only thing Bronze truly believed, really at this core kept sacred, his singular axiomatic principle—his awe of women.

Yet against women, from the beginning of time and with relentless regularity, men have committed acts of absolute horror—some because of animal attraction and some because of a need to control and some for greed, but mostly a man sins to destroy his awe, and with it, that awful feeling of powerlessness.

And there's nothing lower than that.

And whatever deformity of a god pulled the strings that made Bronze and his universe go round and round must be as low as they come—absolute bottom.

Just like me, Bronze thought.

And as he thought this, whatever dam of drunkenness held back the pain in his head burst forth and a sensation of pure violence screamed through his mind.

The pain screamed, *Come with me.*

And Bronze cried. Right there in front of old Bruce Schwarz.

BRUCE SCHWARZ LOOKED DOWN at Bronze's collapsing face. Instinctively he sat down next to him on the couch and put his arm around him while Bronze tried desperately to control his emotions.

Bruce felt the tug of that old love stirring. He couldn't help himself, as much as he might want to. What was it like for Bronze, for any friendship of straight men? Could they feel for each other as Bruce felt for Bronze? Could they really love so entirely separately from that thing within that blessed Bruce with seeing beauty in his fellow man? Oh, and Bronze was a tragic beauty. A doomed beauty. The dark hair and curving art nouveau lines of his face were imbued with their own haunting light—moonlight reflected upon a black river.

Was this how Bronze felt for this woman? The same way Bruce felt for Michael? An unquenchable longing that made you feel just like God's first angel simply to be able to feel your longing so deeply, so painfully? Could it really be the same across the gulf of genders when there was so much room for misunderstanding among men alone?

Since age seventeen, Bruce Schwarz had borne the word *FAG* carved in evil slanted writing that you now couldn't read amongst the wrinkling softness of his forty-year-old belly, been beaten half to death by a cop with a baton outside an East Village drag bar in '81 only to limp away down an alleyway full of brown and green broken beer bottle glass as the man's malevolence had turned toward a fleeing queen tripping in high heels, seen half his friends and his one true love shrivel in upon themselves on the way to slow death. Yet Bruce had come to accept that his eternal betrayer—unrelenting empathy—would never die within him, no matter how much pain it caused him. He still had warmth in his heart for Bronze after all these years, all this distance from the time when they had been true friends, unself-conscious in their friendship. And, despite the utter lunacy of it, in that big wet broken red heart of his, Bruce still had sparks of sympathy for the plight of the heterosexual.

21

HOPELESS DISCIPLINE
IRIS

"So, should we just go ahead and make this a weekly thing?" Bruce asked with a sly smile over his cup of Constant Comment tea.

I laughed, offered him honey that he waved away, and then sat down across from him at my round kitchen table, squirting an ample portion into my own cup.

"I do always enjoy gabbing over a spot of tea. My girlfriends, such as they are, are mostly busy with kids and piano recitals and soccer practices or whatever it is that they do these days."

"Me too, and while I have a regular tea partner, I couldn't imagine a worse one than Lawrence."

"The cashier at the antique shop?"

"The one and only. All beauty and not a hint of a sympathetic ear for his aging elders. Still spends every night flitting about DuPont Circle. Looks at me as if I were about 105 years old. I shouldn't be so harsh. He's got a sharp eye for Canton and stemware. The voice of an angel too, if you would believe it—but if I have to hear him shouting along to Madonna's 'Borderline' in the store one more time, I just don't know what I'll do."

"Are you sure I can't get you something sweet to nibble on?"

Bruce waved his hand and shook his head.

"So, how's the patient? What's the prognosis?"

Bruce shook his head again, more slowly this time. "Physically fine. A little worse for wear. I got him off the couch and onto the bed. He's sleeping it off. But I'm worried. I really am. Carolyn—that poor girl—but why did it have to involve him? After all he went through with the Keaton killings ... Can I ask? What was he like last night?"

I looked down at my reddish tea and fiddled with the handle as I tried to mentally order the details of an event that seemed more vision than reality.

"I'd been sleeping only lightly. At first, the knocking at my front door seemed like part of a dream, but when I realized I was in fact awake, my first thought was panic—that it was vandals attempting to lure me into opening my house to them. I went to my bedroom window and looked down to see Bronze, waving away a woman that called to him from his apartment.

"I threw on a bathrobe and ran down to him, fearing some terrible news. When I opened the door, the smell of booze hit me like I had walked into a Kentucky distillery.

"I said 'Bronze?', completely startled to see him like this.

"His face didn't look at mine but seemed pointed somewhere around my knees.

"'She's dead.'

"'Who?' I asked, but then it immediately came to me.

"'Carolyn ... I wanted you to know.' Then he finally looked me in the eyes and said 'I'm sorry' before those eyes dropped away again and he turned to go back down my steps toward his apartment.

"I'm not sure on what impulse it came to me or even really all that I meant, but without thinking, I called out to him. 'It's not your fault.'

"He looked back at me with this big drunken smile and

said, 'Of course it is.' And just kept going down, all the way from my door to his apartment and to the woman waiting for him."

I stopped the story there for some reason, lying by omission.

Bruce was looking around the room. "The lamp you bought from me looks nice there ... I didn't make note of it last time I was here, I was so frazzled ..." He looked back at me with water in his right eye that didn't quite overtop the lid into tears. "I'm sorry, Iris. We'll just have to pray it doesn't end up like last time. He's older now. Wiser, right? We do get wiser, don't we? Ha, it's times like now I wish I still had religion. My mom would be here warding off the evil eye for all of our sakes. I don't know. I suppose I can guess how he feels ... You know about Michael, yes?"

I nodded. "Bronze told me. I'm so sorry, Bruce. Oh god, I never know what to say."

"What's there to say? I don't know what to say either. There's nothing to be said or done. Michael's been dead a long time now. I accept that. Maybe I'd even date again if anyone showed a bit of interest. You'll let me know if you hear of anyone, won't you?"

He smiled, those drooping eyes lifting for a moment with wrinkles all about them before they slowly sagged back down and the smile disappeared.

"But that isn't really true, is it? Really, I cannot accept it."

Bruce's eyes became unfocused. He seemed to fade within himself. I became hyper aware of every little noise in the room —the cycling of the air conditioner, a bird rhythmically chirping outside, the creaking of my floorboards, and the rubbing of my thigh against the chair as I unconsciously shifted my foot from heel to toe and back again.

"How do you go on, then?" I asked finally, if only to fill the oppressive silence.

That quickly fading smile flashed across his face again. "*Hopeless discipline*, darling. Hopeless discipline ..."

He took a deep breath, his eyes flicking across the ceiling until they settled on my face again.

"I wake up at the same time each morning—early. I don't rightly know why, but just like burning goat fat or whatever. It is pleasing to the Lord if you get up early. It's good luck to get up early.

"I try to move very elegantly from the first moment I arise. I place my feet softly on the floor from the bed. I do not jerk my back straight but float to standing. I move like a dancer cast in a background part with no dancing. Understand, this is not natural for me—it takes great discipline of mind.

"I drink a glass of pure water. I limber my body up. I dress in an outfit laid out the night before. Then I, without any hesitation, pierce the veil of my front door into the cool morning air and begin to run. The run has its little challenges. There are three hills—the second one's quite a monster. I take them on each day to the best of my ability.

"After, I stretch, and I don't skip steps in my stretching. I shower in water that is neither hot nor cold, because even though I love to stand there in very hot water, I know that that is not best for my skin or the general feeling of my body throughout the day.

"I eat breakfast. I go to the shop. If I'm honest, Lawrence runs most things at this point—really only leaving me to the financials and to help out when there's a rush, which almost never happens. So I make sure I know my craft. I read and learn something new about the decorative arts. Then I read fiction. I never went to college, but I like to think I could be awarded an English degree at this point. I read all of the classics. I read Dickens, Proust, Eliot, Faulkner, Woolf, Hemingway, Fitzgerald, all of them—I read newer stuff too. And I enjoy a lot of it, but in my mind, I am thinking—this is part of the discipline, this is for your mind as the running is for your body.

"There's a pull-up bar in the backroom of the shop. I'm sure it's the only one in all of the antique shops in all the world. Whenever I feel I am drifting, I do pull-ups or drop to the floor for push-ups or sit-ups or whatever ups I can think of.

"At night I make dinner. I try to improve my cooking a little each night. I try to push my knowledge of technique. I put on some great work of music while I cook. A piano concerto or a famous jazz record, *Kind of Blue*, that sort of thing—and, like the fiction, I often enjoy this, but I am thinking all the time, joy is not the point. The point is the discipline.

"I eat my meal. While I eat, I watch a rental from Block-buster. A work of cinematic art. A black and white classic. A foreign film, perhaps. Again, an education of another kind.

"I make sure I stay up a couple of hours before bed so as not to get heartburn. I write in my journal. I might practice the piano a little. I clean. If it's nice out, I'll take a short walk around the neighborhood. Then I get into bed.

"Even while I'm falling asleep, I think, I may be enjoying the feeling of the warm bed and the cool pillow and the soft sheets, but really I am trying to have another kind of education—I'm trying to induce lucid dreams and improve my ability to remember my dreams so as to gain another dimension of insight. And I will build this capacity up within me as well, just like the running and the reading and the cooking and all the rest of it.

"Then I do it again.

"I do all this because I cannot accept.

"I do it because I am an exile in this universe that has denied me Michael, which of all its wonders was the tiny little corner of the universe that I loved the most—the only thing or person that truly granted me the feeling of what it was like *to love*.

"And once that feeling was inside me, it was never going to leave. I was irretrievably changed. And it took him from me ... it fucking took that from me.

"No. I am not on good terms with the universe. We have irreconcilable differences."

I had no idea what to say, but, as if without consulting me, my hand reached out across the table and took Bruce's hand. I squeezed his hand, then he squeezed mine back. Then we were still and there was just the warmth of Bruce's hand and the smell of tea. And there was silence.

LATER, AS I HUGGED Bruce and said my goodbyes at the front door, I caught sight of Mark Roth sitting in his unmarked car parked across the street from my townhouse.

I lit a cigarette and watched him as he scribbled something in his notebook, completely unaware of me.

What was he up to?

I imagined scenarios, attitudes, adventures. I imagined walking over to Roth's car and rapping my knuckles against his window. He would be startled to so suddenly see me leering down at him, blowing smoke through pursed lips. When he opened the window, I'd say something clever and provocative, give my best go at a dangerous dame vibe if only to set the mood, as if I could slip away from myself for a time, lose the responsibilities and demands of relentless thought and become a stock character in someone else's story.

But Roth was already opening his door and walking toward me or my tenant below.

And as Roth walked and I watched his stiff movements, I thought of the part from last night I had left out when talking to Bruce.

How as Bronze went down his stairs, he stopped again and spoke to me from below, hidden by the stairs between us, his usually warm voice harshened by drink.

"Iris ..."

"Yes, Bronze?"

"Iris ... you know I lived in Japan once. Back in the judo days. Feels like a dream or a story I read. But I really did.

"I even got close to speaking the language OK. It went *whumph* from my mind afterward. For years I'd hear some Japanese tourist speaking in their native tongue and all the sounds would seem so familiar, so understandable, but they'd form no meaning in my mind. Infuriating. If I really focused, I could pick up a word here or there, but I could never follow the greater meaning.

"These days Japanese doesn't sound like anything to me. As random as any other language I don't speak. Except I can remember that once—once when I was young ..."

And then he was silent for what felt like a long while. I imagined him swaying a little there under the stairs. Then I heard the door open and close.

And I wonder why, of all things, I couldn't tell Bruce that part.

I'm not even sure what Bronze was really trying to say. The drink had likely blocked the necessary synapses from carrying his confused thoughts to his mouth with any clarity. But without the drink he wouldn't have spoken at all, I suppose.

Something about being young.

I remember that too—being young. I remember what it was like. And I don't aggrandize it. I remember it too well, maybe. The pain of it.

But now my nerves are burned out and I don't think I could ever hurt like I did in those days again.

And it gets so that when some great pain does manage to

break through the Novocain of experience, it comes on like an old friend dropping by unexpectedly. You sit down with the pain and over cups of steaming tea remember back to those long-gone dragging hours when you felt all the time and so acutely the pain of longing, like there was nothing else in the world, like a full body bruise, like an animal ensnared in the metal teeth of a trap, like desperation.

Now you know that in those days you could have walked down any of a thousand roads. Now you're trapped on just one. And it'll end where it ends.

You're young and in pain. Then you're old and hopeless.

That's what Bronze was saying.

I think.

If I had to guess.

22

A COMMISSION

MAY 12, 1997

Dusty yellow light filled the living room, made the room look like an old sealed basement or attic cracked open after years of neglect.

The pain was gone. There was just the feeling of cotton stuffing his head instead of a brain. Everything was flattened out. Nothing mattered all that much. You could do a thing or not do a thing. You could go left or right. North or south. Drink or not. Listen to Roth or only pretend to.

Go with Carolyn and die. Stay here and ferment.

All was equally righteous and vile.

Bronze sat in the dog chair and drank lukewarm coffee out of a mug that read "X-Files" on one side and "The Truth Is Out There" on the other. Roth and Iris sat together on the couch, the permanent indent on Bronze's usual side causing Iris to list towards Roth as if she were leaning in, about to rest her head against her lover's shoulder.

Roth was uncomfortable. Iris was uncomfortable. Bronze just was.

He decided to try to move things along. Roth needed help and didn't know whom he could trust. Except for Bronze.

Because Roth had been there in '88. And Roth had seen what Bronze had seen.

"Anything you say in front of me, you can say in front of Iris." Bronze sipped his coffee, thought of a hundred reasons why that statement was absurd. "Well, within reason."

Roth rubbed his hands together. "Of course, of course. I just thought Iris might not want to get too ..."

"Mark, not only has Iris offered to work as my unofficial assistant—I assume for experiential reasons related to the research for her next novel, a sort of Tom Wolfe saturation journalism thing, making any expenses she might accrue throughout the whole process Schedule C tax deductible—but she is also a moneyed interest of another kind, seeing how if Metro PD does indeed commission me as consultant on this case, I might actually be able to pay next month's rent."

Roth stopped rubbing his hands and threw them up in a gesture of surrender. "I, of course, leave it to your discretion." Then, turning to Iris: "Iris, your work with Bruce Schwarz looking into those back files on Kopes has been invaluable. We apparently don't have anyone half so thorough at our office. Can't thank you enough. My next appointment after this is, in fact, with this Senator Crawford to look into your tip that he's rumored to have hired Roger Haake. I hope you can keep working some of these political connections for us as well as the Kopes family business dealings. There's just too much material out there for us now that we have possibly four connected murders. And just since Kopes's death, there's been another eleven presumably unconnected murders around DC that Metro PD has to work ... it just never ends.

"That being said, the information I'm about to discuss does not leave this room."

Iris nodded. Bronze noticed a look of hunger on her face to hear a class of secrets she'd never been privy to before. He hoped she wouldn't be too disappointed. Secrets were always better in your imagination. The reality of them was just another headache.

"Mark, I'm happy to help in any way I can. And Bronze, stop bringing up the rent. We can just call a moratorium until everything's more ... settled."

Iris meant to be kind, but the idea that Bronze would be her charity case pricked at an ember of anger within him. He had made the bad joke about the rent. And he had been at least half serious under the sarcastic tone. Down deep somewhere there was a small voice within him crying out muffled noises that sounded something like "You're lost again." But the real Bronze, the Bronze that held tight to the controls in his old noggin, knew he'd always been lost. And always would be. So what was one more indignity?

Meanwhile, Roth had dropped a large file of documents labeled "Kopes, William Friedrich Jr." on the coffee table and gone back to vigorously rubbing his hands.

"Starting with Billy Kopes. The autopsy report has come back from the FBI. He died of strangulation. Amongst the postmortem injuries from his time in the Potomac, there are clearly defined markings on the neck. The coroner says these are hand marks, and based on the apparent placement of the thumb and fingers and the consequent array of nail marks, he was strangled from the front by someone face to face with him."

Roth put his hands out in front of him, thumbs overlapping, fingers forming an encircling gesture, open at one end where a neck might slip in.

Dropping the gesture, Roth kept his hands busy again, now massaging his knuckles, first one hand, then the other.

"Bronze, you were right from the beginning. This was murder.

"There are what appear to be indications of a struggle—

bruising along the knuckles, a fracture in one of the fingers, bruising on the hip and lower back as if he was thrust backward against a desk or to the ground.

"We don't have any prints or blood or any other identifiable material associated with the assailant. It's possible that all of this material was lost in the waters of the Potomac. But it's also possible that the assailant carefully removed such evidence and purposefully placed Kopes into the river as part of his attempts to avoid detection. We're lucky Kopes washed up as soon as he did. If the body had been exposed for significantly longer, which was the likely intention, we may not even have been able to determine the cause of death."

Roth paused his self hand massage a brief moment and then began again with even more rigor.

"As you are both aware, both Roger and Carolyn Haake have also been murdered. Both died from gunshot wounds. Forensics has determined that a Heckler & Koch PSG1 semi-automatic sniper rifle was used in the K Street shooting targeting Roger Haake. No bullets were recovered from Carolyn Haake's body, but based on her wound pattern, we are confident the same rifle was used. No prints or forensic identifiers of the assailant were found by the Austin PD.

"Yesterday, after failing to reach James Howell several times for further questioning by telephone, a patrol was sent to his apartment. He was found dead there, tied to a kitchen chair, with significant bruising and broken bones in his hands consistent with torture. Like with Carolyn Haake, no bullets, no prints or any other usable forensics from the assailant were discovered. The FBI's ballistics team believes a silenced pistol was used to kill Howell.

"Zachary Jackson, Carolyn's other lover, has been moved out of his apartment to an undisclosed location known only to the federal marshal's office. But not too far away in case he's needed for more questioning. Jackson has motive and a weak alibi. But he lacks any firearms training, and upon inspection there was no bruising or wounding of any kind to indicate he may have been Kopes's assailant. And nothing about him that would indicate the means to hire a skilled assassin. He willingly gave over bank records, and there was nothing out of the ordinary in terms of deposits or withdrawals. But who knows? He's part of the same political world as Kopes and Haake and Howell. So maybe we just haven't found the connection yet.

"Getting back to Howell. There was a call placed from Carolyn's hotel in Austin to Howell's apartment. Based on this call, the ballistics evidence, and common sense, we believe the same man killed Carolyn and Roger Haake as well as James Howell—that Howell was a tool to find Carolyn Haake's location and was killed once he'd served that purpose.

"This same killer may have also murdered Billy Kopes, but, as I'm sure you've noticed, the modus operandi of that murder was distinct from the others. Strangulation. No gun. Close quarters. More personal. Messy ..."

Upon hearing the revelation of Howell's murder, Bronze let his head fall forward, barely tracking the rest of Roth's monologue. He hadn't known how the assassin had found Carolyn, but the greater part of him had assumed that he had never managed to lose him during their wild escape a week earlier. That as he and Carolyn had taken the highway west, he had missed some patient, nondescript follower, a silent predator taking each turn with him, stopping down the road from the gas stations he chose or maybe even filling up next to him, watching them talk through the back window of Bruce Schwarz's Volvo, watching the slightly swaying faded maroon of their drawn motel curtains, watching him leave her at a bus station in Cincinnati so ugly he couldn't even picture it anymore, instead it was just a sound that buzzed in his head like amplified static, and then he, Bronze, disappearing like a broken soldier fleeing a lost battle into a dark woods while that other stayed and watched her buy the next ticket to Austin, sat near her on the bus and watched her sleep, watched her check into her downtown hotel, watched her move about a strange city, waited for her to be alone, to let her guard down, to think she was safe, to fall into a dream of some other life, watched hope light across her face, watched her and watched her and watched her and then ...

But that wasn't what had happened. The assassin hadn't waited at all. Hadn't watched her more than it took to find her, to see her walking back to her hotel alone down some darkened alleyway and ...

Roth had moved on to telling them what they knew about the assassin—that the CIA called him the Machine. That they didn't even know where he was from, but that intelligence and an FBI psychological profile suggested a harrowing upbringing. Possibly a war-torn country. Possibly Soviet oppression. Maybe one of our own cock-ups. Roth read aloud the last chilling lines of the psych report. "His upbringing was torture. While there is no basis for ruling out psychopathy, severe childhood trauma leading to acquired sociopathy is probable. He is utterly indifferent to suffering. He was born into a world of constant terror and sees brutality and horrific events as the natural course of things. Controlling the violence is the only way he feels any sense of control."

Bronze raised his hand for Roth to stop. "What do you think of this name—the Machine?"

Roth stopped massaging his hands for the moment. "I hadn't thought too much about it. I suppose it's fitting given his methods and demeanor. He's cold, calculating, and without morals, sentiment, or remorse."

"I don't like it," Bronze said, seeming to fully focus on Roth for the first time, not really knowing where he was going with his objection until it tumbled out of him. "It's a metaphor, and one must be careful with metaphors. Iris knows what I mean. She knows all about metaphors and their dangers.

"I see the connection. He behaves like a machine. We, the collective we of humanity, created him with our callous atrocities, like we might create an Abrams tank or an atomic bomb. But if we call him a machine, he can't be killed ..."

More than that, Bronze realized; to try to kill a machine was to become like Captain Ahab chasing his white whale, full of a great sickness that turns beasts into men or men into beasts. And now in this day and age, as the world began to relentlessly fill with computers and robots and programs and scripts, men were instead turned into machines and vice versa and back again.

More and more society's thoughts twisted away from people as individuals toward systems, mechanics, abstractions, cyphers and codes, worlds within worlds. Unstoppable *progress*. A glacier sliding down a smooth groove of history indifferent to Bronze's opinion.

"Calling him a machine separates us from him. Since we don't know his name, let's just call him 'the assassin.' We should remind ourselves that he is human, that he is one of us, he is a part of us ... As much as he was made by circumstance, as much as he might tell himself otherwise—he chooses what he does. Just like you. Just like me. And knowing full well the whys and the wherefores and all the rest, I choose to kill the motherfucker."

Roth now sat stone still, staring at Bronze, hands rigid on his lap. "And how exactly do you propose to do that?"

Bronze just shook his head. He hadn't got as far as *how*.

Roth gave a quick curt nod. "My job is to work the Kopes case. The big picture's being coordinated at a higher level.

Bronze, I know you're invested in the Carolyn Haake angle. Our resources are stretched thin working everything here in DC. Frankly, we don't have anyone I'd trust more than you to send down to Austin. I'd like to hire you to go down there and see what you can see. The Austin PD doesn't have the full context surrounding Carolyn's death. Maybe you can pick up something they missed."

He paused, seemed to focus in fully on the almost frenzied intensity thrashing within Bronze's eyes.

"Bronze, you come within a mile of this Machine, this assassin, whatever name you want to give him—you call the police and you wait. You remember '88—you remember the last time when you should have waited but didn't. And Keaton was just a run-of-the-mill whack job. This guy's a whole different level."

Bronze leaned back in his chair and sipped his now-cold coffee from his X-Files cup. "Aye aye, whatever you say, Captain. But if I'm going to do this right, I need to see the Howell crime scene first. Then I'm gone. Just get one of your desk jockeys to buy me a ticket on the first flight to Austin."

23

THE CLOAKROOM

MAY 12, 1997

A couple hours after his meeting with Bronze and Iris, Mark Roth found himself in a small hideaway office dominated by a dark wooden conference table surrounded by tall black leather office chairs. The wall decorations were ornate in the style of revolutionary American kitsch: a huge mirror, framed in swirling flourishes of gold leaf; a bronze statue of an eagle in flight; an old framed flag with a circle of stars; a painting of George Washington looking off into the distance; a painting of Thomas Jefferson looking piercingly ahead; a painting of John Adams looking ambivalent; and in the far corner, a modern American flag hanging limply.

Crawford sat across from Roth along with his bland and bespectacled chief legal counsel. Crawford had a dour look on his senatorial face. As far as Roth knew, he was primarily famous in DC circles for looking like everyone's generic mental picture of a senator, for his great shock of white hair, and for his penchant for randomly punctuating his circuitous locutions with sharp gesticulations of thumb and forefinger. Little mention was made of any great list of legislative accomplishments or flights of oratorical sublimity.

They had been talking in a roundabout fashion for too long and Roth was growing weary of Crawford's winding and loopy-sounding avoidances of anything approaching a substantive answer. It was time to hit him directly with the information Iris had uncovered in her research.

"What is your relationship with Roger Haake?"

"Haake ... Haake ... Kyle, do we know a Haake?"

The chief legal counsel, apparently Kyle, responded, "I believe Detective Roth is referring to the late Roger Haake. Senator Crawford has cause to meet many of the individuals who make up the Washington establishment. Until his recent demise, Mr. Haake was a prominent member, not unknown to those in this office."

"Yes, Roth, not unknown."

"So, Senator, just to be clear, you are admitting you knew Haake, then?"

"Roth, please. Kyle just explained the whole thing. He says he was unknowable. We couldn't have known, you see. The consequences, I mean. So many young men lost in the jungles of Kuwait. And for what? Just so Johnny can get his Coca-Cola for a nickel and three quarters? It defies reason and, what's more, good old-fashioned American common sense. Roth, the American people—the American people are a decent hard-working people. They don't want to fly off to South Ceylon or North Siam just to punch some two-bit Commie in the jaw. We've got to get back to our core values. Family. Manufacturing. Agriculture. Freedom. Wiping the sweat off your brow and drinking a cold one with the boys while the missus fires up the sirloins. Yes, and I'll say it, even lighting up some fine Virginia pipe tobacco and patting little Suzy on the shoulder. She's worked hard all semester to get those grades. Come hell or high water, she's going into town to that county fair this year and you bet your doggone she's going to get to ride that tilt-a-whirl. We'll have big old hogs and thin-waisted women strolling daintily in their lace and dresses and parasols. This is a real country, Roth. A beautiful new and ancient land. God-given and God-inspired. And God watching over us too. You're not going to take that away from these people. I won't let you, dammit. These God-fearing men and women who work with their hands and make the car you drive and the burger you eat. No sir, not while there's breath in these old lungs, by God."

It finally struck Roth somewhere between the reference to the "jungles of Kuwait" and "North Siam" that Crawford was quite far from his right mind to say the least. Somehow his staff must have been keeping his diminishment more or less under wraps. But the other politicians—they had to have known.

Then the first implications hit Roth.

Billy Kopes had known.

Billy didn't think he had a good chance against Crawford in '98. No, he was *guaranteed* victory. So why was Haake working for Crawford at all?

Roth nodded at Crawford. "I couldn't agree more, sir. I think that's all I need from you at this time. If you can spare him, I'd like Kyle here to stay behind to answer a few more questions."

"Roth, I want you to know I salute what you and the boys in blue do for this country. You can have Kyle for all the time in the world. God bless you."

"God bless you too, sir."

Crawford achingly made his way out of the room while his legal counsel's eyes anxiously flitted about as if he was looking for a door to dash through.

Roth was going to have to get tougher with him.

"Kyle." Roth looked long and hard at the legal counsel. "Kyle what?"

"Browning."

"Mr. Browning, it is clear that Senator Crawford did not

himself contract with Roger Haake for the senate campaign in '98 or, in fact, make any strategic campaign decisions. But we know that someone in his office did. You, I presume. I would like to know very clearly and in minute detail exactly what was going on between the Crawford office and Roger Haake. If you are feeling reluctant, I am more than happy to take you down to the station."

Browning's legs began to bob and shake under the desk. "That won't be necessary. Yes, you're right. We, uh, we were working with Haake. And the things we were asking him to do ... please, I know they weren't strictly, um ... well, they were in a gray area. But you have to understand, it was only a matter of a few days before Kopes hired him out from under us. We didn't act on any of it! We just listened. And Haake was playing us the whole time. He was only using us to bid up the price of his services to Kopes."

One of the great advantages of having a reputation as a detective is that you were so often overestimated. It appeared that Kyle Browning assumed Roth knew something he didn't— that Haake had moved on from Crawford to work for, apparently, Billy Kopes again. But how did that make any sense? Why did Roger Haake hire Bronze to photograph Kopes with his wife if he was working for Kopes all along?

"Mr. Browning, I see no reason to press forward with issues of campaign malfeasance in light of our current murder investigation; that is, so long as you're fully cooperative. What I'd like you to tell me, as precisely as possible, is why did Kopes hire Haake?"

"Well, I couldn't really say why Fred Kopes hired Roger Haake. The same reason I'm sure you've heard a thousand times. Everyone knows Fred hated his brother."

24

THE LAST LOVER

MAY 12, 1997

B ronze had spent four hours staring uselessly at the bloodstain on James Howell's carpet, at his bathroom, at his kitchen, at his bed, at his pictures of himself smiling with golfing buddies or walking with an air of importance down marbled halls next to dark-suited politicians.

There was nothing there.

Well, maybe there was something there that a Sherlock Holmes or a Philip Marlow would have seen, but not Bronze. And maybe there was some better version of Bronze that would have seen that missing clue too if he weren't two whiskies deep by the time he arrived.

Eventually he was just banging his head against the wall, going over the same ground again and again with no plan to hunt down some novel crawl space behind the laundry hamper, no secret safe in the wall to search, no critical insight of which knickknack was odd or which pair of worn tennis shoes was out of place.

The uniformed cop that had let him in on Roth's orders had started out leaning against the threshold reading the sports section of the *Washington Times* but, as time stretched on and on, had eventually devolved into just staring at Bronze with bored cow eyes. He seemed to be reminding himself over and over that he was getting paid to stand there and do nothing. And that beat a lot of other horseshit a DC cop could be doing.

The cop's stare reminded Bronze of four hours earlier, when he had first entered the front door of Howell's red brick apartment building. Bronze had felt a different pair of eyes on him then. For all the boredom of Officer Cow Eyes' stare, this other stare had burned with intensity, but by the time Bronze had tried to get a good look at its source, there was nothing but empty air and sunny sidewalk.

It was just a passing moment of discomfort. He shouldn't have given it as much thought as he did. Bronze had long ago learned that the calibration of the alarm bells in his mind was out of whack and that they sounded with far too much sensitivity. But now, hours later, as he walked through the building's lobby lost in thought over how thoroughly the assassin had covered his tracks, he gave Officer Cow Eyes a lazy salute and pushed through the glass doors out onto the street only to feel those same intense eyes again.

He told himself it was nothing. But still, he walked away from the upscale apartment building with a slight uptick in his pace and heartbeat, a small dose of adrenaline releasing into his bloodstream.

Two concrete and glass blocks from Howell's building, he peeked back over his shoulder. There was a man following about a block behind.

Maybe.

He was imagining it, in all likelihood.

He turned right and went another block and half, cars grumbling by, the distant pounding of a pneumatic drill breaking a sidewalk somewhere blurring any hope of hearing his supposed stalker.

He dared a quick glance behind ... the man was still there.

The man just happened to be going in the same direction. In the glare and haze of the sun, the man didn't seem to have a single distinctive feature, might not even have been the same man. Maybe he was seeing different men. There just always happened to be one man or another behind him. Always *exactly* a block back ...

The assassin.

Maybe ... and if it was, well, just the man he was trying to find.

But if it really was him, that killing *machine*, did Bronze even stand a puncher's chance? Earlier, he had carelessly proclaimed he'd kill the man, but now the full weight of Roth's words came back to him: *And how exactly do you propose to do that?*

Bronze's heart now truly pounded, his hands were sweating, and the muscles of his upper back began to tense and prepare for what may come. But what good would muscles be when the assassin's bullet struck? No, his body would not be placated by whatever wishful thinking his half-drunk, half-hungover mind concocted. No, eyes had been waiting for him at Howell's building and now they stalked him. Predator and prey. And Bronze on the wrong side of that equation.

At the next intersection, passing a homeless drunk atonally shouting "In for a penny, in for a penny" over and over again, Bronze suddenly deviated from his path, taking a sharp turn to the left when he had appeared to be going straight.

He hustled down two blocks, doing his best to make his hurried pace seem in the realm of normal. Another block and he began to dare to feel relief. He consciously slowed his pace again. Felt his heartbeat start to respond, felt his muscles loosen a bit.

His hands still sweated.

Hoping to start to get back on the right path home to

Georgetown, he took a right at the next intersection, where a stopped Mercedes blasted deafening gangsta rap through open windows.

It was then, crossing the sonic chaos of the street, that he truly saw him. Definitively saw him.

He was a block back, wearing dark sunglasses with metal frames that glinted in the sun. And he distinctly turned his head to follow Bronze's sudden change in direction.

Adrenaline now poured freely into Bronze's blood, his heart rate jacking way up again.

He did not yet start to run but picked his pace up to an almost half jog, as fast as he could go while maintaining the barest illusion he was still walking.

Was this the assassin, then? He'd killed Carolyn and now he was coming for Bronze.

Bronze wished he had Officer Cow Eyes with him now. But if it really was the assassin, what could either he or Bronze hope to do?

He turned left at the next block, straight at the one after that, left again, almost random movements, looking for an alleyway, some place maybe to double back ...

Then it hit him. If it was the assassin, he'd be dead by now. He had had the drop on him this whole time. This was not the kind of man who hesitated over a clean shot.

If the assassin had been looking for him, why would he have been waiting at James Howell's place? Bronze was easy enough to find. His address was listed under Private Investigator in the Yellow Pages. No secret about it.

And true, it was a cliché that the killer always returned to the scene of the crime, but Bronze didn't think the assassin was much for that particular cliché.

No, now that he thought about it, he had spotted his follower too quickly. His pursuer was much too clumsy to be the assassin.

So who? Someone else who wanted him dead? Some other player in this madness that he couldn't begin to fathom? Bronze tried to think through it all logically, but his mind was racing too fast, redlining RPMs, cycling muddled nonsense with no answer in sight.

Then he took another left turn and stopped dead in his tracks. The last block had been a meaningless DC stretch of tree-lined concrete, but now ...

In an instant, as abruptly as his panic had come on, it vanished. Disappeared into something much worse.

His mind took a hard right on a dime. Suddenly he didn't give a shit who was following him.

Somehow, in all those random movements, his unconscious had taken him here.

He was the cliché; he was the one returning to the scene of the crime.

He began to move without conscious intention. He drifted over to the exact place it had happened. Traced where the walls had once been with his steps, walked as if under water, in slow motion. His mind emptied out, and an icy black tumult of unfathomable memories slid about all around him, just beyond thought, slick as a snake and ready to bite the moment he dared to flee.

Let the follower come. Let the bullet or fist or accusation come. *Who fucking cares?*

Rain started dripping from his scalp and running down his face. He stood there at the spot thinking nothing. Just breathing. Just managing to get from one heartbeat to the next.

At some point, it had started to rain.

ONLY A PARKING LOT NOW.

The noontime sun had beaten down on the cars and pavement and now they steamed in a late afternoon rain shower. The smell of heavy raindrops hitting the hot pavement was that of childhood summers. It was the smell of flowers pushing through dirt, of cool iced tea after hard physical labor, of slow and steady thoughts full of calm revelations.

Here, that smell was an obscenity.

Bronze hadn't brought an umbrella or hat or coat. His blue dress shirt and white undershirt were both soaked through, and he shivered despite the heat.

Somewhere to his left, he was vaguely aware that a man in metal-rimmed sunglasses had stopped and was watching him. But that seemed a very small thing.

So that's what it came to in the end—a parking lot. No memorial. Nothing to mark the spot. Where did one look for the blood and torment?

He looked from car to car, from cracked pavement to the blank concrete of the payment booth to the rusted-out toll gate. Was it just Bronze or did the whole place hum with death and turquoise?

Bronze closed his eyes, but there was no relief. Out there across the distance of his black mindscape formed the hard, implacable face of Nakatani. The impossible opponent. A machine of precision brutality. The true judo master.

Just as he had twenty years ago, he came for Bronze without hesitation. His movements were blurred lighting that left blinding after-images burned into Bronze's eyes. His arms were a deafening thunder, cascading blows onto Bronze's ears and neck and everywhere, finding him at his softest and most vulnerable. His iron hands gripped and ripped at Bronze— everything was alternating empty black and searing light, an ugly wall of ringing noise, rough scraping sandpaper on soft skin and flowering bruising broken pain. Yes, the world was violence and it smelt of burning sulfur. There was no air to breathe, but there was the desperation for clean air, so Bronze gagged and choked and had not even the strength to cry out.

It all somehow tasted of turquoise.

Then, just as suddenly as he was pinned, he was released, gasping in heaving breaths of hot, swampy air.

Nakatani was just a cover. A repressive hallucination. Now all illusions fled and his true enemy came for him.

The one that had turned this place into a parking lot. They'd had to tear the building down after Keaton's murders. In the collective wisdom of the capital markets, only the mundanity of a paid parking lot could seal away those memories for the efficient collection of profits.

But Keaton would never really be sealed away. Not from Bronze, anyway. Especially not here. He was all around him. Yes. There he was. There was Keaton's face twisted in madness as he came for Bronze, the only light now the glinting steel of Keaton's knife. Bronze made to wrench his body away, but Keaton came at him from every direction in which he so desperately turned until the knife pierced him and Keaton grotesquely flung himself inside the wound he had cut through Bronze's abdomen, the ultimate violation, possessing him, disappearing into his bloodstream like a vicious venom, racing to poison his heart and brain, filtering down to a cellular level, turning every element of Bronze into a vector of corruption and disease.

Bronze snapped his eyes open and tried to keep them open. He looked at the faceless parking lot. He tried to look at the faces of the dead women who weren't there. The women he should have saved. (If he was honest, he didn't need to be here to see them. No. *They're always there, aren't they, Bronze? No matter what games you play, no matter what elaborate distractions you devise, they're always there waiting for you. And all they do is thirst.*)

Keaton had thought women made him weak.

He was right.

Not for the reasons he supposed. But he was right ...

Villainy and madness. Words couldn't describe that evil. *Keaton* ...

To even try to describe Keaton's evil was to create an obscenity. Words sanitized. Villain? Villains could be so many things and some half charming. Same with madness. There could be flashes of genius in a mind of madness. And violence thrilled on the big screen after all, didn't it? Thrilled Bronze as much as any other. What thrilled like violence?

Other than sex?

Or better to say what thrilled like sex other than violence?

But to place even a hint or merest implication of the words *charm* or *thrill* within spitting distance of Keaton was blasphemous, true obscenity—the watering down of the unspeakable reality of evil in this world.

Why had he come here? Were these nightmares of Keaton just that or something more sinister? Had Keaton truly cut his way into the core of Bronze's being all those years ago? Did he live on in Bronze's head? Really *live*? Was Bronze's mind a home to that mad demon? Was that his burden—to make a prison of his mind? To trap that mad psyche within himself? And if Bronze were to die and Keaton's soul was released, would even he be forgiven? How long could Bronze stand to live on in the role of jailer? How long could Bronze hold on to him in there before he went mad himself? Or perhaps he had gone mad already, long ago?

The man watching Bronze had taken his sunglasses off in the rain.

Yes, indirectly a weakness came from women, but it was born in a man's heart. *Love.* But really it was just another kind of breaking. Another loss. Love again and again. Each one just as strong as the day Bronze first felt it, accumulating and building like one of those great mountains of heaped trash that would soon connect and swallow the world whole—endless oceans of old plastic, soiled cardboard, used diapers, and rotting food. Hemingway said that the world breaks everyone and afterward many are strong at the broken places. Bronze liked the quote but knew the real truth. Yeah, the world broke everyone and at the broken places, well, it just kept on breaking them there over and over again. Right where it knew you were soft and weak.

The mistake a *villain* like Keaton made was to imagine that the breaking could be stopped. That there was some external cause of their suffering that could be undone in violence. Better to direct that violence back at yourself. The weakness in you could only be destroyed when you destroyed whatever it was that made you *you*.

How much better would the world have been if Keaton had just stepped off a bridge somewhere? Bronze too for that matter.

And Keaton was a part of Bronze now. Buried in his *I*. Part of every drink he took, every woman he failed.

The man watching Bronze now finally walked toward him, slowly, as if on stiff legs, as if wary that his prey had so easily given up.

Bronze thought again, *Let him come.*

"Was she sleeping with you too?"

Bronze looked at the man who had followed him. Up close and without the sunglasses, he saw his smooth, handsome face, his weighty bearing, his air of scholarly seriousness. He knew exactly who this man was.

"Zachary Jackson?"

"You were, weren't you?"

"What the hell does that matter?"

A rage passed over Jackson's face and his fists balled, ready to strike.

Then he sagged, relaxed his hands, rested back against one of the gray parked cars while rain pummeled down on them both. He looked out of his mind. *With grief?* Yes, even after all he had learned of Carolyn's affairs and after stalking Bronze all day, his first question revealed his still-raw jealousy. But it wasn't just grief; there was wild fear in his eyes as well. Of the three men Bronze had seen her with, this was Carolyn Haake's only living lover. So why had he shaken his protective detail to stake out Howell's place?

Jackson looked up at Bronze, then away into the falling rain, staring at nothing. "It was Kopes, you know."

"What? What do you mean?"

"Come on, detective man, can't you see it? Kopes killed Carolyn. Or hired someone to do it, anyway."

"Kopes is dead."

Jackson looked bemused. "Not goddamn fucking Billy Kopes. Fred Kopes. Or that other one. Peterson."

Jackson stopped suddenly. "Goldberg, have you been drinking? Shit, it's not even two p.m."

Bronze ignored him. "How do I know you didn't do it?"

"The same way I know it was Kopes. Who else has the money to hire an assassin like the one that took out Roger Haake? Who else has the connections? The Kopes family business, man ... shit, they're basically arms dealers—one genteel step removed, maybe. With all that new competition out of the former Soviet Bloc, those boys have learned to play rough."

"But why would they want to kill Carolyn? There's no motive. Why Roger Haake, for that matter? Did they think Roger killed Billy? Was Fred Kopes out for revenge? If so, why kill Carolyn too? Your theory doesn't make any sense."

Jackson just shrugged. "I don't know. I just know that family's fucking evil."

How much of this was politics? Was a political operator like Jackson so used to seeing the other side as evil, he'd lost all perspective on the term? Had matters of opinion become crimes to him, and had one crime come to look more or less like all the others, no matter the scale, the intent, or the viciousness?

But there was something in what Jackson had said—some phrasing that struck Bronze as off. "What did you mean, 'that other one, Peterson'? What's Harold Peterson got to do with it other than being a Kopes errand boy? What did you mean phrasing it that way, 'that other one'?"

Jackson smiled for the first time and shook his head. "Jesus, you didn't do your oppo research, did you?"

"Oppo research?"

Jackson kept on shaking his head, full of arrogance and anger. "Opposition research. Dig up dirt on your opponent. Billy was a shitbag Republican and I'm a dyed-in-the-wool pansy Democratic operator. I knew everything there was to know about any dirt out there that might be useful on Mr. Billy Kopes. Stuff to drop on him when he was in a tough race. If—more like when—he ran for higher office. Most stuff you use right away, but there's a few juicy bits you hold back for when someone goes for the presidency. I'll tell you the last thing I'd lay on him in a general election, right at the end of October, right when it counted the most, and it ain't the affairs and it ain't the cocaine. It's Harold *fucking* Peterson."

25

CLOSED CASE

IRIS

No one recognized me at the Barnes & Noble. In fact, hardly anyone looked my way at all. The staff of twenty-somethings gabbed with one another and listlessly moved books about, seemingly at random. There was a loud mother at the front of the store where they kept round tables stacked with promoted new releases; she was barking orders at her slight, bespectacled daughter of about ten or eleven, who kept trying to get away from her and head down some darkened aisle—Science Fiction or Mystery, anywhere she could be alone. The rest of the customers milled about, eyes on the shelves and away from each other, also hoping to be left to themselves, hoping they would not be judged for whatever odd book should catch their fancy.

I was one with them.

I wandered around the new release hardcovers, running my hands over the dust jackets, letting the names pass through my mind like staccato found poetry: *Timequake, Underworld, American Pastoral, The Perfect Storm, Sex and the City, Cold Mountain* ...

Beyond the new releases, there was a wall holding this week's *New York Times* bestsellers, separated by category and filed in order of their success: *Pretend You Don't See Her*—Mary Higgins Clark; *The Partner*—John Grisham; *The Ranch*—Danielle Steele ... I grabbed the Danielle Steele out of professional interest.

After that, I was off to see how many copies of Henry Gordon's *The Long Dark* the store had in stock and whether they had been discounted with a 50% off sticker and pitched into the bargain bin by some indifferent Gen X employee.

THE RAIN BEGAN HALFWAY through my walk home. I hadn't brought an umbrella with me, so I hustled along with my Barnes & Noble bag awkwardly swinging from my hand. At first it was just a thin drizzle, then big smacks of individual drops.

I glanced down at Bronze's darkened window as I hustled up the stairs and managed to make it into my house before the rain started in earnest. I dropped my only slightly wet bag of books on the floor and plopped down by the window at the back of my living room, watching the rain streak against the glass with increasing violence.

Bronze would have liked this weather; he was always complaining about the sun and heat. If he were here, he could have been out in this rain somewhere, wearing a long dark raincoat and romantically smoking cigarettes under the eaves of some dilapidated concrete building, looking lost in infinite depths of contemplation.

But instead he was sniffing down a trail in Austin, where it was even hotter than it had been here at its worst, where the sun never let you forget for a moment what it really was—a hydrogen bomb.

Out the window a flash of light and seven seconds later—thunder rumbling the walls of the house. I counted the seconds between the flash and the sound to calculate the distance of the lightning strike, just as I had as a little girl watching from my old rambling house in Virginia.

I calculated the lightning had struck about one and a half miles away.

I should be writing. I should go to the solarium and pick away at the keyboard. There were always a million excuses. Always some freshly conceived distraction.

I should write. And I even got up and made my way toward the stairs, but I knew what I'd do once I got up to the solarium. I would leave the lights off and lean back in my chair and watch the rain fall against the glass skylight and shiver to see the lightning dance about the heavens.

I drifted up two flights of stairs, head filled with visions of a black sky splitting in flashes of electric blues and seething whites and rivers of water washing down the glass dome in the ceiling.

But when I got there, low gray clouds dimmed the lightning show to mere bursts of diffuse light. Still, the clouds could not stop the sound of the thunder. So I sat in my chair and closed my eyes and listened to the sky bang and shout and roar, again and again counting the seconds between the light and the noise.

In the dark of my eyelids, the blank flashes of light began to form blobs of green and purple. They undulated with the sound of the thunder. I found I had a loose control of their formation and movement. I could will them into something resembling a green rabbit or a purple wolf for a second or two before they fell apart into formless color. Maybe if my mind was stronger, I might shape them into a human face. Perhaps Roth's face as it had looked holding his hands in front of him imitating the strangulation of Kopes or Bronze's face as it had looked from my front door as he swayed, full of drink, and told me of Carolyn's death.

But these shapes and images were far too sophisticated for me to arrange. I gave up the game and opened my eyes, my vision landing on my desk, and there in front of me, next to my keyboard, was the last memoir chapter Bronze had given me.

The chapter detailed his investigation into Rachel Boyd's death and ended just before the Richelieu Massacre.

Would he ever be able to write about that? The Richelieu Massacre.

People would buy it. As sick as it was to say, Bronze could have a bestseller if he wanted—all he would have to do was walk again through memories of hell.

I picked up the chapter and began reading again. Rachel Boyd's death was one in a series of killings later linked together as being committed by a single serial killer, Caleb Keaton. Bronze, then an investigative reporter for the Metro section of the *Washington Post*, became involved in the case after Keaton began writing insane missives to the *Post* and Boyd's former Georgetown roommate came to Bronze, begging him to help find the killer.

In the chapter, Bronze describes the roommate at length. One senses that they'd built a deep connection, or perhaps he had merely become fixated, developed a one-sided fascination with her.

Her name was Alyssa "Lysa" Stackhouse. She was Black and tall, with a high frizz of corkscrew hair pushed to one side forming an asymmetric halo about her head. She was the daughter of a dentist from Rockville, MD and majoring in psychology at Georgetown. Stackhouse had read about Bronze's stories investigating cold cases, especially the Cortez murders, and come to believe he could succeed where the police had failed.

And she was right—before she came to Bronze, the investigation into Boyd's death had gone nowhere, was lost in a fire-hose of late '80s murders linked to the crack epidemic.

Bronze described how Lysa had attended Rachel's funeral in Massachusetts at an old Protestant church with white wooden doors on the pews where Rachel's parents sat shell-shocked and her two brothers oozed palpable rage, muttering dark dreams of what they would do to the killer when they found him.

Later, at home for summer break, she couldn't stop crying for days. Her parents brought her sandwiches in her room and she stared out the window at the ancient oak trees rustling in the wind, thinking nothing.

As if to add insult to injury, her birthday came along just a week after the funeral. She had loved throwing elaborate birthday soirees once, but now the whole concept of celebrating yet another year on this earth seemed infantile and meaningless. She tried to put on a good face at dinner for her parents and little sister, but before the cake had been brought out or the presents opened, she had to excuse herself up to her bedroom to silently sit with her back against the side of her bed, staring at the darkness between the slats of her closet doors, thinking about the number 84 and how someone could keep on stabbing another person that many times. Let alone someone with Rachel's big toothy smile.

Eventually she ran out of tears. She felt like her brain had been shot full of Novocain.

Then, over breakfast the next day, she had seen Calvin Goldberg's byline on an exposé detailing the truth behind the Greengate Robbery and remembered all the other crime stories she'd read by him. She got her dad to drive her downtown that very afternoon so that she could offer Bronze all she knew about Rachel and the days leading up to her murder for some small hope that at least one man would continue to investigate the murder.

As I read what Lysa Stackhouse had told Bronze about Rachel again, I stopped dead at a detail I had previously passed over without any notice, having originally read the chapter before Billy Kopes's death.

Rachel had been a congressional intern that year to a Democratic congressman from Massachusetts named Paul Piccione.

Another *congressman*.

The coincidence was too much. What was Piccione's relationship with Billy Kopes? Was there some connection there? Could Rachel Boyd have known Kopes?

But Keaton had killed Rachel Boyd. The case was over and done with. This had all happened nine years ago. Still ... it was too strange, one too many points of contact between the cases.

I thought of that old box down in Bronze's apartment ... There would be everything he had on the Boyd case down there. But Bronze wasn't there and was, as far as I was concerned, unreachable.

I, of course, had a key to the apartment. I had offered to help with the grunt work of the case, but there wasn't really anything for me to do at the moment. He had told me to go in and look through those boxes down there once before ... With this automatic assassin killing everyone with seemingly any connection to the Kopes murder, could I really wait to get explicit permission again? It would feel so strange to walk down there in the dark and rain, this time with no Bruce Schwarz, completely alone.

I HADN'T BOTHERED with an umbrella for the few steps it took me to get from my door to under my stairs on the flight down to Bronze's door, but I should have; even that seconds-long exposure to the rain had half soaked my hair and left rivulets of water running down my shirt at the neck.

I stumbled into the darkness of Bronze's apartment, having to throw my weight against his stuck front door, kicked my already wet shoes off, and turned a couple of lamps on. The boxes on Billy Kopes were still strewn all about. Before I moved to tackle them, I headed into Bronze's bathroom to attempt to dry my hair and neck.

The light in the bathroom was fluorescent and harsh. The mirror reflected me back in this light hyper-clinically, like a patient on a table ready for exploratory surgery. There was a sprinkling of facial hair around the sink's faucet handles, a red can of Noxzema Sensitive Skin shaving cream, a cracked, curving bar of Dove soap, and a green bath towel half faded with use. Seeing no other towels at hand, I wrapped my head in Bronze's bath towel and rubbed my hair vigorously, trying to mop up what I could from my neck and under my shirt.

Before I knew what was happening, the smell of the towel almost laid me on the floor, filled me with a feeling of semi-intoxication. There was a slight whiff of must to it, but otherwise it was pure Bronze. I almost looked about, wondering if he'd just walked in. The smell was Bronze but a concentrated solution; a dab of the towel here or there and you would have smelled Bronze as you might smell him from across the room as you made him coffee, but at this dosage it was like you were wrapped in his arms about to fall into bed.

I replaced the towel and found myself wandering out of the bathroom into the bedroom. It was like the towel had been a ceremony of induction. I now lingered in Bronze's most private space as if the smell of the towel had imbued me with some sort of intoxicated diplomatic immunity.

I sat on the very edge of his bed, which was made up with sheets and blankets, the bed coverings ordered but not with great precision—not fully squared away, as my father would say. There was no indent in the pillow, as if he had fluffed it up in the morning after sleeping. On the nightstand was a haphazard pile of three paperbacks topped with a quarter-full pack of Chesterfields next to a velvet-lined cufflink holder filled with gold, silver, and many-colored silk ball cufflinks. I looked from the nightstand toward the closet, and my eyes drifted toward the gaps in the wooden slats of the closet doors and into the darkness beyond. I thought of Lysa Stackhouse in her bedroom after Rachel Boyd's murder.

It felt as if there was a weight to that darkness, a gravitational pull, a dampening of thought, a submergence of ego. The darkness waited for me with perfect patience. What dread tools lived within that darkness, what unthinkable thoughts, what visions ...?

My intoxication subsided, and with it, my temporary immunity was revoked.

I would have to open that terrible old box again.

I stood up and ran my hand over the blanket at the edge of the bed, smoothing out the ripples I had made.

IN HIS MEMOIR CHAPTER, Bronze discussed several details of the Rachel Boyd case. Being a crime reporter, he had seen a string of brutal stabbing deaths come across his desk. That in itself was not so unusual—a husband stabbing his wife, a brawl outside a bar taken too far, a botched robbery. But as Bronze looked into Rachel Boyd's murder, he identified a line of similar slayings. As he wrote in the chapter, "When looking for the through line, the connection, the flash, the big eureka, the sameness in all the differences—it must be the *right* sameness. The right sameness hidden amongst a million illusions. It amounts to a grotesque game of aesthetics, a feeling of letting go of yourself and seeing the world with colors shifted to reflect the drives and distortions of some strange psychotic mind."

The killer was hunting isolated women at night. He was stabbing them to death on abandoned streets. He was closing their eyes with gloved fingers. And he seemed to be building toward something, each murder increasing in daring and ferocity.

Then came the letters to the *Post*. The killer had some obscure demented goal in mind—probably a convenience, an illusion to justify his lust for violence and all-consuming hatred of women.

Rachel Boyd seemed to fit the profile. Working late at Piccione's hideaway congressional office, the last person confirmed to see her alive was Jason Fuller, Piccione's senior legislative aide.

But there was always something not quite right about the Rachel Boyd murder. In connecting the dots to Keaton's other killings, Bronze had been able to create a map of the linked slayings, and Rachel Boyd's had been one of two outliers in a pattern that ultimately centered on an underground but, in certain circles, well-known brothel—the notorious Madam Richelieu's. Bronze had worked the case, reading Keaton's deranged letters over and over again until he had determined that he truly was planning something bigger, which Bronze came to realize too late was an attack on the brothel itself.

Keaton had come to believe that most adult women were the agents of a vast conspiracy set on dulling and drugging his mind and those of other strong-willed men in order to keep them bound in a kind of psychic slavery. His theory was intricate, elaborate, and completely insane. Women fell into different classifications: a small set of Alpha Witches who worked directly with the ruling class cabal and appeared as talking heads on TV, actresses, political figures, and madams, and a much larger set of women who were programmed with subliminal neurolinguistic messages and possibly drugs in the water supply to become what Keaton called Disassociated Beta Slaves, or Betas for short—all of whom Keaton considered to be prostitutes in one form or another.

As I looked through the old box Bronze had kept on the Keaton case, I found whole notebooks full of his thinking and musings back in '88. While in his memoir chapter he alluded to some unique aspects of the Boyd case among the other killings, his contemporaneous notes revealed sizeable gaps.

Rachel Boyd was not dressed provocatively. The other victims usually had short skirts or low necklines or both. Rachel Boyd had recently had sex, and an autopsy revealed vaginal injuries. There were no signs of rape in any of the other Keaton murders. Mark Roth, who had been Metro PD's lead detective on the case, had emphasized in his notes that Rachel Boyd's eyes were wide open when her body was discovered. No gloved hand had closed them.

Something else strange in the autopsy report too. Different from all the others and remarked on as almost a curiosity, irrelevant seeming at the time, but in light of the Kopes killing, my breath caught and my hands began to shake like the first time I'd opened the box and found Caleb Keaton's letter.

Unlike all the other murders, there was some uncertainty as to the precise cause of death in the case of Rachel Boyd. The eighty-four stab wounds would seem to have been clear enough, but the coroner noted that markings on her neck and oddities about the tissue damage resulting from the stab wounds may have indicated that Rachel Boyd had actually expired from strangulation and not the knife wounds alone.

Something came to me, something half remembered from

days earlier, searching through all those boxes Esther McNamara had gifted Bronze ...

I ran to one of them at random, ripped off the top, and poured the contents onto the coffee table, ignoring the text and rifling through the pictures ... This wasn't it ...

I remembered that the boxes were ordered by date. I flew about them reading the tops until I found the one from 1986, emptied the contents onto Bronze's couch this time, and raced through the pictures until I saw it.

I wasn't crazy. *Jesus.* What did it mean?

26

PRESIDENTIAL SUITE DREAMS

MAY 12, 1997

T he Hay-Adams was a grand square block of a hotel overlooking Lafayette Square and the White House within. The front façade granted the hotel a sufficiently imperialist flavor that a nineteenth-century British viceroy would feel no embarrassment striding into its white-ceilinged lobby full of arches and chandeliers. The hotel was built on the site where poor Clover Adams had committed suicide, and it was said that she haunted it still, that you could catch whiffs of an almond smell from the potassium cyanide she had ingested wafting about the floors, but all Roth could smell was money.

Fred Kopes, Billy's older brother and current CEO of Kopes Industries, had been staying in the Presidential Suite of the Hay-Adams Hotel while overseeing Billy's funeral arrangements and serving as the family's interlocutor with Metro PD.

Roth was met at the door to Kopes's rooms by a thick-necked bodyguard jammed inelegantly into a black suit. He was shown into a living room and directed to sit in an awkwardly deep and sagging couch, while Fred Kopes sat haughtily in a stiff chair and Harold Peterson paced the room behind Fred.

Fred Kopes was forty-eight and thick shouldered, his fine hair thinning slightly at the front and combed back. Most of it was still light brown, but at the temples he'd gone quite gray. He wore a haphazard blue blazer, cuffed and pleated khakis, a white shirt pressed outward by a barrel-shaped gut, and a loosely tied red Hermes necktie with a garish print of golf balls and clubs.

Billy Kopes had had an elegance to his appearance that was completely absent from Fred. If Billy had been the high school football team's quarterback, Fred would have been left tackle. And Fred looked as though he would indeed have reveled in the crash and tussle of a football scrum. There were flashes of menace lighting up his small brown eyes and a casual air of ready violence hanging about him like an ugly smell. He looked as though he had long ago given up trying to be handsome but instead substituted a cultivated appearance of undeniable primal force, a man to be trifled with at one's dire peril.

But, for some reason, it was Harold Peterson and his steady, silent pacing in his blue chalk-stripe suit that caught Roth's eye more than the obviously bullying posture of Fred Kopes. Peterson was in his early fifties and had been Billy Kopes's chief of staff ever since the younger Kopes brother had been first elected to congress in '86. Before that, he had been an executive with Kopes Industries, working directly with Billy and Fred's father, William.

Billy had been elected to congress at only twenty-seven years old, and if he hadn't met his untimely end, he'd have been on track to be elected to the senate before he turned forty. And from there, who knows—perhaps ambassador or secretary of state or even the presidency in due time. And with Billy's eventual ascendancy, Peterson would have risen in stature too. Maybe never to the heights available to the Kopeses of the world but far higher than a Mark Roth could imagine.

Now those hopes were dashed. How much had Peterson lost in Billy's death?

Could there have been anything to gain?

Roth had finished with the pleasantries and began his questioning in earnest. "Mr. Kopes, why did you not mention in your initial statement to the police that you had hired Roger Haake?"

Fred squinted those small eyes even further than their resting state. "Haake was working for Crawford. We thought it simpler, easier to bury any embarrassing issues that may have resulted from Haake's work with the senator by hiring him away before he looked too deeply into Billy's life. Hardly seemed relevant to Billy's death. Routine political maneuvering, all in all."

Roth raised an eyebrow at that. "But you still had him set up an operation to use Bronze Goldberg to spy on Billy's love life?"

Kopes cocked his head to the right, seemed to be calculating how much Roth already knew, how big of a lie he could get away with. "Haake might have gone off script. It was his wife. He was probably jealous. Angry. Wouldn't you be?"

Roth was silent a moment, thinking it through. What was being obscured in that statement? "But how would that have played out for you in the end? It seems that Haake already knew his wife was having an affair with Congressman Kopes. Why seek documentation?"

Kopes leaned back and took a long breath in and out, the out breath making such a loud sputtering noise that Roth knew beyond a shadow of a doubt that he must snore unmercifully at night. "If I had to guess, I suppose Haake might have gotten the idea that he was actually helping us in the Kopes family by revealing the affair. I hate to speak ill of the dead, but let me be frank with you, Roth, Billy was a fuck-up. He never really worked a day in his life. Peterson here pretty much ran things ..."

Roth noticed a small catch in Peterson's pacing at that remark.

"Billy wasn't going to make it at a higher level of politics. But he was arrogant. He needed to be ... gently urged aside."

Fred formed a pyramid with his meaty hands on top of his belly, then opened them in a gesture of *this is just the sad truth.* Roth studied those hands—no marks or bruises.

Had he seen Peterson's hands? Would any bruises have faded away by now?

"Haake was likely mining the situation with his wife to provide that prompting. Better to allow someone with the *appropriate* qualities to take over a run for the senate in '98. Billy could have been allowed to keep the congressional seat. But we needed someone with a steadier hand in the senate. Someone who might have a real shot of doing something significant there —maybe even going to the next level. Billy could still be useful in the house. No one intended to take that away from him. So long as he saw reason in the end."

Now it was Roth's turn to lean back in the uncomfortably deep couch. He saw where this was going. "And this person who would run for the senate and crush an old man verging on senility—that would be you, I suppose?"

Kopes nodded without hesitation or the slightest hint of shame or self-deprecation. "And why not? I've been running a Fortune 500 corporation for close to a decade. I've done deals all over the world. It's a dirty secret, but you won't find the real American diplomats in the State Department. It's the American businessmen. We are the ones who really protect American economic interests. It's the businessmen who strike the real deals that bring dollars back home to this country—that grow our GDP, grow our power and standing in the world.

"It was me that would be a good fit for the Senate Foreign Relations Committee. Not Billy. I've already met the major players in Europe, Asia, Latin America. The Republican party doesn't want to elevate some do-nothing congressman. They want someone who's been in the private sector, who knows what the big cruel world is like when the rubber hits the road. And Billy ... Billy was a dilettante."

Kopes paused suddenly. Had he realized he was drifting? Saying too much? His eyes focused back on Roth, boring into him now.

"He was also my brother. We might not have been the closest of brothers, but I would have relished having a Kopes in both chambers of congress. Maybe in the end it could have brought us closer together. Dad would have been proud, I think.

"But someone took that from us. And I assure you, the Kopes family will stop at nothing to see Billy's killer brought to justice."

Was that a hitch in Peterson's step again? Was Peterson watching Roth watch him?

WHEN ROTH GOT BACK to the station to put in a request for a second look at the alibis of Fred Kopes and Harold Peterson, there was an urgent message waiting for him from Iris Margaryan. He called her back immediately.

"Mark, I've got the picture that proves it. I've got it right here!"

"What, Iris?"

"The Rachel Boyd case."

"Rachel Boyd? What does Rachel Boyd have to do with anything? That was almost a decade ago."

"Mark, you remember that Rachel Boyd was an intern for then-congressman Paul Piccione, right? You remember she was last seen at his office, right?"

"Uhhh." Mark closed his eyes, remembered a pock-marked face. Jason Something. An aide to Piccione. He was the last to see her. That's right, it had been at the congressman's office. "Yes, I remember."

Iris began talking extremely rapidly in her excitement. "I've got a picture here of Billy Kopes on his first day as a congressman in '86. He moved on to a better office after his first reelection in '88. But his first office ... In the picture, he's standing in the hall with Harold Peterson and his dad. His office back then was right across from Piccione's—right across from where Rachel Boyd was last seen!"

Mark Roth felt his stomach go cold. "But Keaton ..."

"Go back and look at the autopsy. Look at your notes on the case. She'd been raped. Keaton didn't rape. Her eyes were open, Mark. Before the massacre, everyone Keaton killed, he closed their eyes.

"Keaton's murders were in the papers. Everyone knew about a rash of stabbings ... Mark, someone hid her amongst his victims. She didn't even die of those stab wounds ... they were post-mortem. She was strangled, Mark. Strangled just like Billy Kopes."

Roth hung up the phone in a daze, staring blindly into the middle distance, the gears of his mind turning and turning and turning ... He didn't even notice his secretary, Mrs. Miller, walk into his office, looking down at the yellow legal pad she used for taking notes or dictation.

"I forgot to include it with the other message. Bronze Goldberg called too."

Roth turned to her, but his mind was still focused on what Iris had said. He had to ask her to repeat it twice before he processed it. But it still didn't make any sense.

"Bronze called here collect from LaGuardia before his flight to Austin," Mrs. Miller began again in exasperated tones. "He said something like: talked to Zachary Jackson. Kopes brothers.

Harold Peterson. Jackson. Kopes. Peterson ... son? There were a lot of Kopeses and sons in there. He was quite rushed and unpleasant and slurring his words too, I might add. Anyways, should we take the collect charges out of his bill or just eat them?"

27

A HOLE IN 6TH STREET

MAY 13, 1997

B ronze was on 6th Street in Austin, TX, standing in the shadow of the Driskill Hotel, smoking and sweating.

He had no idea what he was going to do.

He'd shown up. That was about all he could say for himself. That and it was 1:15 p.m. and he hadn't yet started drinking for the day. A temporary victory at best. The smell of last night's booze oozed out of his pores. The Driskill bar was calling his name again and he was going to let it.

Shit, there had to be something, though. Something here somewhere.

Something in the mechanics. He had two points of a line. May 9th the assassin is in Washington, DC at James Howell's apartment. May 10th he's in Austin, TX killing Carolyn Haake. The assassin had had to fly here. He had to have used a name, present ID. He needed to have stayed somewhere overnight.

Somewhere in the mechanics of all that, in the banality of the logistics, there must be something, at least some small detail to find.

Bronze threw his Chesterfield down and stamped it out. No

point in standing around. He knew one spot the assassin had been. *The* spot.

He left the protection of the Driskill's shadow and walked to the place Carolyn had been found, an alleyway just off 6th Street between San Jacinto Boulevard and Trinity Street. The spot was only about a five-minute walk from the Driskill, but in the heat, it was enough for Bronze to sweat quite thoroughly through his shirt.

His immediate thought upon arriving at the alleyway was that there was not a chance in hell Carolyn would have walked this way willingly. It was an entirely alienating space that no woman in her right mind would walk down at night. It consisted of the unadorned backs of buildings, dumpsters, pipes, fuse boxes, and small heavily locked doors for bringing out the trash. The exact spot Carolyn had been found—slightly north of a manhole cover in front of a broken-down wooden fence with winding razor wire running along the top—was probably the cleanest part of the whole alley, Carolyn's blood having been meticulously sanitized away.

Perhaps the assassin had lured her back here somehow. But she would have been firmly on her guard; what lure could possibly have worked? Or maybe he had shown her the gun, demanded and threatened her into coming with him. But that was also unlikely to work. All the streets except for the alleyway would have been at least modestly busy. Carolyn could have simply run or screamed. And why kill her with the rifle he'd used on Roger Haake and not the silenced pistol he'd used on James Howell?

No. There was only one possibility. He had shot her some-where else and carried her here. And Bronze doubted very much he had used a car. She would have stuck to populated areas. The practicalities of arranging to shoot her, then getting her into a nearby car, then parking that car somewhere around this alley, taking her out and dumping her here made it just too unlikely.

So what had he done? Bronze leaned against the white cement back of some bar or restaurant whose colorful front faced 6th Street and closed his eyes.

What would *he* have done?

He would have learned her routine the night before—a dry run. Then he would have waited for her at some vulnerable juncture. Carolyn's hotel was on 5th Street and Trinity. 5th was just too busy, but Trinity might not have been. If Carolyn had walked home at night on Trinity and he had waited for her somewhere with a clean shot at the spot just where she passed the alleyway ...

Bronze walked the length of the alley to Trinity Street, looking at the ground as he went, not sure exactly what he was looking for, sticking whenever possible to shadows, going slow, hoping and failing to minimize the sweat that continuously poured out of him.

Looking all around when he exited the alley onto Trinity, he realized there weren't any places of business directly facing the street that would be open past dinner. Opposite the alleyway there was just a parking lot.

Yes, with his silenced rifle the assassin could have shot Carolyn after she turned off 6th Street and was walking down Trinity, then he could have run to her pretending to help. *Oh dear, my wife has had a bit too much to drink.* That kind of thing. He might only have been in the open with her about a half dozen paces or so, probably throwing her dead arm over his shoulder, propping her up like a passed-out drunk girl, then into the alley, dropping her on the ground like a piece of garbage.

Her blood would have been all over him then.

Had Austin PD checked the dumpsters for bloody clothes?

Bronze hadn't seen anything about that in the case file. It was too late now. The trash would have been emptied.

He could try to trace the trash to the dump ... but that was a long shot.

Out on Trinity Street, there was no shade from the sun that beat down on Bronze without so much as a wispy cloud for protection, turning his skin a hot lobster red, boiling his thoughts into confusion.

He squinted and looked upward.

Almost all the buildings were two stories, squat and dirty looking, holding loud bars within. The assassin could have been up on the roof of one of those buildings. For him, the shot would have been easy enough, but he couldn't have gotten down in time through the bar crowds, couldn't be sure he could move her body to the alley.

Bronze twisted his torso and neck away from the direction of 6th Street. Over past 5th Street he could see her hotel. Fairly far away, but given what he'd seen of him, the assassin could have made that shot too.

But again ... too far away to be sure of getting to the body in time.

He continued to look around and found himself staring at a three-story apartment building just behind the parking lot. He wasn't really sure why he was staring at it. The roof of the building was no good for the assassin's purposes. The building wasn't as far away as the hotel, but like the bars, it would have taken too long to get down from the roof and cross back to the spot where he must have shot her. And if he'd gone into one of the apartments on a lower floor, there would have been a report —someone would have seen him or found something amiss. No way he could have done that unnoticed.

Then Bronze saw it.

What his deeper brain had been looking for subconsciously.

There was a fire escape in the recessed center of the building. From the second-floor level of the fire escape, you could have an angle on Carolyn Haake turning off 6th Street and walking down Trinity. And you could be down off it within seconds.

Bronze headed over to the building, feeling almost faint and thoroughly drained of fluids by the relentless sun—completely dehydrated. He climbed up the black cast iron stairs. When he got to the second level, he looked out. He curled his hand to form a tube and sighted down it until he found the spot where the shot would have traveled. He measured the angle to where the bullet would have passed through Carolyn on its way to carve out an indistinguishable hole among all the others somewhere on 6th Street.

Yes, the assassin could have easily made this shot.

Bronze whispered "Bang," then quickly raced down the stairs, then out across Trinity to the spot he'd just been, at the head of the alley where they'd found Carolyn.

Seven or eight seconds, maybe. That probably wasn't too long. Unless someone was walking right next to her, even if someone was close, it would have taken five seconds to process her slumped over, then at least another five to decide what to do. And then there would be the assassin, already there, picking her up, waving any curious passer-by off with a phony smile, then dumping her in the middle of that back alley.

Out with the trash. Just another piece for the scrapyard. Junk. Refuse. Bury it in dirt. Throw it into the sea. Burn it to ash and smoke.

Yes. That's what he would have done.

This was the spot, then. The last spot she'd been alive. The real spot.

The spot the spot the spot.

Bronze took a long, slow breath.

Was Carolyn's imprint here anywhere? Some kind of essence? Or that of her killer, maybe? Some black, unctuous, slick slime in the air?

Shouldn't we leave something behind in the place where we die or where we kill?

Bronze thought about the killing fields in Europe, the places where the dead had mounted up over the centuries as Charlemagne, then Napoleon, then Hitler swept out their arms and demanded senseless battle. In those lands saturated with blood, surely the call of the dead could be felt. But was one death too fine a thing?

Bronze leaned against the nearest building framing the sidewalk. There was no shade anywhere here. His eyes watered from the straight, sharp light all around and the heat that came off the bruised street in undulating waves.

This was the spot.

It seemed like something.

Bronze had another point on the map of the assassin's travels. This one quite precise.

But when he made inquiries at the apartment building and parking lot across the way, he found that they had no working security cameras.

It was a dead end.

BRONZE DRAINED TWO GLASSES of ice water before he moved on to scotch and soda paired nicely with a pack of Chesterfields. The Driskill bar was a square rotunda of dark wood under a copper-tiled ceiling. The bar was beautifully stocked. The barstools were comfortable and boldly backed in cowhide, which helped, along with the mounted longhorn heads on the walls, to disabuse any confusion as to which state of the union one currently found themselves in.

It was still too early for most people, and the only other customer at the bar was a heavyset man in a ten-gallon cowboy hat who eyed Bronze for a half minute before saying, "Not from around here, huh?"

"No, I'm from the great District of Columbia. Washington, DC."

"Washington, DC! Boy, you're a long way from home."

"Don't I know it. Yourself? You from Austin?"

"Austin? Not a chance. No, sir; I'm from Dallas, Texas and *all* that that implies." At that the man tipped his hat to Bronze, lifted his glass of whisky on the rocks, and took a swig. Bronze reciprocated the gesture and drank off a long sip of his cold, fizzing, peat-flavored drink.

"Well, Mr. Washington DC, what's your line? Don't tell me you're a politician. Got the look for it, I suppose."

"Not me. Far from it. I'm a PI."

"PI? Like a private eye? A private dick?" The Texan laughed as he said that, a big rolling chuckle that shook the considerable mass about his middle.

"That's right."

"So, you in town on PI business, then?"

"I am."

"You get your man yet? Get your man *or* woman, I should say. It is the nineties, after all. Can't be talking like a caveman no more. Haven't seen a woman working no oil field yet, though. Matter of time, maybe."

"Not yet."

"What's the problem, then? Too wily for you?"

"Something like that ... I'm just sitting here thinking about it. I suppose I'm not the first to try to find the answer at the bottom of a drink ..." Bronze gave the Texan an unhappy smile. "It's just one of those things. I know who. I know when. I know where. I even figured out how, but it didn't help at all. I'm not any closer to finding him."

"Mmmm," said the Texan, drumming his fingers on the table. "What about the why?"

"I've got a rough idea. Nothing too special. Never really is. The man was hired to do a bad thing. So he did it. Not the kind of man to think too much about the why beyond that. Part of what makes him so effective."

The Texan was nodding and drumming his fingers on the bar, increasing the firmness and pace until it became almost like a low roar of thunder off in the far distance.

Suddenly he stopped, picked up his drink, and swiveled toward Bronze.

"Reminds me of something. Something between the how and why. You know they mingle sometimes. Get mixed up and lost within each other ... Hmmm, mind if I tell you a little story?"

Bronze shrugged. "Please do. At our age, hearing a good story is the best thing that can happen at a bar."

An infectious smile lit up the Texan's face. "Man after my own heart. Well, let me tell you something that happened when I was a young man. Left my heart in Texas for a time, so to speak, out sowing the old wild oats a bit. At one juncture I spent a spell in the merchant marine. Nothing fancy, just an able sailor. But I saw all the ports of Europe and the Caribbean too.

"One time we're cruising along north of Havana. It's nighttime. A big ole full moon, though. I can still see the moonlight shining down, rippling along in the black waves. We come upon this boat out there in that moonlight. Dead in the water. It's a sport fishing boat. The kind rich folks own or charter in those parts to go try to get a picture of themselves hooked up with a blue marlin.

"We try hailing the boat on the radio. No response. We drive up close to it, try hollering at it. Nothing. We get up *real* close to it, don't see nothing happening on board. No lights, no sound. Couple of us jump down off our ship and board the thing like old-time pirates.

"It's spooky on the boat. Like it's a ghost ship or something. We look all around the deck—nothing. We go below, and ... well, there it is.

"The boat's got a little galley, a head, and a tiny little bed. On the bed is maybe a sixty-year-old guy dressed in a double-breasted navy blue blazer—you know the kind, with all them big brass buttons—and he's got pressed white khakis on too, and someone has gone to the trouble of slitting his throat for him. Ear to ear."

The Texan tapped a finger against the side of his head. "Can still see it like it was yesterday." He took a loud, gurgling sip of his drink, wiped his brow with a handkerchief, and continued.

"So, we radio in the coast guard and we get delayed some hours having to stick by the boat and answer questions, and the captain's right pissed off because we're going to wind up way behind schedule. But we don't mind so much on the crew. Gave us something worth talking about for a few days. We'd be out on watch and speculating.

"*How they do it?* They on board with the guy, slit his throat and some other boat come along at a prearranged time and pick 'em up? They couldn't have swum, could they? *Why they do it?* Were there drugs on board? Documents important to the Castro regime? Spy stuff, maybe? Was it revenge?

"There was this guy on board with us in those days. He said his name was John something. But we all called him Boss. The captain didn't like that, affront to his authority, but he knew it was good to have a guy like Boss around—someone that'd seen and done as much as old Boss had. And he'd done a lot, let me tell you. This was about, say, '71, and Boss is in his mid-seventies at least. No one knows where Boss is from originally; we didn't know if he was Cuban or Sicilian or a Swede with a long deep tan. But he'd been everywhere in the world you could be. Some of the guys insisted he'd fought in both world wars, but no one could agree on which sides.

"Someone says, 'Boss, why'd you suppose Mr. White Khakis got an early ticket to St. Pete's?'

"Now, Boss didn't say much, but when he did, we all listened as sharp as we could. Ain't nobody had stories like Boss. And it's the night watch. We're deep away from land. The stars out everywhere and the air is very still. We all crowd around Boss, leaning in, waiting for him to answer. Boss just shakes his head, says, 'Boys, so strange to kill a man this way, no? Obvious *how*. Cut his throat, leave him floating. Not so strange why. Money. Revenge. Power. Always the same whys. But why this how, huh? That's why you talking so long. Why this *strange* how? Like life. All life, you see. *How?* Physics, chemistry. *Why?* Religion, philosophy. Thinking thinking thinking. Boring boring boring. Make you fall asleep. But real life, real living—*why this strange how?*'

"Then this big smile splits Boss's face; he's missing half his teeth at least; the other half is yellow, brown, or green. And Boss lifts his arms up to the sky, gesturing at all the stars burning up above so breathtakingly bright out there in the dark of the ocean. He's pointing and waving and smiling that big smile like he's saying, 'Right there! There's the answer!'"

It seemed to Bronze that the Texan now had that same smile Boss must have had back in '71, only he still had all his big white teeth intact. And he was making the same gesture up at the sky, only above them wasn't stars but the elaborate copper tiles of the Driskill bar ceiling.

And Bronze thinks, *Why this strange how? Why kill a man that way when there are so many different ways to kill a man?* And then he thinks about the assassin. He thinks about how he killed

Roger Haake and James Howell. Nothing too strange. He wanted Haake dead, he shot him. He wanted information from Howell, he tied him up, got it, then shot him. Carolyn ... he wanted her dead, shot her ... *picked her up and carried her away* ... She hadn't been shot in the alley like Austin PD presumed; she'd been shot on Trinity and carried to the alley ... The assassin shot her with a rifle from far enough away that no civilian would have been able to track him if he had just left her there. He could even have shot her from further away without a problem. Would have been safer.

But instead he'd gotten as close as he could, then went to her, carried her somewhere no one would see, then dropped her there with the trash, useless to him ...

So why this strange how?

Bronze smiled back at the Texan. A real smile this time. "My friend, I think you might be a genius."

The Texan let out a roar of laughter. "Mr. Washington DC, you just been stuck with them politicians too long. I tell you what, you come on up to Dallas some time, you look me up. We'll have a grand old time—Dallas style. You can tell the missus about me being a genius and all."

Bronze bid the Texan farewell and used the hotel phone to call Austin PD. No, they hadn't found Carolyn's hotel key on her person. *Why? Is that so unusual? Maybe she just forgot it.*

Bronze made them get out the inventory from her hotel room. Went through it line by line. There was something missing. Something they wouldn't have had any reason to know about.

Bronze was practically bursting, remembering her packing as they fled her house what seemed a lifetime ago. "You sure you didn't find an unmarked videotape?"

"No, sir, I'm sure. We don't have a record of anything like that. No videotape at all."

In his excitement, Bronze slammed his hand against the wall near the phone, drawing a stern look from the concierge. "She had a videotape with her. The son of a bitch went back to her room!"

Bronze hung up on the Austin detective. Called Mark Roth.

Before he could say anything, Roth was interrupting him, saying he had been trying to get in touch, asking him about Harold Peterson.

"I told your secretary. Didn't she tell you? Harold Peterson is half Kopes. He's Billy and Fred's half brother. Daddy Kopes screwed the maid or something. Big Bill himself. Jackson says they think they've been so clever about hiding it, they don't know the info's out there. Apparently Jackson and his political friends squirreled it away to use against Billy."

On the other line, Roth was swearing a blue streak in excitement.

Bronze went on. "That's not the half of it. I know why they killed Carolyn. I know where the assassin went after Austin. I know how we can track him ..."

After Bronze had explained, Roth said he would call his friend Leo Rossetti of the FBI immediately. They had to act fast before it was too late.

Roth and the FBI now had the best lead Bronze could hope to give them.

Finally—time for the real professionals to step in.

The mad energy that had filled Bronze ever since he'd found out about Carolyn's death sloughed off him like dirty bathwater down a drain. There was no peace; he just felt like a burned-out husk. But it was over, at least.

He picked up the phone again and booked the next flight back to DC. It was out of his hands now.

~

THERE WERE A FEW hours to kill before the flight.

He went back to the bar. The Texan was gone, but more people had started to file in and there was a pleasant buzz.

He got a Manhattan to celebrate.

Then he got another and started thinking of Carolyn. He switched to straight scotch.

It was out of his hands now.

It was over ... There wasn't much for Bronze to do anymore, was there? And Carolyn ...

He vomited in the Driskill lobby bathroom. Would have missed his departure if the flight hadn't been delayed. Hardly remembered the cab to the airport or the flight back to DC except vomiting again in the cramped bathroom of the plane and the harsh sucking sound of the toilet flushing it all away, but he sobered up enough to remember the cab ride bringing him back into town past the monuments at night, lit up and ghostly in a soft white light.

28

THE CLIENT

MAY 14, 1997

T he assassin knew Peterson had a gun. He could see it in the stance of his hips and the awkward drape of his hands about his waist.

But Peterson couldn't see him out there in the dark. The assassin had picked their meeting spot for this purpose, for its shadows, for all its many angles of approach.

The assassin didn't quite smile, but there was a flush of satisfaction in his cheeks to watch Peterson trying to play it cool but instead jerking his head about every other second or so, trying to catch the assassin coming.

The only members of the human race the assassin had more contempt for than his targets were his clients.

Peterson stood at the head of an ersatz platoon of seven-foot-tall stone soldiers, America's latest monument to its wars of empire—the Korean War Veterans Memorial. The soldiers wore ponchos and stalked through a field, misery written on their faces. What could be more American than causing a war through ineptitude, expanding it through arrogance, bogging down, giving up, leaving it in a tortured stalemate that mutilated a culture, and then recalling the whole affair as some tragic sacrifice?

There was no one else at the memorial except for Peterson. It was night and dark and no one in America cared to remember the Korean War.

Peterson stared ineffectually at the giant soldiers and the dark gaps between them.

He could put a bullet in Peterson from here. Clean, right through his forehead, blasting out the back of his skull. Reasonable punishment for bringing a gun to this meeting.

He could stalk up behind him without Peterson ever knowing he was there until he pressed the point of his pistol against the occipital bone, just where his spine met the back of his skull. He would whisper in his ear to hand him the account number where he would find the back half of his payment, *slowly, easy does it, oh yes, I know all about the gun*. Then, once the account card was in his hand, he would slip the pistol along his head to point now at the right temple, pull the trigger, drop the videotape on his body. Just another DC political suicide. Place was lousy with them.

He could dispatch Peterson in a thousand ways, but better to let him live. Peterson wasn't acting just for himself. The assassin had a reputation to maintain if he wanted more business to come his way. Sure, if Peterson really dared to pull that gun on him, he'd execute him without the slightest concern. Probably have to execute the whole Kopes family then. Maybe their whole company. He *did* have a reputation to maintain, after all. One way or another.

The assassin stepped out into view and walked toward Peterson, straight in his line of sight. He would just have to let Peterson play it however he was going to play it. He would be fair. He would give him the chance that they all could walk away from this thing.

Or there would be a lot more killing to do.

Either way was fine. He was as fair as a typhoon. You either got out of his way or you failed to. Either way was fine. Either way, it meant nothing to the typhoon.

Suddenly seeing the assassin, Peterson started, jerked his head toward him, hand instinctively clutching toward his gun.

"You brought a sidearm," the assassin said by way of introduction as he walked unhurriedly toward Peterson.

Peterson's hand twitched away from the gun at his waist as if in embarrassment, as if his mother had caught him playing with himself. But then the hand steadied and started to drift back.

"Didn't you?" he replied.

The assassin closed the remaining gap between him and Peterson, coming to stand about six feet away.

"It is my job to carry weapons. That is the natural course of things. On the other hand, when a client brings one to a meeting, it is *unnatural*. The implication is that he does not trust me. Or worse yet, that he is not to be trusted. Which is it, would you say? Who is *not* to be trusted? You or me?"

Peterson swallowed. Streaks of sweat began to fall from his temples. His eyes danced all about the assassin's shadowed frame, at his hands, at his waistline, at his eyes, looking for some advantage, and failing that, from where the blow might come.

The assassin continued. "Nothing to say? You have grown so *taciturn*." He drew the word out, let it hang there. "I remember when we met in London you wore a *loud* suit. Remember that? The Rivoli Bar? You ordered a *loud* cocktail. You asked me to do a rather *loud* thing. Do you not remember?"

The assassin shook his head as if he were a disappointed parent. "Now you have grown so quiet. I suppose you are letting that hand that jerks back and forth from your concealed pistol do the talking. But a word of advice on firearms, Harold. If you do not know how to handle one, the person you are most likely to injure is yourself."

Peterson went rigid. Tensed his jaw, ground his teeth. Seemed to reach a decision. "Stop fucking around. No one asked you to kill Howell. We didn't know if you'd gone off the reservation. Like a *rabid* dog."

The words hung in the air for a dangerous second, then Peterson held one hand up in front of him, palm out, like he was trying to calm a slathering, growling, teeth-baring canine. The other stayed at his waist. "But all's right that ends right. You brought the videotape?"

"Howell was necessary collateral damage. I warned you that could happen. In fact, you ought to recall—I *emphasized* it."

Peterson had gotten control of himself now. Forced a hardness into his face. Angled his head back in a look of arrogance, like he was looking down his nose at something he feared smelled of rotten fish. But at the same time he finally let his hand slide away from the gun at his waist and kept it away.

"The videotape? Remember? You were *contracted* to bring the videotape."

So that's how it would be, then. The assassin pulled the black tape from his coat and handed it to Peterson. Peterson, for his part, kept his hand well away from his gun, dug into his coat, and delivered the account card to the assassin.

No last confrontation. No more killing. The job was done. One more night in the hotel and then a plane back to Europe tomorrow. First to the banks in Switzerland, then to Berlin to let his contact know he was available again, then to London once more.

Back to London again. Back to waiting.

Peterson was walking away now. The assassin called out, "I wonder, now that you have it, are you going to show it to Daddy?"

There was a hitch in Peterson's step, but he kept his cool. Never hinted at turning around.

The assassin dropped his hand from his pistol.

No more killing, then. For now.

29

RED SAGE

IRIS

My agent, Mitch, called while I was staring at myself in the mirror applying lipstick, getting ready to leave on my mission with Bronze.

"How's Loretta's latest novel coming along? Ready for the big game yet? Pre-season? Training camp at least?"

"Loretta's day to day, Mitch. We discussed this."

"What are you telling me, Iris? You're not punting, are you? It's not ... Jesus ... not a turnover on downs, is it? Iris—you know just as well as me, you can't score if you don't shoot."

I looked at my face in the mirror as I listened to Mitch. The face had grown strange with the years, the eyes settling down deeper and deeper as the youthful collagen had vanished. Under the eyes had appeared dark blue shadows followed by a sprinkling of tiny red splotches that marred my cheeks—a million different little adjustments, each almost unnoticeably subtle but adding up to create an entirely different impression when viewed altogether—just here, thinness where there had been the plumpness of youth, and over here, softness where there had once been straight, sexy lines.

As Mitch prattled, I stared further into the abstract visual that, for others, *was* me.

This strangeness was me.

I suppose I look like myself now. I don't know how long it will last, but right now I finally look like me. When I die, this is the me they will remember. The picture they'll use in the obit.

There's a sameness to the beauty of youth just as there is a sameness to the aged. But right now I am fully me. All the bells and whistles have been stripped away, all the weirdnesses revealed in full. You either like me this way or you don't.

When you're young, what makes your face your own—an odd twist to the lips, a wandering tooth, a jag of the nose, one eye smaller than the other, a mole, a scar—the boys who find you attractive pass it over, thinking just below the level of consciousness, *Perhaps that's not so bad; I can deal with that, the rest is OK*, but there's that one boy who steals looks at you all year in algebra class who thinks, *What is that* thing *about her, that* mysterious *thing?*

Well, now it's out and there's no hiding it.

"Iris, are you listening to me?"

"I am—more or less. Look, Mitch, now's not a great time. I'm working on something I think you'll like. But Loretta's injured reserve right now ... Don't worry, don't worry. I'm working on it right now ... words are coming ..."

BRONZE USUALLY WORE blazers or sport coats, but I had hardly ever seen him in a full suit before, let alone a tuxedo. But here he was, resplendently attired in rich black and stark white, standing at the bottom of my stairs as if working up the courage to come up and knock. When he saw me in my dark green floor-length dress (the only dress in my wardrobe that even got close to black tie appropriate this time of year) and struggling in high heels, he jogged up in his shining black shoes to offer me his arm.

He looked good. His arm felt like iron.

And he didn't smell of booze. At least not yet.

We slowly made our way down the stairs as I leaned most of my body weight on him.

"Nice dress. I don't think I've ever seen you wear something like that before."

"You don't look so bad yourself. I'm no connoisseur, but I'm guessing that's a very expensive tux."

I couldn't help briefly rubbing the fine wool of the jacket between my fingers. Bronze had gone silent. I looked up to see him giving me a look like the cat that ate the canary. I let my hand drop from the fabric.

"Your dress almost matches our ride for the evening."

I looked around our street, confused. I had assumed we'd take a taxi over to the event. It couldn't possibly be ...

"Ms. Margaryan." Bronze gestured to the deep-green sports car parked in front of our respective homes. "Let me introduce you to the 1997 Porsche 911 Turbo S in Metallic Forest Green. One of the last of the air-cooled 911s."

"How?"

"Roth arranged it. It's on temporary release from city impound. If you're twenty-six, living in a studio apartment in northeast DC, and just sold $250,000 worth of Colombian cocaine to an undercover federal agent, the cash purchase of this vehicle is not recommended. However, I think it should do nicely for us this evening ... One's got to take their wins where they can find them."

I shook my head. Boys with their toys. I ran my hand over the cold, clean metal of the exterior while Bronze opened the door for me.

"So, Mr. Bond, do the headlights convert into missile launchers?"

"No, but there's a six-CD changer."

"THE TUX WAS FREE."

"Huh?"

I was lost in the rumbling vibrations of the engine, feeling the power of the Porsche as we smoothly took the winding turns and circles of the DC streets. I was lost in anticipation of this evening and its implications. Triggered by the Porsche, I was distracting myself, out of touch with the now, thinking of fetishes, a long-standing professional interest.

I had started out thinking of car fetishes. But my thoughts soon drifted into all the major ones: women's underwear fetishes, buttock fetishes, computer fetishes, flower fetishes, motorcycle fetishes, naval fetishes, and the granddaddy of them all—the foot fetish. Although in late twentieth-century America, the surgically augmented breast fetish was perhaps giving the foot a run for its money. Were we all so at the mercy of the whims of culture that our very sexual desires, our most individual fantasies, morphed with the times? Foot binding in China argued yes. Marilyn Monroe and Jayne Mansfield argued yes. Heroin chic argued yes.

"You asked about the price of the tux earlier. It was free. My father made it for me. Did you know my father was a tailor?"

I shook my head.

"Yeah, the tuxedo is a funny garment, meant to make men look like background decorations to the women. It's an almost entirely standardized outfit—no vents, single button, jetted pockets—and when there are choices, they're mostly binary—

peaked lapels or shawl collar, cummerbund or waistcoat, black or midnight blue.

"Yet you'll never find an off-the-rack tux that's quite right. It seems like willful negligence on the part of the big brands. So bespoke is the only way to go if you're cursed with knowing too much about tailored menswear. My father constantly made tuxes his entire professional life, for bankers and lawyers and CEOs and idle heirs and politicians. My father's fingers were callused and creased and scarred with tuxes. Tuxes put me through college."

We parked two blocks away from the Red Sage, a palatial restaurant and DC's most *en vogue* setting for the political elite to conduct unofficial legislative dealings in surroundings of opulence and excess. The Bushes ate here. The Clintons eat here.

Tonight it belonged to Fred Kopes, Billy Kopes's older brother. He had rented it out for a kind of political memorial for Billy. Tonight DC's elite would come and kiss the heavily moneyed Kopes ring, make phony speeches about Billy, and most of all, jockey over who would take his place at the top of the running for the GOP's senate nomination in Virginia next year.

Only to find out the answer would be Fred.

I had been to the Red Sage once, years before, with George on a double date that doubled again as a business meeting for George. I'd gotten the mushroom goat cheese enchiladas and a giant margarita, which were as advertised and helped make up for spending half the evening quietly listening to George's business associate—whose name I couldn't remember but whose permanently arched eyebrows from an overly aggressive face lift were forever etched in my mind's eye—tell *me* at length about *his* theories on the book market.

Tonight, though, we were here on a mission from Roth.

Simple enough. Watch Fred. Watch out for Harold Peterson.

Bronze had broken open the case on the assassin. I didn't yet have all the details. But from Bronze and Roth, I had gathered that the FBI had been able to recover surveillance video of him going into a back facilities entrance of Carolyn's hotel in Austin. While they didn't get much of a picture of him, they were able to clearly read the plates of the car he drove away and were able to painstakingly track his movements from her hotel. He hadn't gone to the Austin airport but to the San Antonio airport, only about an hour and a half from downtown Austin, then onto a flight back to DC. Then, from there, they tracked down the taxicab and the driver who had driven a rather strange, frightening man with an odd accent back to his hotel. There were a few gaps in the itinerary, but they were fairly certain to have him pinned.

He was unlikely to remain at the hotel long. They had to act immediately. Leo Rossetti and his team in the FBI were moving on the assassin aggressively. While Fred Kopes had his party, the assassin would soon find himself dead or in custody.

And then maybe Bronze could start to move on.

Meanwhile, Metro PD was tailing Harold Peterson while Roth was following a last lead, doing a last piece of due diligence. He was heading down to the Kopes estate in Virginia to see what additional evidence he could gather on Peterson from Big Bill Kopes. They knew Peterson had been there at least once during the last few weeks. But more importantly, they knew he had been on a flight to London on May 4th, immediately following the murder of Billy Kopes.

It was there that Roth and Rossetti believed that Peterson had contracted with the assassin who had killed Roger and Carolyn Haake.

The dangling question was, had Peterson been acting alone or was he working on orders from Fred Kopes?

By the hearty grin Fred gave all those coming to shake his hand at the front of the restaurant, whatever his involvement, he didn't betray the least bit of worry.

I HAD BEEN HOPING for something to happen. I wasn't sure what —some adventure, something light and fun with a hint of sexiness. The night had started so promisingly with the tuxedo and the Porsche, but Fred Kopes was just about the most boring mark one could imagine. We ate hors d'oeuvres and drank champagne—at least, I did. Bronze stuck to soda water and lime, which I was relieved to see. We watched Fred gladhand and thump about, imposing his force of personality and almost tangibly visible wealth on all those around him, supplicants who depended on the financial benedictions of the Kopes family.

As the night dragged on, it became more and more clear that there would be no action here. The action was with the FBI. It was with those tailing Peterson. Maybe even with Mark Roth hunting evidence down in Virginia. If Fred Kopes was involved, we were not going to catch him out tonight.

Here the only intrigue was politics—the inane and constant squabbling for power. And for what? As Bronze and I chatted by the bar, we could agree on the stupidity of that. Why this constant seeking of the most boring forms of control? The chance to hold one's hand to the lever of bureaucracy, just as thousands more fought you, pulling on it every which way, while the lever itself stood mostly still.

Why seek control at all?

Was it fear? Was it the feeling that life had no purpose, but that if you could one day make yourself president, then you might feel as if yours did? So you became a congressman, then a senator or governor or whatever, but the pursuit would never stop at anything but failure unless you made it that last final step to the presidency.

Eventually Bronze remarked, "We've got to get out of this damn town. It's doing us no good."

I nodded. "But where should we go? Are you saying we should run away together?"

I meant the comment to be breezy and amusing, but no sooner was it out of my mouth than I realized my mistake. He'd run away with Carolyn already, hadn't he?

Bronze looked down at his feet a moment, then straight into my eyes. "Look, about Carolyn—"

"You don't need to say anything, Bronze. I'm sorry to have reminded you. You don't owe me anything."

"But maybe I'd like to ... owe you something."

Something in that phraseology struck a false note in my ears. "Is that what love is, Bronze, owing and owning?" Again, I meant to be light, but it seemed I couldn't keep an undertone of accusation out of my voice.

He shrugged. "No. Not at all. But, Iris, you're a little intimidating where love and romance comes in. You know that, right? You're one of the world's leading experts, I mean—according to the book sales, at least."

I couldn't help but almost spit out my drink chortling at that. "Me? I think you wildly misconstrue romance with the romance novel."

He didn't seem to know what to say, and I heard myself continuing as if observing us from a remove.

"Look, in this country we have two forms of popular art that masquerade as romance: the romantic comedy film and the romance novel. And don't get me wrong, I love both, because I, like most people, I would assume, love to escape. But that's what both of these art forms are really about. Escape. The romantic comedy is about escaping to the time of ritualized courtship leading up to that one transcendent moment"—I gestured quite wildly with the hand that wasn't holding my champagne glass— "and the romance novel is about after that. After you're trapped. Spoken for. Stuck and pinned. Looking for the exits, if only in your mind. If only for a moment. Yearning to transgress all the places you are bound. The romance novel is a necessary balm, an escape hatch, but escape ... escape is most certainly not *romance*."

It was then that I heard a feminine voice intruding on our conversation, soft and velvety but undergirded with a strength and confidence I could only dream of. Before I even turned, I saw the change in Bronze's eyes.

The woman said, "What *is* romance, then? *I* would certainly like to know." It was Esther McNamara and her husband, Chris. I laughed and quickly did my best to steer the conversation to more mundane topics.

That seemed to work. They were pleasant enough people. And our conversation too was pleasant enough. Interesting and charming, as far as these things go.

But the way she looked at Bronze, I got the feeling that she felt I was somehow stepping on her territory. She—there with her husband, no less—seemed to put out an almost imperceptible vibration that she had marked Bronze out for future safe-keeping.

Or perhaps I was seeing things. Projecting my own insecurities onto her, my own jealousy rearing up from some dark place within.

But even if I were to give her the benefit of the doubt, there was no mistaking Bronze's eyes.

He was in love with her.

And had he managed to fall in love with Carolyn too? In less than a week? What about ex-wife Ellen? What about all the other women he had fallen for over the years? In Japan and New York and God knows where else? What was love to Bronze, really? It seemed the lightest thing for him. Cast about without consideration.

And maybe there was some flicker of love growing in him for me. Had been blossoming slowly over time while he lived below me, watching movies together, making jokes, growing through all these little moments we shared. But what did that amount to really?

Did love just pass through Bronze with the randomness of mood? Did he go through his morning in love with me, then Carolyn in the afternoon, then Esther in the evening? Or did his loves swirl about more rapidly than that, even? Did they click by like frames in a film reel, so fast, he couldn't even track the feeling from one moment to the next?

While for me, love moved at a glacial pace, like sediment accumulating, achingly slow, building inch by inch a mountain range over millennia. Static to the human eye. Frozen in time. A silent prison stuck in ice.

WE HARDLY SPOKE on the car ride home, the Porsche covering the silence with the shifting whines of its engine. The evening had been a bust. Harold Peterson had never shown up. Fred Kopes had never varied from his bland politician's act. The moment of greatest drama was when he made a speech, ostensibly to discuss Billy's life and accomplishments but really the point was to build up to an official declaration of his candidacy for the senate, to "carry on Billy's legacy," as he put it.

When we arrived home, Bronze walked me up to my door. I leaned on his arm again as I had at the beginning of the evening, but my earlier excitement was gone. Instead, there was only a dead feeling in my stomach.

But when we got to my door, he bent his face down to me. For half a moment I stood there stunned, unable to comprehend what was happening, until I realized that this was meant to be a kiss.

I turned to the side and placed my hand against his chest and felt his heart pumping away there. The kiss landed harmlessly on my cheek.

But wasn't that what I wanted? Wasn't that exactly what I had hoped for when the night began?

"Bronze, I'm not sure ... I feel ... confused. Maybe this isn't the right time. Recently your life has been—"

He nodded solemnly before I could finish and interjected, "You're right. I'm sorry. I understand. Goodnight, Iris."

I quickly went inside and shut the door, then leaned back against it. I could hear him take a step or two away, but then he paused, stood still for what seemed a long while before returning to knock on the door.

I opened it, about to say something—what, exactly, I can't be sure. But he raised his hand to stop me before I could get going, and something about the look on his face made me want to stop.

"I think we need each other," he blurted out.

"You and me specifically? Or would any port in a storm do for you, Bronze?" I almost flinched, surprising myself with the caustic tone of my words. Did I really feel as angry as I sounded?

He just shook his head. He seemed resigned. Tired.

"I don't know. I don't know how it all works—destiny and soulmates and love at first sight or learning to love or chemicals in the brain or evolutionary imperative or whatever explanation you want to come up with. I don't know about *me*, even. I don't know if I'm strange or typical. I don't have the slightest idea about any of it. After all these relentless years of *it*.

"We've both been around. I know we've both felt love before. I don't know what that feeling's like for you, but for me, it has just become this deep hurt that I'm here and all the women I've ever loved are somewhere else. Even if they're standing in the same room, like Esther tonight, they've gone away from me now. Even if I never really had them and only imagined it, it hurts all the same. And that pain isn't going away. I've waited on it and it just isn't going away.

"But I can't shake the feeling that there's something in you, some *good thing*, that I'm missing. That I couldn't dream you up in a million years because I just don't understand the first thing about what that *good thing* is, because I couldn't possibly imagine it without seeing it with my own eyes.

"And I don't know what I've got for you. Probably nothing. You want something fixed in place. Something solid and unchanging for you to desire. What you want is a man, and I'm not sure I know what a man is. But I know it's not just a black pit of wanting. It's not the endless vacillation of *desire* and *shame*, of desire and *fear* of desire.

"It's something else completely.

"Maybe I've got my own good thing that you don't have. Maybe not. *Probably* not. Maybe I see you living in this big, beautiful house all by yourself. I see you talking with your friends, and you're clever and you're entertaining and you hide yourself away. Even in your writing, you hide, piling pseudonym on top of pseudonym. I think, 'Maybe she doesn't quite see herself for what she is. Maybe I can show her how she looks through my eyes—how beautiful she is in everything she does. And if I can do that, then I don't know ... maybe there's some point to me after all.'"

Later, alone in my bed, I think about how I should have let him in.

He looked so vulnerable in that moment. There really was a

part of me that wanted to let him in and do what I could to comfort him. But the part in me that controlled my mouth told him that I needed to think more about it. It was too sudden. We could talk more in the morning. It was all too much for tonight.

And, wide awake in bed, I hated myself for my indecision and cowardice. Stewed in my racing thoughts like a slow-acting poison. Thinking of all my regrets. Of all my excuses.

As I lay there, it occurred to me that my regrets stemmed not from overindulgences or infidelities but from the denial of pleasure for some "righteous" cause or other. Those denied pleasures haunted me. Haunted me with all the moments of intimacy I had avoided. All the moments I had had like tonight, where I let a spark that could have turned into a kiss hang and hang without ever acting—hang until it died.

And while those missed moments stalk my thoughts, my actual indulgences and pleasures fade from my mind—are at best black and white sketches. I think of all those sparkling chances that will never pass my way again. They sing to me at night like sirens.

I know the truth. I turned down the feast of life to merely watch it, and I will starve filled to brimming with unspeakable visions.

But not again. Not this time. I can't let it pass me by again.

I throw on my clothes, run down my stairs and out my door and down again, down to the basement apartment at the bottom of Bronze's stairs.

There's a big stupid smile on my face.

Only I'm too late.

30

SEMI-AUTOMATIC

MAY 14, 1997

He heard their footsteps in the hall. They were trying to be quiet—leopards stalking prey. To him, it sounded like a stampede of buffalo.

He had had to compromise on the hotel and the room he chose. He needed a place he could be anonymous. One of many walking in and out. In quick reach of downtown DC. But these considerations meant that egress in an emergency would be difficult. Still, he had outlined a plan for escape as best he could.

He always did. And ninety-nine times out of a hundred, all that planning was for nothing.

But you didn't do it for those ninety-nine times. It was the one time that got you. He had seen rivals in the business come and go. They didn't plan for the one time.

He did.

The room had a small balcony. It was on the top floor.

The front door was the only way in or out.

He grabbed his pistol, holstered it, grabbed his rifle, and stepped out onto the hard ceramic of the balcony floor, closing the sliding glass doors behind him but leaving the blinds open, so that when he stepped over the iron railing onto the thin ledge between rooms, the balcony would appear empty.

They were gathering at the door now. They would come in with a team of about eight. There would be backup down the hall. There would be backup in the lobby and outside.

He pressed the length of his spine against the smooth outer wall of the hotel, nothing but a fifteen-floor drop in front of him. He calmly took the scope off the rifle and slid it into the pocket of his jacket. There would be no need for it this close up, and there was a slight chance it would get in his way.

He imagined that some rivals scoffed at him for picking the rifle he did. The Heckler & Koch PSG1 was only of average accuracy when compared with modern bolt action rifles. Some in his field had an obsessiveness bordering on petulant connoisseurship over the accuracy of their rifles. As if an assassin was simply a long-distance sniper in some military unit. Sure, the PSG1 was just OK at range versus something like a bolt action Sako TRG, but the PSG1 was semi-automatic.

There was no way in hell you could do what he was about to do with a bolt action.

Crunch!

They smashed the front door in.

Even for him, it took every ounce of restraint he had relentlessly drilled into his nerves to wait the two seconds it took the first couple of FBI agents to race in—to go on waiting until the rest of the assault team would be maximally bunched at the door, then ...

He quickly swiveled on the ledge, turning to the left and his balcony, his right leg pirouetting out over the empty space in front of the ledge, up and over the balcony railing, the PSG1 brought to bear on the four men rushing through the door.

He ignored the two already in the room and looking in the wrong directions.

He fired, shooting rapidly right through the glass of the balcony door.

Pop! Pop! Pop! Pop! Pop!

He didn't bother to check the results of his shots; he was already turning to the closer of the two FBI agents already in the room, trusting he'd disabled the four at the door.

The agent was half a second slow bringing his own rifle toward him, and in that half second, the assassin put one shot right through the bridge of the man's nose.

Pop! ... Pop!

A half beat after his shot, another shot rang out from his right. The other FBI agent in the room was good enough with his reaction speed and almost good enough with his aim. The bullet came within a few inches of taking the assassin in the chest, but instead it passed through his right bicep at a diagonal.

Still, the shot through the arm was enough to throw the assassin backward. With only one foot on the balcony and the other on the thin ledge, it might have been enough to send him out into the open air to free fall into the black night.

With everything he had, he twisted himself to the right, so that his momentum slammed his right hip against the near, outer corner of the railing, and, after a moment when he almost went windmilling over the railing to splat fifteen floors below, he instead ricocheted off the iron rail, fell forward, and landed on the hard balcony floor.

He managed to hold on to the rifle in good order as he fell, and no sooner did he land than he put one shot into the offending agent's knee; the agent dropped to the floor with a crunch like a tossed sack of rocks. The assassin put two more rounds in him then, passing within millimeters of each other straight through the man's left cheek.

Then he was already twisting the PSG1 back to the left toward the front door, firing two rounds of suppressive fire that didn't hit but made the agents attempting to file in jump back from the open door.

He crawled back into the hotel room right through the shattered glass of the balcony door, hot blood dripping from his arms. He had killed the first two agents in, and there were three down on the ground at the door. He might have clipped one or two more, but they had managed to drag themselves back out to safety.

They'd be formulating a new plan now. Calling in reinforcements. It was his chance to get out, but first ...

One of the three he'd shot at the front door was still breathing—fragile, whimpering little breaths.

He crawled to the wall to the right of the door, grabbed the still-alive agent, and dragged him a little way further in, where they were no longer in view of the doorway. He cradled the rifle in his right arm and with the left he took out his pistol and pressed it hard against the FBI agent's temple.

"How?" he demanded.

The agent limply shook his head.

"How? How did you know where? Was it Peterson?"

The agent began whimpering pleadingly, "Please don't kill me, please don't kill me ..."

"Then tell me how."

"We traced you from Austin. Bronze ... Bronze Goldberg ..." *That drunk two-bit voyeur Haake hired?* It didn't make any sense.

"Who? Who ordered the hit, then? Which agent?" What asshole-fuck in the FBI thought they could go after him? They should have known better. He would end them hard. He would slaughter them like rancid swine.

Bang!

One of the agents in the hallway had crawled toward the door so as to almost have an angle on him but not quite; the shot went wide. He leaned forward and fired three shots at a shadow on the gray hall carpet that must have been the agent, not knowing whether he hit anything.

But before he could reset himself, he was suddenly tackled backward, and arms were wrenching at the rifle cradled in his elbow. The agent was not half so hurt as he had pretended to be.

The assassin tumbled back against the wall, the rifle coming loose from his weakened grip, but before the FBI agent could bring the rifle around against him, he swung his pistol up and shot the man from under his jaw, the bullet coming right up through the top of his skull with a *thunk* and a spray of brain and bone.

The man slumped over in a heap.

He holstered the pistol again, grabbed back the rifle and repositioned it in his arms, came up onto his feet once more.

When he burst out into the hall, he came with his rifle blazing, running through the rest of the clip. He shot for speed and suppression, to get the agents ducking for cover, but he knew that with his endlessly trained reflexes and aim, he'd probably hit at least a few times.

One of them managed to get a shot off at him, but it went wide. He fled, dropping his empty rifle, and dived into the stairwell caddy corner to his room. He got lucky; any backup in the stairwell must have pulled out to support those in the hall or take the wounded down to safety. They hadn't yet had a chance to position themselves again properly.

And besides, from their perspective, where could he go?

He got off the ground and raced up to the roof, just one flight up. The whole reason he had stayed on the top floor and the reason he had picked this particular hotel now came into play. The hotel abutted right up against another building that was just about a floor shorter. It was easy enough to sprint out along the roof and jump down onto the other building.

The next building after that was several floors shorter. Too much of a jump to take without risking a broken ankle. But he had worked that out in advance.

He went down the stairs from the second building's roof, rapidly racing down four flights. It was an empty office building at this time in the evening, and his clanging footsteps seemed to fill the whole hollow building with violent noise. Once out of the stairwell, he ran down a half-lit hall to the bathroom at the far end, went in, opened the window, and dropped out of the window onto the roof of the shorter building.

From there he took the elevator down into the basement of the third building, into its private underground garage, and emerged out the back end of the garage driving a hotwired BMW. With the chaos he had created and the speed of his flight, he was far enough away from his hotel that the FBI would not figure out where he had gone before it was way too late.

HE MADE A MAKESHIFT bandage out of a sleeve of his shirt for the wound in his bicep. He pulled the glass out of his forearms and wrapped those up as well, looking like a failed suicide. The hotel had been in Rosslyn, but he did not encounter any FBI as he drove over the Francis Scott Key Bridge and down into Georgetown.

When he got to N Street, he parked and discovered there was no one home at Goldberg's apartment or in the townhouse above. It was simple enough to pick the apartment lock, slip into the dark living room, close the door behind him, and wait with his back against the wall, his silenced pistol at the ready.

It was about half an hour before Goldberg came home. He blathered on annoyingly with the woman who lived in the townhouse above, while the assassin was forced to continue to silently wait there, primed and unmoving.

Finally Goldberg came down the stairs, taking the steps in a slow, staccato rhythm.

The assassin lifted the pistol and poised to fire.

BRONZE OPENED THE DOOR, sighing loudly, thinking of Iris, already replaying in his thoughts all that they had said to each other.

He saw nothing in the dark of his apartment before the assassin put a bullet in him.

PART III

SING, GODDESS

Wrath: Sing, Goddess, the wrath of Achilles
Black and murderous
—Homer, *The Iliad*

31

WRATH

JUNE 14, 1988

All was black—murderous and cold. Then visions. In the darkness, he saw it all again. In the darkness, he and Keaton were one. Bronze saw what Keaton saw. Felt what Keaton felt. Would it loop again and again for all eternity? Was this hell, then? If God works in mysterious ways, what then of the Devil?

Behind the first door was a man in his late middle age, naked, lying back on circular throw pillows, propped up on his elbows, eyes solemnly watching a rotund Disassociated Beta methodically performing fellatio on his thin gray penis. Caleb Keaton briefly noted the morbid stretch marks on her bare white ass before aiming his shotgun at the center of that large target and pulling the trigger. The sound was deafening even through his earplugs and the thumping, pulsing beat of the music everywhere. The force of the blast turned her backside a speckled red and threw it in a somersault over the man, who screamed as her jaw clenched shut in shock.

All the better for him. At least he would be saved from future temptation.

The woman was whimpering and trying to crawl away to the corner of the room, as if there was safety there. The previously torpid man sprung backward, eyes wider than oceans, the blood from the Beta whore's ass streaming down his face to the nonexistent musculature of his chest and the sagging skin of his stomach. The remnants of his missing appendage sprayed pulses of blood as if he were urinating.

There's trauma in revolution. Oh yes, brothers. Only through pain will your eyes open.

Sighting down the barrel, Caleb turned the shotgun to follow the Beta's pathetically slow movements. Time to put her out of her misery once and for all. He depressed the trigger again. The movement stopped and black blood leaked from a dozen more pinpricks in her back. She looked like a lumpy leaking sack of blackberries.

As soon as he was reasonably sure she was dead, Caleb turned quickly on his heel and went back out the first door. No one was in the hall. After hearing the blast of the shotgun in that first enclosed room, Caleb had worried that even with the loud music and Madam Richelieu's thick soundproofed doors, the element of surprise would be lost, but his luck held.

With quick sure movements, he reloaded the shotgun. While the removal of the previous man's sex organ was a satisfactory outcome, he knew that, going forward, he would have to do more to avoid innocent male casualties. Although, of course, there was only so much he could reasonably do.

And there were those men, those in the heart of the Cabal itself, who were as irredeemable as the women.

Through the next door two fat men were fucking a diminutive woman on a bed. She lay on her back, her thin body almost seeming to disappear into the puffy white bedcovers. One man held her legs up as he took her, while the other arched her head back over the edge of the bed and thrust himself into her mouth.

Caleb yelled, "Halt! Police!"

He smiled as both men leaped backward, hands up, ready

excuses on their lips. Caleb waited as the woman more slowly rolled herself off the bed and stood up. If it weren't for her overly plucked and shaped eyebrows that formed a long thin line over her oval eyes, she might have been beautiful. At least in that dim light. Caleb wondered briefly if she was even eighteen, but it was always so hard to tell these days.

She looked at him almost hopefully for a split second until she saw his cheap plastic Ronald Reagan mask. The men were a half second slower on the uptake, their excuses dissolving into confused nonsense. Despite his earlier resolve, the frenzy was in his blood, and Caleb briefly considered executing all three. But his will held and he merely blew the woman's head off with a single blast from the shotgun.

A strange slow-motion stillness filled his vision with dilated time as he imagined her headless body would fall to its knees as she had certainly done so often in life with the vibrations of Cabal and Coven echoing in her mind, but instead she fell back onto the bed with arms outstretched, feet hanging daintily in the air. Behind her, black chunks of skull and a spray of blood coated the white bed in a beautiful arching pattern that filled Caleb with an almost unbearably bright white light of satisfaction.

Out and on through door three. Here the threesome was reversed as a diminutive man with rimless spectacles and a halo of wispy hair tried to handle the attentions of two obese women wearing identical platinum blond wigs. Caleb got one with a head shot, but the other flinched and he only took her pendulous left breast off with his first shot. Between her hollering and incoherent gyrating movements, he was only able to open up her undulating stomach with the next blast, spilling red blood and yellow fat. He was forced to drop his shotgun then, grab his pistol from the holster at his belt and proceed to finish her with a close-range head shot while she screamed "I knew! I knew it!" for some unknowable reason.

As he left, he re-holstered his pistol, reaching behind him to grab the semi-automatic assault rifle strapped to his back.

The rifle worked just fine through door four, where a Black man masturbated in the shadows while watching a pale white woman dancing in white lingerie. Caleb was able to cleanly put two rounds through her chest without incident. But in the next room his rounds went right through a redhead, killing her male partner as surely as her.

He felt a twinge of guilt, but you have to break a few eggs to make French toast or whatever the saying was. And when he was once again forced to kill the man in the next room, who, after his well-built brunette Beta Slave was eliminated with an efficient two-tap to the heart, ran screaming at him covered in blood, his fire-hydrant-shaped phallus bobbing half erect in the open air, Caleb no longer felt even a hint of guilt. So little, in fact, that when he left that room to see the voyeur Black man from a few rooms back walking shirtless toward him with some kind of makeshift blunt weapon held in front of him like a sword, he didn't even bother to try to scare him off nonviolently. He just took aim at his head, missed low, and caught him in the neck.

Caleb watched with a feeling of deep relief as the man grasped at his neck and slumped against the hallway wall, vainly attempting to hold back the fountain of blood spraying in all directions. It was strange, this relief. Strange that he seemed to find an almost satisfaction in the men he was forced to kill as opposed to the demented, pseudo-human women that it was so necessary to eliminate. It was a feeling he would need to examine at mirror time. But not now—now there was still the madam to take care of.

Would she give up her masters? Would he finally find his

way to the central core of the Coven—to the very Cabal itself? His heart thrilled to think of it.

Behind the Ronald Reagan mask, his face was sopping with sweat that now bit cigarette burns into his eyes and turned his vision into a shattered river of bubbling celluloid. He ditched the mask and rubbed his eyes until the world returned to him, his true face now gloriously revealed.

BRONZE WAS TOO LATE. The front door of the hidden brothel was incongruously ajar; behind it, a heavily muscled bouncer lay in the fetal position on the carpeted floor, his dead hands clasping at his open belly, trying and failing to stop the jumble of his intestines from spilling out.

The lounge was empty. Heavy music thumped. The smell of spilt whisky and sharp citrusy perfume still lingered in the worn upholstery of the red sofas and chairs.

There was a bar in the lounge and behind the bar, a phone. He called Roth on his direct line and got his young partner instead. Roth was in the car. He would radio him. He would radio everyone. They were all coming. Hang tight.

Except they were too late. Bronze had been too slow to figure it all out. Even when the evidence had been staring him the face for days.

Yeah, hang tight, sure, but then how many more will die?

Bronze grabbed a full bottle of vodka off the bar shelf, intending to use it as a makeshift weapon if need be. He left the bar and pushed through the beaded curtain separating the front lounge from the hallway where the real business was conducted.

Through the first door on the left, he could barely see in the low light of the room, the blood on the walls looking almost black in the dimness, but he could make out the red of the blood that pooled around the mutilated groin of a dead older man who lay upon the bed. Bronze stepped into the room, noticing something over in the corner, to the side of the bed. He stared at her for several long beats before he could even process that this was once a human being.

Bronze's hand went to his mouth; he doubled over and vomited through his fingers. Still half bent over and dripping puke from his left hand, he stumbled back out the door into the hallway.

He wiped what vomit he could off his hands onto the wall. When he got to the second door, it was shut. Perhaps Keaton hadn't got to this one yet? Or maybe he was still inside?

Bronze raised the vodka bottle above his shoulder with one hand, gripped the knob with the other, and threw himself into the room ready to do quick violence to Keaton.

Nothing. Just stillness. Then he saw a pair of bare feet hanging over the end of the bed facing him.

"Miss," he whispered through grinding teeth. "*Miss!* You've got to get out of here."

When she didn't respond, he stepped further into the room.

He looked down at her naked body, arms stretched out to the sides. Where her head should have been, there were only red stains spreading out from her neck in a widening cone.

She looked so small and fragile there. He wanted to go to her and pick her up and carry her out of this place.

It was too much.

He lost control of the coordination of his body and sank to his knees. He was too stunned to cry.

From his knees, he could see only her dangling feet.

He stared at them.

He stared, and his stare felt like some bastardization of prayer—a lamentation and a plea for forgiveness.

She had turquoise nail polish on.

He thought of her in her room putting on the polish. He thought of her in a store picking out the color. He thought of her walking down the street on the way to the store, no one noticing or caring that she came from this place. He thought of all the people who knew what this place was and did nothing, and that if the cops had come here at all, it would have been to arrest her, not to set her free.

A black rage filled him. A red wrath. He rose back to standing. Raised the vodka bottle once more and went to find Keaton.

He didn't need to go far.

As he opened the door to leave, there, standing in the hall waiting for him, pale face plastered in sweat and blood, was Keaton, pistol aimed vaguely in Bronze's direction.

He screamed, "Where are they? Where's the Cabal? Tell me! *Tell me!*"

Keaton's mouth foamed and his hand shook. So great was his fury, Bronze saw that he was not concentrating on aiming the pistol. There might be a chance if he seized the moment.

Bronze swung with all his might, bringing the vodka bottle down hard, aiming for Keaton's head. Keaton dodged to the right, too slow to avoid the bottle completely but getting his head clear enough that the bottle only smashed against his neck and trapezius.

The blow from the bottle was enough to cause Keaton to drop his pistol and fall to one knee. But, jackrabbit quick, he pulled out the trusty knife he kept strapped to his ankle and came up hard with it, stabbing Bronze between groin and hip bone.

Bronze fell back against the hallway wall. Keaton pulled the knife out and Bronze slid down the wall till his ass hit the floor.

Keaton menaced him with the knife jammed up against his throat, face pressed close against Bronze's face.

"Where? *Where?*"

Bronze had no voice to say anything.

Keaton screamed, now not even forming words, spit flying into Bronze's eyes. Then he reared his head back and smashed his forehead into Bronze's nose. Metallic blood spewed immediately into his mouth. Then the forehead smashed again; less well aimed this time, it hit Bronze in the mouth, then the next thrust clanged hard against Bronze's own forehead. Bronze figured Keaton might have dazed himself, since he dropped his grip on Bronze's shirt and stumbled away, gathering up his pistol from the floor, muttering incoherently to himself as he made his way back through the wall of beads into the red lounge where so many men had sat and waited for the varied delights of Madam Richelieu's.

Maybe he had died right then. Maybe all the rest was part of the same torture. Maybe Keaton's face had smashed through his and they had truly merged. Maybe his soul was poison.

No. Remember Bruce. Bruce had been there in the end. Like a guardian angel. Roth too. He remembered ...

Bronze limped his way out of the brothel and, by some miracle, made it to an antique shop, where he collapsed from blood loss and Bruce Schwarz waited for him in the back. Roth and a veritable platoon of police had caught up with Keaton a few blocks away from the brothel, trailing a stream of blood, his face painted red with the stuff. Keaton had got a shot into Roth's shoulder before Roth put one in Keaton's head, then the rest of the cops lit the already dead Keaton up, emptying clips and turning him into a shapeless, leaking bag of flesh.

Roth wound up on the same trauma floor of the same hospital as Bronze.

They both stayed awake all night, staring into the dark,

hearing the same medical machines chime and beep and cry out over and over again.

Bronze remembered.

When he had gotten out of the hospital, he had researched the stories of the dead women he had found at Madam Richelieu's. He remembered the articles he had written detailing their lives.

The paper had edited them down and buried them in the back.

But he had done it—even though it was meaningless in the end.

Each story was unique, but they fit together as a piece, like songs with rhyming melodies.

Each song resounded with the wrath of men.

32

UPSTAIRS, DOWNSTAIRS

MAY 14, 1997

When Bronze came to, reality was no improvement over his memories.

His arms were duct taped down onto the arms of the dog chair at his elbows and wrists, while his hands gripped hard on the carved dog heads. His legs were taped at the ankles and knees to the chair legs. His mouth was duct taped shut and he struggled to breathe, sucking in air with great billowing puffs of his nostrils. Blood ran down the front of his white shirt from the gunshot wound in his shoulder and down his black left pant leg from where the assassin had shot him in the knee as punishment for his first screams for help.

The assassin was in the kitchen. Bronze could hear him opening and closing cabinet doors and, strangely, the sound of ice being cracked into a bowl, then finally running water.

Bronze noticed the crisp precision of the assassin's movements as he emerged from the kitchen carrying a large Tupperware bowl full of ice, which he placed on Bronze's beaten-up coffee table. Then he returned to the kitchen and brought out a pitcher of water. A final trip resulted in a steak knife, a metal meat tenderizer, and a small wooden cutting board. All were neatly arranged on the coffee table, although he did not go so far as placing a placemat underneath the pitcher of water or the sweating ice bowl.

The assassin leaned back against the arm of Bronze's couch. If he weren't tied down, Bronze would have been able to reach out and throttle the bastard without even leaving his seat—had he any strength left.

The assassin spoke in a calm, cold voice that mixed a tinge of an upper-class English accent with a strange tonal lilt that made him sound utterly alien to any particular country on this earth.

"Now, Mr. Goldberg, I know the current circumstances are difficult to accept. But here they are. You are defenseless and I am going to kill you in the next few minutes. To be precise, I am going to shoot you in the head with this pistol."

The assassin leaned over and patted the silenced pistol that he had laid on the coffee table before going into the kitchen.

"I am here for two related reasons. First, through the result of your actions, a team of FBI agents attempted to kill me tonight. They, as you can see, were unsuccessful. I have a reputation to maintain, primarily so that such attempts are not made with any frequency in the future. Therefore, as the precipitating party, I must see that you are put to death with all due speed.

"Second, I know that you informed a particular member of the FBI of my location—an FBI agent with status enough to order the hit. I would like you to tell me who that high-ranking FBI agent is. Such an operational decision was detrimental not only to my interests but to the interests of the FBI and the United States government as a whole. You likely believe that you owe this personage some portion of loyalty, but I assure you that their poor decision-making in this context is indication enough of someone who ought to be immediately removed from any position of authority. In this regard, I understand that you probably do not yet see things my way, but you will be doing your country a service to reveal this person's name to me. Now I am going to remove your vocal restraints, and I would like you to remember the wound in your knee."

The assassin ripped the tape off Bronze's face in one quick motion. The pain was instant and sharp, but it did not come anywhere near the level of the foul, stomach-churning pain rising from what remained of his kneecap.

"Who is this FBI agent, Mr. Goldberg?"

Bronze wanted to say something defiant, to put all the rage he felt into words, to tell this embodiment of evil exactly why he was so mistaken, why his every action only served to dig his soul deeper into a hole he would never escape from. But Bronze was in too much pain and too weak for any of that. All he could do was shake his head in a motion more like a controlled swoon than an act of defiance.

"No? No, you will not tell me? I am afraid this sets us down a dark path. Well, level one, then."

The assassin replaced the tape over Bronze's mouth, careful to smooth the edges down with a prim fastidiousness, then moved in an unhurried manner to the coffee table and retrieved the steak knife and cutting board. Then, in a sudden blurred motion, the assassin grabbed Bronze's left hand and jammed the cutting board between his hand and the dog head carving. Bronze instinctually balled his hand into a fist and made a futile renewed effort to fight against his restraints.

The assassin wrenched Bronze's fist open and drove the steak knife down through the top of his hand with such ferocity that it penetrated not only the hand but halfway through the wooden cutting board as well.

Bronze screamed again, vision completely falling away for several seconds, as did the pain of his other wounds. For the length of three breaths or so, the searing pain from the knife was all he could register.

When he could see once more, the assassin had removed the tape over his mouth again and was slapping his face.

"There we are. There we are. What is the name, Mr. Goldberg? Tell me the name."

Bronze spat, but even in this he failed, as he was too weak to eject the liquid from his mouth much past his chin, where it fell to dribble down his neck.

The assassin moved to replace the duct tape over Bronze's mouth when Bronze appeared to try to say something.

"Yes? What is it? What is the name?"

"... *yuliekt* ..."

"That's it, you can tell me now."

"... *you like it* ..."

The assassin shook his head. "What does that mean? What is the name?"

Bronze breathed a huge gulp of air into his unobstructed mouth.

"You think you're cold-blooded ... but you like it ... They said you were a machine ... but you only play at one ... You want everyone to hurt as you have ..."

The assassin roughly slapped the duct tape back over Bronze's mouth and stared into his eyes quietly.

"OK ... As expected, I suppose. We will begin level two. And as you experience level two, I would encourage you to keep the following thought in mind. As bad as level two is, level three is rather a deal worse. Level three involves an organ vastly more sensitive than even your fingers."

With that the assassin grabbed the pinkie finger of Bronze's left hand, the one pinned to the cutting board with the steak knife, and, swinging full strength with the meat tenderizer, crushed the pinkie's middle knuckle.

Bronze's scream was muffled by the duct tape. Tears streamed from his eyes. But before he could even fully process the pain, the assassin smashed down once more with the meat tenderizer, destroying the middle knuckle of his ring finger as well.

Between the two gunshot wounds, the knife straight through his hand, the two obliterated knuckles, and the total body fear, it was simply too much. His nervous system burned out and he passed into unconsciousness.

The assassin noted the state of his victim, placed the meat tenderizer back down upon the coffee table, and poured the pitcher of water into the Tupperware bowl of ice. Once he'd gotten a good mixture of water and ice, he thrust the contents of the bowl into Bronze's face.

Bronze came to with a shock and a spluttering sound, ice-cold water running down his nostrils, choking and drowning him.

He was once again blind, his eyes stinging from the ice water, ice cubes having slammed against the entire surface of his face, freezing water seeping down his shirt collar. He harshly coughed up the burning water flooding his throat and nasal passages.

"It is important that you realize, Mr. Goldberg, that there is no escape for you. Not in taunts or pleas or unconsciousness. Even if you were to have a heart attack, I would revive you and continue your torture. There are no options. All that is left is for you to say the name of your colleague in the FBI, and then, and only then, will you be allowed to die."

ROTH FOUGHT TRAFFIC all the way down from DC until he hit Fredericksburg, Virginia. There he turned off the highway down quiet country roads watched over by empty fields and the occasional sleeping cow. Even when he got to the Kopes estate, it was another mile of driving down a private road before he arrived at the driveway leading to the main house—the one where William Kopes resided.

Roth lowered his window as he drove down the one-lane private road, hoping the breeze and the smell of the country would sharpen his tired mind before he attempted to intrude on a personality like William Kopes. There was the smell of the warm country night, the heat slowly sliding away from steamed grass and underbrush, a breeze that didn't quite cool. And at the last second, just before Roth was about to head up the final driveway, that breeze carried a sharp birdsong: *Ree-ree-ree-ree-ree!*

The sound startled Roth into looking more closely into the night at what lay ahead down the road. Out there in the distance, he saw it. *Shit.*

Cardinals didn't sleep much at night. But when they called before sunrise, they called in warning. He killed his headlights and pulled to the side of the road.

Harold Peterson's red Mercedes was parked in front of Kopes's garage.

Peterson must have slipped his tail. Or someone had let him go on purpose. But then, why had he come here? Fred Kopes was up in DC still, announcing his senate campaign.

Roth walked over to the Mercedes as quietly as he could, staying off the gravel driveway and instead walking on the wet grass next to it.

William Kopes's house was enormous, like the country seat of some grand old English noble family, built in stone and complete with turrets. The palatial garage was like a house unto itself, and it was said to hold a vast collection of expensive cars, from the Model T to the latest Ferrari. And past the garage, further from the main house, was a much older structure—a small entrance to a tunnel that went down deep below the big

house. It was out of that tunnel that the estate's long-ago abandoned work of tobacco farming had been conducted. And it was
from there that Harold Peterson emerged, walking hurriedly
toward his Mercedes.

THE KNOCK CAME JUST as the assassin grabbed Bronze's middle
finger, meat tenderizer poised to swing.

A woman's voice called out. "Bronze? Bronze, are you there?
Look ..."

Bronze yelled "Iris! Run!" with all his might and squirmed
mightily against his restraints. The voice was muffled and the
words indecipherable, but the banging and scratching of the
chair against the floor were audible through his front door.

"Bronze, is everything OK?"

Iris began to turn the doorknob. Bronze screamed and
screamed into the tape, in danger of running out of oxygen, face
turning deep red.

The assassin shrugged, retrieved his silenced pistol, aimed
steadily at the door, and as the black silhouette of Iris
appeared, fired a round with his inescapable and inhuman
exactness.

Bronze thought he had run out of tears, but as the assassin's
round left the chamber of his pistol, he wept and cried and
violently jerked his body, prayed and cursed God in the same
breath.

ROTH SAW PETERSON coming too late. He tried to hide by
ducking down on the far side of the red Mercedes, but Peterson
had already spotted him.

Peterson hesitated a moment in confusion, mouthing "Roth?" Then louder, "Shit!"

He awkwardly pulled a gun from his jacket, the grip catching briefly on his coat before he was able to wrench it free, then fired a volley of bullets toward Roth. But Roth had already hustled halfway around the Mercedes and now he dove to the ground behind it, Peterson's bullets zipping off, flying far astray, poorly aimed in the meager evening light.

Roth pulled his own pistol out and rose to his knees, maintaining his cover behind the Mercedes as best he could. He was able to look in time to see that Peterson was already running back into the tunnel.

There was nothing for Roth to do but follow, running as best he could on old, stiff legs.

PERHAPS THE SHOT was more difficult than the assassin was expecting, looking out from a lighted living room into the dark night outside. Perhaps it was the gunshot wound in his bicep from his earlier encounter with the FBI that threw off his aim. Perhaps he saw Iris's sapphire eyes flaring wide and some small rebellion within him hesitated to kill so quickly such a creature.

Perhaps he just happened to miss for once.

Looking into the light of Bronze's apartment, Iris registered the full horrible tableau in an instant at the same moment the assassin's bullet buzzed past her head so close, it clipped her hair.

Iris turned and ran.

Up Bronze's stairs, she took a step toward the empty, weakly lit street but knew she would be a sitting duck in the open. If she turned the corner and went up the stairs to her house, she'd at least have the protection of her stairs as cover for a second or two and the chance to slam her front door shut, perhaps buying enough time to phone the police.

She turned on her heel, taking the corner up the stairs, hearing a two-tap of bullets ricocheting about her feet.

THERE WAS NO LIGHT in the tunnel below the Kopes mansion. Outside, the evening was dark enough, but the tunnel was pitch black. And as Roth pulled up from his hobbling run and walked slowly down into it, the darkness descended even further, becoming a total blackness that made Roth think of his greatest fear—that, like his father, his glaucoma would one day take his sight completely. That he would be left in this complete darkness forever.

His heart was already a piston pounding in his chest, but now it began to rev toward a redline, became a fluttery blur as if he were sprinting down the football field a half pace in front of a tackler, as if he were racing through the jungle with bullets everywhere firing from the unknowable darkness between the trees.

Peterson knew this tunnel. Roth did not.

There was nothing else to be done; despite the risks, he needed to turn on his flashlight to have a chance.

When the light came on, it lit up what looked like empty horse stalls imbued with the cruel ambience of ancient jail cells.

He swept the light one way and then the other.

And in the second sweep ... a flash of movement, followed by the quick report of a pistol firing bullet after bullet in his direction.

THE ASSASSIN TURNED to Bronze after Iris made her miraculous but inevitably temporary getaway.

"Very unfortunate." The assassin shook his head. "We will go ahead and skip to level three once I have dispatched your unlucky neighbor."

With that, the assassin walked swiftly out of Bronze's apartment, slamming the door shut behind him.

For a moment, all Bronze could do was breathe and hurt.

She was coming to see you. She was coming because you made a fool of yourself. She was coming to try to relieve your embarrassment. Now you've gotten her killed. You let her play at detective because you wanted her, even when you knew what had happened to Carolyn. And now Iris is dead too. The best thing you could have done is die long ago. You were given everything in life and you turned it to ash and shit and death.

Bronze rapidly sucked air in and out of his nostrils, full of snot and ice water, hyperventilating, vision blurred and muddied.

He saw her dying. He saw the bullet taking her in the head, in the heart—the light going out of those eyes ...

A colder, calmer voice rose within him: *If you don't stop panicking, you'll lose consciousness again. Do you want her to die without having even tried?*

One slow, full intake of breath came to him like manna from heaven.

Then visions: a vast city of lights sparkling electric in the night, strange symbols elegantly curling, delicate trees whispering in a gentle wind, the sharp ripping forms of wrestling transfigured to dance, perfect flowing movement beneath sacred swords, demure eyes beckoning behind silk screens, kimonos and quiet, a lonely temple, a softly singing stream, honor, loss ...

He remembered again the old technique. He tried to master himself, to master his breath and mind.

One breath. Two breaths. Three ...

Then once again he saw himself fighting Nakatani all those years ago, but not through his own eyes this time. Staring down from above. They etched geometries with their feints, striking in sudden claps of thunder, locking together like rushing water, grappling and straining, attack and defense and counterattack, a sinuous ballet, a covalent binding of bodies, minds, consciousness—force and counterforce, esoteric energies, a new exotic physics. No winning or losing.

Only beauty.

He breathed.

He focused on something concrete. He focused on the ruins of his left hand.

Bronze leaned his head down toward his left hand, tilting his hand and with it the cutting board toward his face. In taking the duct tape on and off his face and so haphazardly slapping it on that last time and then going on to throw the bowl of ice water over his head, the assassin had loosened the edges of the tape over Bronze's mouth. Leaning his head as far as he could, he was just able to rub the edge of the cutting board against the loose edge of the tape stuck across his mouth.

Every rubbing motion of his face jostled his broken fingers and agitated the knife through his hand, causing it to saw against the bone and tissues there.

The first three rubs got the tape to curl back on itself ever so slightly. The fourth pulled it back a bit further. On the fifth, the tape caught on the board and Bronze ripped it off two-thirds of his mouth with one hard jerk of his head.

But he had been overzealous and the motion wrenched the sharp edge of the steak knife another quarter inch through the remaining flesh of his hand. He cried out once more, but his energy was so far gone that the sound was more like a barely audible whimper. He would have to be more careful; if he tore through the rest of his hand and the knife and cutting board fell to the floor, he would be finished.

Bronze leaned his head once again over his left hand. He opened his mouth wide, reaching forward with his jaw to its furthest extremity, and placed the knife handle as far into his mouth as he could get it. He didn't for a second trust the strength of his lips to do the job, so he bit down as firmly as he could, feeling at least one molar crack against the hard wood of the handle.

When he had the knife firmly in the grip of his teeth, he forced himself to push down with his broken left hand against the cutting board, pain roaring and every animal instinct in him pleading that he relent.

With the board now firmly fixed between his hand and the dog head carving at the end of the chair arm, Bronze took one deep breath in through his nose and, on the exhale, jerked his head and neck and torso upwards with tremendous force. The torque against his neck was vicious; one of his cervical vertebrae let out a violent cracking pop.

The knife moved upward but did not come free from the board.

Bronze breathed two big breaths in and out of his nostrils, trying to regain his strength and thinking of Iris. Thinking of Carolyn. Thinking of the poor girl behind the second door at Madam Richelieu's.

He jerked upward with all the strength still left in his body.

Too hard.

The knife was wrenched from his mouth, scraping along his broken teeth, his head flying up and to the right, snapping hard as his torso slammed into the back of the armchair.

By some miracle the knife was still in the board, but barely, tilted at an angle now and digging into the torn flesh of his hand.

Bronze quickly leaned his head back down and gripped the knife between his front teeth, his lips pressed against it for support.

While before he had jerked his body, now he lifted upward with steady force, moving his head from side to side, working the knife back and forth in the cutting board, trying to move his hand with the motion of his head, but there was no fully avoiding wedging the knife further into the sides of the wound, opening it up further and further until ... the knife came free of the board and he pulled it out from where it pierced his hand, almost laughing in triumph and the madness of pain.

With his broken left hand he slipped the now loose cutting board away to fall to the floor. He used his mouth to place the blade of the knife in the pinch of his still functioning thumb and forefinger. Then, working it about between fingers and mouth, he reoriented the cutting edge to face toward his body and the duct tape at his wrists.

Once the blade was positioned against the edge of the tape, he held it as firmly as he could between his molars once more and began to saw against the tape ever so steadily. First the hard edge of the tape gave way, then more quickly the inner threads, until finally it weakened enough that he was able to wrench his wrist against it and tear the last portion free.

Again came the mad laugh, unrestrained and earnest this time.

He grabbed the knife by the handle now between his thumb and forefinger and went about freeing himself from his remaining bonds.

When he had finished and finally stood up from the dog chair, his body broken and bleeding, he almost lost control, swooned, and fell to the ground. But by some grace he maintained consciousness, if only barely. He knew every second counted if he was to have any chance of saving Iris, but in all likelihood she was already dead.

Either way, he was entirely outmatched as he was, bare-handed, and one handed at that, against the assassin with his pistol. And he could hardly walk with the bullet wound in his left knee; he had to lean on his right hip and throw his left leg forward while supporting himself on his furniture or walls, and even this with great pain.

His only chance was surprise and the wakizashi sword that had lain dormant in one closet or another for the last twenty years. So, each step an unbearable agony, Bronze limped back into his bedroom, opened the closet, and pulled the blade from its unadorned dark green scabbard, then limped out of his front door.

When he saw the stairs, he realized there was no way he could make it up both flights to Iris's door. He'd lost too much blood. His left kneecap was shattered. There was no point anyway. He could barely move his left arm from the bullet in his shoulder, and his left hand was completely useless.

He tried the first step, supporting himself on the banister as much as he could with his right arm while also managing to hold on to the eighteen-inch samurai sword. Still the pain in his knee seared through his nerves in great thundering pulses.

He needed to go faster. Iris was either already dead or soon on her way. But the pain was so great, he feared passing out again. But if he was too slow, the result would be the same anyway.

Bronze hesitated. It seemed to him that a great black pit opened in front of him. Blackness and empty, endless falling. *Madness.*

But in that madness, even more strangely, there was a kind of superposition—he didn't quite see Carolyn's face in the void in front of him, but the idea of her came to him as vibrantly as a vision, and Esther too, and then Iris, left all alone to face that monster in her house, and then more faces too—all the women he had known and loved, the idea of them was there in front of him ... and once he had come to love them, had he not carried them about within him forever after, like open wounds?

And was there not a kind of strength in all that pain and beauty? *A strange power.*

He was already walking up the stairs without even realizing that he had decided to go on, the pain flying through his body and brain like a distillation of all the pain that had come before, forty years of the stuff, every old wound gracefully opening like flowers in a sudden spring.

It was as if the more pain Bronze let in, the more beauty he could see in front of him. It was as though the pain were white light and he the breaker of light, casting it all about in the mad colors of this world. Every gut-wrenching, searing step, every moment he chose pain was a moment he continued to live, and the world he saw lived on too, with its million lights and colors and the impossible melancholy of its fleeting beauty.

Bronze chose pain. Step after step. On and on. Until he almost fell as he raised his leg to take the next one and found himself stumbling on the landing before Iris's open front door.

THE BULLETS FLEW at Roth's flashlight, one even smashing into the lens, shattering the glass and knocking out the light, plunging the tunnel back into total darkness.

If Roth had been carrying the flashlight in front of him pressed up against his gun like cops did in movies, he would have been deader than disco.

But Roth had remembered his training all those years ago; he held his flashlight in one hand, up and away from his body, knowing that if some asshole shot at him in the dark, they'd shoot at the light.

The shot that took the flashlight in the lens twisted the thing out of his hand hard, jerked his wrist, and sent a painful vibration down his hand and forearm. Still, he fired back immediately.

Eight shots into the dark, four directly at the point of the muzzle flash and then four more, all at points surrounding the flash.

He heard Peterson fall to the ground like dead weight.

Then no more sound.

He kept his gun at the ready in one hand; with the other he felt in front of him, waving it about, making his way to the tunnel wall to his left. When he got there, the surface of the wall was hard and cold against his hand. He slid himself along it, slowly placing one foot in front of the other.

He kept going, listening intently for any sound, any chance that Peterson might still be alive or that there was someone else out there in the dark.

Finally he put his foot down in front of him and felt it squish into something soft. He kicked it. It was Peterson's hand. No reaction. He was dead, beyond any doubt.

He moved on, kept on sliding down the wall, on past Peterson until he came up against the far wall at the end of the tunnel and felt his way along it to the door. Opened it and slipped into a finished basement that, though only dimly lit, filled Roth with an immense relief to be out of the pitch black.

Ahead there was a twisting set of iron stairs leading up from the basement into the mansion proper.

Roth stepped ever so cautiously up the tightly turning stairway, heading up from the basement into the distant light of a room above, gun held out in front of him, leading the way.

As silently as possible, he exited the staircase onto a landing.

The hallway itself wasn't lit, but the light was coming from a cracked door a few feet ahead.

Slowly, slowly he moved toward the door, hearing for the first time strange muffled cries.

He moved more quickly now, worried about what might be happening, gun pointed at the cracked door. He was mentally preparing himself for the moment he would burst through when he stepped on some weakness in the floor, which let out a loud creak.

A voice called to him.

"Harold! What's taking you so long? And what's the point of this second video? It's not what you said at all. It's just some whore getting fucked."

Roth rapidly flew through the door, gun first, only to see William Kopes sitting in a chair, looking like a combination of Billy and Fred—strong and hard like Fred but with Billy's handsomeness still apparent, even now in his early seventies.

Roth quickly assessed his hands. No gun in sight, no weapon of any kind. The knuckles of both hands were green with bruises. He had a fading black eye too and a long scratch on his neck.

Before Roth had burst in, he'd been staring intently at a large TV screen. On the screen, Carolyn Haake, maybe ten years younger than she'd been at the time of her death, was having sex with some man Roth had never seen before.

"The fuck ..." Kopes began to say.

"Hands up!" Roth yelled.

Kopes slowly complied, saying nothing.

Training the gun on him the whole time, Roth moved around and handcuffed him. While he cuffed him, he saw Kopes's eyes darting again and again toward his VCR.

Roth left Kopes in his chair, one eye on him and gun still pointed in his direction, and moved over to the VCR. There was an empty unmarked videotape sleeve on top of it, as well as another one, similarly unmarked but this one containing a black videotape.

He hit stop on the Carolyn Haake porn video. Ejected it. Put it in the empty sleeve. Took the other video out of its sleeve, put it in the VCR, and pressed play.

BRONZE PASSED OVER the threshold into Iris's house, his eyes wide open and desperately searching.

Through the hallway he could see to his left stairs ascending to private rooms he had never ventured into before. In front of him and to the right was the entrance to the kitchen. His sight-line into the kitchen was blocked on the near side by the hallway wall and was framed further down by the counter at which he had sat days ago and watched Iris make him coffee. Out ahead, past the counter, was Iris's welcoming living room with its soft, clean couch and matching chairs.

All was perfectly quiet. There was no movement but Bronze's labored, limping walk.

Unless he was all the way up in Iris's solarium, the assassin had surely heard Bronze at this point. He was either waiting silently in the kitchen or he was upstairs. Either way, Bronze didn't see how he could have much hope. If the assassin was upstairs, he'd have the high ground; he'd be able to see Bronze coming from the top of the stairs and simply shoot him from a distance while Bronze attempted to charge up the steps.

If he was in the kitchen, he would wait there pressed against the wall, gun poised, ready to shoot Bronze as soon as he walked forward far enough to appear in the kitchen opening.

Bronze had an idea. It wasn't much, but it was something.

Iris had a coat rack just inside her front door with a navy

raincoat hanging from it. As silently as he could, he removed the coat, then repositioned himself close to the hallway wall.

He breathed. Steadied himself. He thought back to walking out onto the mat to face Nakatani, his heart in his stomach and his stomach like a fist.

Bronze knew all the rules of judo. All the rules of wrestling too. What you could and could not do. What mattered now were those things you could not do. Those weaknesses of the body other men had not pondered, those acts so horrible that other men, men who'd not fought hand to hand over and over again, would never think of in the heat of the moment.

And he knew one other thing too. When you made your move, you did not hesitate—you went hard and fast and with everything you had.

So Bronze charged forward two thundering steps down the hallway, his destroyed knee lighting up with vile pain.

Then, just before the opening to the kitchen, he braked hard and threw Iris's raincoat out in front of him.

The stinging sound of two silenced pistol rounds zipped through the air and tore two holes through the coat.

A woman screamed.

Then came Bronze, crouching low and quick as a cobra, broken kneecap fragmenting into a hundred more pieces as he ran without thought of the pain or the consequences. He was just a flying head and shoulders, and thrust out in front was the point of the wakizashi sword.

The assassin's head cocked to the right a split second to look behind him at the screaming coming from the cupboard below the sink, then he snapped it back at the real threat and fired, seeing only a blur of motion.

The bullet missed high; the assassin not anticipating Bronze charging so low in a double leg shot, *morote-gari*, a torpedo, a comet, a kamikaze aimed full speed at his legs.

The assassin's reflexes were trained to impossible precision. He was just in time to deflect the blade from piercing his thigh with a sweeping block from his left arm that flung the blade wide. It stabbed deep into the brushed metallic refrigerator door.

But there was no way to halt Bronze's momentum, and they crashed together into a heap on the floor.

Though the assassin's right arm had been flung wide and smashed to the ground as Bronze had knocked him onto his back, he had managed to keep hold of his pistol in his right hand, while Bronze's wakizashi blade was solidly stuck in the refrigerator door.

Bronze's left arm was too weak and too slow from the gunshot wound in his shoulder and the torture of his hand, so he had no protection as the assassin began to sweep his right arm back to fire a close-range unmissable shot.

Bronze lifted his head and torso and right arm and did the thing you couldn't do in judo or wrestling or any style of fighting short of a death match.

He thrust his right hand down hard, with all the force left in him, thumb first like a makeshift nail into the assassin's left eye. The assassin tried to turn away.

Too late.

Bronze didn't quite hit the eye directly; the thumb instead, in a glancing blow, banged off the maxilla bone of the cheek before sinking into the paper-thin skin of the eyelid, crushing the cornea, his thumbnail piercing the eye's outer membrane into the sticky humors beneath.

The assassin thrashed and screamed, momentarily losing himself in the pain and failing to bring his gun to bear. But as Bronze brought his bloodied left hand to the assassin's chin, attempting to steady his flailing head as Bronze ground his thumb further into his eye, the assassin remembered his gun and swung his pistol upwards to kill Bronze once and for all.

Only to find his arm suddenly trapped.

Iris was out of the cupboard under the sink and now threw her whole weight behind her as she pressed with all her strength down onto the assassin's arm, pinning it to the floor.

Bronze looked over at her, catching her eye, and his lips curled in a mad grin full of blood and broken teeth. Then he pushed his thumb down harder and further, the eye now pulverized to liquid, grinding his thumb further and further through the gelatinous structures to the retina and there through ropy strings of flesh and nerve, artery and vein, until the thumb finally ran aground against the orbital bone separating eye and brain.

All the while the assassin screamed and pleaded and begged for Bronze to stop, as desperate and broken as his most cowardly victim.

THE BACK SEAT of Roth's unmarked car wasn't equipped for taking in a hostile suspect. So he handcuffed William Kopes's hands behind his back, tied his ankles together with a length of rope from his trunk, threw him into the back seat of his car, and seatbelted him in. For the first few minutes of the drive to the nearest police station, Kopes angrily strained against his seatbelt as best he could and swore a blue streak at Roth.

When he finally wore himself out, Roth let silence reign for a minute or two. But eventually Roth, who would have given anything in this world for a son, couldn't help asking, "I just don't get it. How could you kill your own son?"

William Kopes relaxed back against the seat. He was calmer now. He had begun to accept his fate.

"My son? Ha. What right did my son have to do what *he* did? Huh? To threaten *me*? My son was born into what I had. Born into it, you see. His whole life teenyboppers and coeds and society women and slut waitresses and cross-necklace-wearing good girls have been letting my son fuck their mouths and pussies and wherever he wanted, whenever he wanted, with open arms and smiling faces. His whole life.

"Did my son wonder at this? Did he question why? No. No, no, no. Not my son. You see—it was his whole life. He was born into it. It was God given. Divine right.

"My son's greatest gift was his lack of imagination. He could stroll his way through life and never for a second imagine what it would have been like to be someone else, to be poor or homely or not from the right family or a bit too clever or a bit too dull or a bit too sincere—what it would have been like to have worked for what he had. Never for a second did it concern him that these women and girls spread their legs for just the merest chance of getting a taste of my—*my*, you understand—my money. All of it. Everything he had. *Mine.*

"My son's schools were paid off. He was given a do-nothing job with our stately old senator, who was paid off. And then paid off again to endorse him for congress. I let my son vote as he wanted for most things—things that did not concern me. And for things that did, Harold would suggest the correct vote and my son had neither the wits nor the imagination nor the interest to argue. Mostly he was flying off to Miami or LA or Las Vegas or wherever he might go for his next screw on *my* dime.

"And my son was tolerated in this. He was, dare I say, beloved. My son's conscience was as clean and clear as glacier water. And everyone loves a man with a clean conscience. Much, much more than they love *good* men. And never the twain shall meet. Don't you mistake it. A good man with a clean conscience is like a hooker with a trust fund. For my son, everyone always had a smile, a kind word, a compliment, a joke, a back slap, a well-met toast.

"And do they love me? Me, who built this country? Who made the machines that made the guns and the ships and the planes and the tanks and the bombs that saved this country from the Germans and the Japanese and the Chinese and the Vietnamese and the Russians and whatever pig-fucks try to come for us next? And come they will.

"No. They say you're an evil corporation. You owe us more money, more taxes. You didn't build that. Your workers—with their sub-100 IQs that moved their arms up and down the same exact way over and over again a thousand times a day just the way you told them to—well, *they* really built it all. Not you who thought of it, acted on it, took all the risk for it, made every decision for it—you are just *capital*. And that's a dirty, dirty word today. You'll see. Within a decade or two they'll be cutting off our heads. And what a party it will be for a year ... two, maybe, until they're living like Soviets and the whole country has turned into a colorless gulag.

"No, I don't need or want their love. And I certainly didn't need my son. He was an appendix at best. Tolerated until he turned to poison, until he dared to threaten me over Boyd, that little meaningless strumpet, and needed to be—removed.

"Look at you, Roth, driving silently, feeling so righteous ... you all owe your comfortable lives to me. To my vision. To my sweat. If I need to snatch one or two away ... well, that's my business. You should look to history. You should learn humility, Roth —learn your place. You and your papa and your mami and your bubbie and all your Jew friends would be dead without me. And don't forget it. If I do it, it's for the greater good. If it serves me, then it's right."

33

JUDGES AND KINGS
THE END OF SPRING

T he hospital had Bronze so doped up on heavy dosages of morphine, he didn't know which face he saw first. Iris and Bruce and Roth floated in and out of fractured visions. Sometimes they seemed to want to comfort him; sometimes they pointed, wild and incoherent accusations on their lips. Sometimes they had tears in their eyes or just lay sleeping, curled up on stiff hospital chairs. Sometimes they appeared to him as children; other times they had grown old and wrinkled and gray and bent. He knew what he saw was half fantastical, but for a long time he couldn't tell where his dreams ended and reality began.

Eventually his brain reattained a sense of coherence, and the first time he opened his eyes and knew himself, it was Esther who looked down on him.

"*Esther?*" he whispered.

She held his right hand in both of hers. "Hey, Boss, you coming around?"

Boss. That name on *her* lips triggered a cascade of memories.

When Esther had first worked for the *Post*, she had started out calling him Mr. Goldberg, which he hated. So, with a sly smile on her face, she'd switched to Boss for a time, a name of her own invention. Then Cal. Then eventually, like everyone else, she had called him Bronze.

He hadn't realized she even remembered that old nickname. He hadn't thought of it in years. It was just like the Texan's old merchant marine friend, he realized. Could she ever have really looked to *him* as a fount of wisdom?

"I was never really your boss, Esther."

She smiled now, realizing he was really, finally awake. "True. Maybe we don't have a word for it anymore. Doesn't *mentor* feel hollow these days? Like a word in some corporate training video. But you were *something* to me, Boss. You know that, right? Despite the other stuff. And you still are too. And not just to me either ... You got to stop letting yourself get beaten up like this ... You're not so young anymore. You've become precious cargo."

There it was. He could see it in her eyes now. He felt a blackness drifting away, an impossible weight lifting. He tried to speak, but there was something in his throat.

How magnificent it was to be forgiven. How terrible too. Knowing the truth of it. That until the wronged truly felt it, no matter the words they said, the guilt was a weight no force could lift, not even God. And now that his slate was wiped clean, it was up to him to keep it that way, and when had he ever done that?

She patted his hand. "I'll get the others. They've barely left your side. But I pulled sitting duty while they finally went to pick up lunch. Especially Bruce and Iris. Poor Iris, she sat there watching over you, not sleeping, not changing out of her bloody shirt. Bruce was the one that finally managed to get her home for a shower. But I still don't think she's slept."

～

THEY FILLED THE HOSPITAL ROOM—BRUCE and Esther, Iris and Roth. He wished it hadn't taken a stay in the hospital for him to gather them all together, but he was glad of it one way or another. For a few precious moments, he didn't think of the past or the future. He hardly thought at all. For a little while he laid down his burdens and let the chatter of his friends wash over him.

Eventually, after jokes and well wishes, Esther made her excuses. She was needed back at the paper. She was covering the William Kopes angle of the story, but, with a wry smile, she promised to keep everything she'd gleaned in her hospital visit on deep background.

When it was just Roth, Bruce, and Iris in the room with him, Bronze's equilibrium broke and the events of the past few weeks roared through his mind in a jumble, totally disordered, the effects preceding the causes, all action random yet laden with meaning—like morning memories of a nightmare. He needed Roth to put it all back together again for him. He needed order. He needed to finally understand all that had happened over the last few weeks.

Roth stood while he explained, rocking back and forth on his feet, rubbing his hands together. His kind eyes drifted from Bronze's face to the various bandages holding his hand and knee and shoulder together.

"Our newly one-eyed friend is in FBI custody. They get first crack at him, but then they'll have to share him with the CIA and others. That's all I know. With all the potential intel locked in his brain, he's the hottest commodity to hit town in quite some time."

"Will he stand trial for murder?" Bronze asked.

"Metro PD and Austin PD are working what channels they can. Eventually, I hope. But the feds are going to try to suck him dry before we get a crack at him. It's all up to our betters to decide at this point."

Bronze looked into Roth's eyes, hoping to find comfort there. "What was the reason, Mark? What set all this in motion?"

Roth looked as if he was trying to will a sympathetic brightness into his eyes, something to take the sting out of Bronze's pain as he reflected on his recent conversation with Leo Rossetti. He and Rossetti had met once again at the Lincoln Memorial but had soon found themselves pacing the length of the Vietnam War Memorial. They had pieced together all that they knew while Rossetti had kept running his hands through his perfect black hair and Roth had limped along on his bad knees, methodically searching the wall for each and every name he knew, his heart breaking again and again as the implacable judge within made sure he walked the whole length, never rushing, never looking away.

Roth was deeply massaging the web between his left thumb and forefinger now, remembering all that Rossetti had told him. Remembering war and murder.

"We have got Peterson's contemporaneous diaries and a trove of other documents from him and William Kopes now. And Rossetti's given me a few tidbits the FBI has squeezed out of their prisoner. So we have been able to draw together a fairly thorough picture.

"It all went back to the Rachel Boyd murder. As Iris deduced, Boyd was raped while working as a congressional intern and killed in the process or shortly thereafter. Her rapist and killer was William Kopes. He was up in DC taking advantage of his son's position and pulling congress's strings to get a Buy American provision passed for the kinds of capital equipment Kopes Industries sold to the Defense Department.

"Back in '88, Roger Haake was contracted by Kopes to assist in wrangling votes, and William, Haake, and Harold Peterson were all working long days and nights out of Billy's office, Billy himself apparently absent on some dalliance. Late one night, old William decides to apply his charms, such as they are, to the beautiful intern he kept seeing over at Congressman Piccione's office. Only she wasn't interested. He didn't take no for an answer. Boyd wasn't stabbed to death like Keaton's victims, as Iris put together; she really died of asphyxiation. William Kopes killed her. Then Kopes enlisted Harold Peterson—who, as we learned, was his illegitimate son—to help in covering up the murder.

"At the time of Boyd's death, Keaton was out there on his killing spree, and by that point a number of vicious stabbings had been reported in the news. So Peterson helped Kopes attempt to cover up the murder by stabbing the already dead Boyd repeatedly, then dumping her body on the DC streets under cover of darkness. You and I then naturally connected, despite some inconsistencies, Boyd's murder with the rest of Keaton's killings. And when Keaton was killed after the massacre, he wasn't around to offer any clarification.

"William Kopes got away with the murder of Rachel Boyd, and Harold Peterson was his accomplice. After the incident, William decided to step back from the company, hoping to lower his profile, to fade into the background just in case. That's why he elevated Fred to CEO. The truth of the matter was that William was still making all the important decisions.

"This was the state of affairs until Roger Haake discovered that his wife, Carolyn, was having an affair with Billy Kopes. Whatever feelings he may have had about that, it seemed that Haake also saw potential strategic advantages. He approached the staff of James Crawford, the senator whose seat was at risk to Billy Kopes in '98, and offered to splash compromising photos of Billy Kopes having an affair with a married woman at just the right time in the campaign. Meanwhile, Fred Kopes saw his chance to blackmail Billy to drop out of the race so that he could get out from under his father's thumb and take what he felt was his rightful place as the family's political face.

"But Harold Peterson catches wind of the fact that Haake is working with Crawford and making shady deals with Fred. Peterson panics. Peterson has suspected for years that Haake may have been aware of what happened with Rachel Boyd and had been holding the information back until it could be best exploited. Which was exactly what Peterson himself had been doing. We often suspect others of our own sins.

"Unknown to William Kopes, Peterson had in his possession a video recording made inside Billy Kopes's congressional offices that had captured Rachel Boyd being pressed through an office door by William, never to come out alive.

"What Peterson fears more than anything is that Roger Haake has a version of the same video, but this one unedited by Peterson and showing Peterson assisting William Kopes with the body. In fact, Peterson's paranoia reached fever pitch when he overheard Carolyn discussing with Billy some damning tape that her husband kept locked in a safe.

"Peterson decides to preempt the situation and gives Billy Kopes a copy of his edited version of the tape, telling him he received it from Roger Haake along with a threat. Billy Kopes assumes that Haake is after him because of his affair with Carolyn, watches the tape, and is horrified to discover what his father has done.

"Now, Peterson probably expected Billy to either go after Haake somehow or acquiesce to whatever demands Haake might make. Either way, by preempting him, Peterson could prevent Haake from finding it necessary to reveal Peterson's involvement in the Boyd murder, or at least cut some kind of side deal with him.

"What he doesn't expect is that Billy isn't quite so cold-blooded as all that and has a bit of a backbone when it comes to the murder of innocent young women, even those that occurred almost a decade ago. Billy calls his father and tells him he knows about Rachel Boyd and that he plans on going to the cops unless Dad has some explanation of why this is all a big misunderstanding. William drives up to Billy's office intending to intimidate him into dropping the matter. When Billy refuses, William becomes enraged and assaults Billy. Who knows, perhaps he didn't mean to go all the way to murder, but his rage gets the better of him and Billy winds up dead. Again, like before, William calls in Peterson to help with the body, which they then dispose of in the Potomac.

"William is aware of Billy's affair with Carolyn and, believing the tape came from Haake, suspects her involvement. William orders Peterson to arrange a hit on Haake and his wife. This is music to Peterson's ears, as he can finally eliminate the Haake threat, and he brightly travels to London to contract with the assassin we have come to know so intimately. We suspect that William Kopes was aware of our assassin through his contacts within the Defense Department as well as those with companies throughout the American and global military–industrial complex. Our assassin may have executed the murder of a number of arms traders in former Soviet Eastern Bloc countries who were selling off surplus Soviet gear and undercutting established brands. It's possible Kopes was aware of the sources of these contracts, which gave him both the information he needed to contact the assassin and also a fair amount of leverage over certain individuals within the US government—certain individuals that are being flushed out by Leo Rossetti and his team as we speak.

"Peterson still suspects Haake had the unedited video of the Boyd cover-up. So, along with eliminating Roger and Carolyn Haake, Peterson also pays the assassin to recover the videotape for him. When the assassin breaks into Haake's home, he finds Carolyn and the videotape already gone, she having fled the city with you.

"On the evening of May 14th, the assassin completes his mission and gives the tape to Peterson. William Kopes is aware of the tape at this point, and Peterson drives down to Virginia to deliver it to him, finally washing his hands of the matter. The irony, of course, is that the tape is not of the Boyd cover-up but the last copy of a porn scene Carolyn shot in her youth that Roger Haake, gentleman that he was, held over her head as leverage. We suspect that Haake never had any idea about the Boyd murder, despite Peterson's paranoia.

"The Peterson edit of the tape that proved William Kopes's culpability in the Boyd murder had been in William's possession ever since he killed Billy, he, of course, removing it from the crime scene after killing his son. We have been able to place one of William's many cars near Billy's home at the time of the murder, and more importantly, we've been able to match the markings on Billy and William to each other. Apparently William had been holing up down in Virginia, seeing no one other than Peterson, waiting for the bruises to fade."

Bronze shook his head, feeling bone tired, like he could barely keep his eyes open. He asked one more question.

"Mark, what did you do with the tape of Carolyn?"

Roth stopped rocking on his feet, stopped massaging his hands, stopped looking at Bronze's bandages, became perfectly still.

"I burned it."

～

AFTER THE HOSPITAL, Bronze went to stay with Bruce Schwarz for a time. He wasn't quite ready to face his old apartment yet after all the violence that had occurred there.

Iris brought everything he needed over to him at Bruce's: clothes and toiletries and paperback novels. When he and Iris saw each other, they talked in friendly, polite tones. But there was a strangeness between them now. Long pauses intruded. Some points of tenderness neither could figure out how to get beyond. She thinking of how she had turned him away, condemning him to torture. He thinking of how he must have looked to her in those last moments of violence, burying his thumb into the assassin's eye, his mind lost in the madness of pain and fury.

He and Bruce took walks together. Seeing Bruce's spartan lifestyle, Bronze began gently pushing him to try dating again. And Bruce would deflect: "But what about you? What about *Iris*?"

One night, after a time, Bronze found himself in Bruce's antique shop after he had closed up for the day. He helped Bruce move various silver plates, carved candlesticks, and lead crystal stemware around to freshen the display, while Bruce kept a dogged eye on him, making sure he didn't try to lift anything too heavy. It was dark out, and both seemed to want to delay braving the shadowed streets back to Bruce's apartment.

Bruce fiddled with the pieces of a Canton set, moving them from one surface to another and back again, never quite satisfied, eventually throwing up his arms in defeat and sitting down at the antique chessboard that never seemed to sell, no matter where it was displayed. Bronze walked over and sat across from him. Without speaking, they started to play, once again bathed in a hundred different shades of light from a hundred ancient lamps.

Bronze had the white pieces and tried an English opening, hoping for a quiet game. Bruce fianchettoed his kingside bishop, and from there the pieces cautiously danced about, looking for safe harbors, but soon they began inexorably crashing into one another, battering at each other's weaknesses, straining for advantage, until Bruce caught Bronze in a sudden checkmate.

Bronze stared at the board, stunned by the move. He hadn't seen it coming in the least—it took a minute or so to work it all out backward, to see how he had been beat.

"I've been reading chess books," Bruce offered with a hint of mirth in his voice.

Bronze nodded, his mind empty except for a light buzzing static, his head moving up and down mechanically on instinct. Then, stillness and one thought—*OK*.

It was OK to lose to a man like Bruce—his old friend.

Good, even.

They had dueled honorably over which king would have dominion over the board and which would fall over and withdraw courteously. Win and lose didn't really matter—both had their own particular beauty.

He saw it now, the clever elegance of the checkmate, and with that new appreciation a sudden unexpected feeling flushed through Bronze, at once terrifying and hopeful.

He had thought his youth long gone already, but now, in this moment of gentle defeat, after all he had been through these past weeks, he could feel it dying truly, passing away gracefully. Somewhere deep in his guts the last weak flames guttered out and went cold. It had been a youth of grand failures. The small victories, such as they were, always temporary, conditional. The losses absolute and final.

But it was over now, he realized. He had passed through alive. And for the first time in his life, he felt sympathy for the man he had been. For his past. He saw within himself what he knew Bruce had always seen. He saw that he had been wrong about the broken places within, although no less wrong than Hemingway. At the broken places he was neither strong nor weak, but instead unique and strange and beautiful for his strangeness.

Bronze looked up at Bruce and smiled warmly, freely. It seemed to Bronze, looking up from the chessboard kings, that they had a chance, after a fashion, to become kings themselves. They held no formal stations, ruled over no subjects, but there were vast territories in their minds and hearts, wilds to be explored, continents for them to organize and nurture, examples to be set.

Despite all they had seen and felt and lost, they still believed in honor.

"Thank you," Bronze said.

Bruce's drooping eyes turned quizzical for a moment, then he thought he realized what Bronze meant. "I've told you, I'm more than happy to have you stay with me as long as you want."

Bronze shook his head. How could he explain it to Bruce? That he was the only one who still remembered Bronze from before, from when he had been new. That all these years he had been a tether that had kept Bronze tied to the boy he had once been, to all that was good within him.

"Bruce, I don't just mean that. I mean ... thank you for it all."

It was only a day after his chess game with Bruce that Bronze made his way back to his old apartment.

It didn't look a thing like he remembered.

Iris had cleaned it all up. And more. Replaced his old couch. Replaced the dog chair. On the wall behind his new gray Chesterfield sofa, she had mounted his wakizashi sword, and above that, his bronze medal was now displayed in a spare but elegant glass frame.

He tried to think about how to thank her properly. About

when the timing would be right. When the wounds would have healed enough, while all along, she worked above him, day and night, finally finding the words to finish her novel.

Sitting on his new couch, he thought of her up there writing. In the end, would he truly find his way into her novel in one form or another? Probably not the hero—maybe if she ironed out most of his flaws and inconveniences. He didn't need to be the hero, though. But he certainly hoped not to find himself the villain.

Maybe he was a friend. He would like that. A friend to the female protagonist, to Iris's stand-in. He could help her on her way like she had helped him. Maybe in her novel there hadn't been so much tragedy and loss. Maybe instead there had been romance and eventual triumph. And maybe there was some world or some fiction as real as his dark apartment where Carolyn was safe and driving far away, convertible top down, belting out some old rock song, her voice lost to the wind. He could see her beautiful face, her sad eyes framed in dark mascara—and there in his memory too were those short moments when he'd seen her free of it.

After Carolyn, they all came back to him, all the faces of the women he had come to love, one by one. He imagined each face was safe and at ease. He wouldn't mind a world where none of them had returned his love. Just so long as they liked him well enough and he was worthy of whatever esteem they granted him. Just so long as here or there he could drop by and see them, chat over tea or coffee until his jaw grew tired and his eyelids drooped. Then he would get up on stiff legs and see himself out as night encroached. Out past their streetlamps or porch lights somewhere, he could disappear into the darkness, and he would know that they were going to be alright. They were all A-OK.

34

A CHORUS OF GHOSTS

I t is done.

The characters are like cracked crystals—shards penetrating each reader with a different breakage, catching the light distinctly. Am I responsible for each of these shards and the feelings that follow? The shards are lodged within me too. Remnants left after each book has gone to print. Ghosts. But as real as your dog or cat. They prowl around the house. A great congress of ghosts—maybe even a chorus in the haranguing Greek sense.

Some sit in my study, some watch over me while I sleep, some are merely attendants watching the door for intruders, some are distasteful to me now, expelled from the court and down deep in the lower floors angrily plotting against me, and there are those, I must admit, who I fall into the occasional conversation with, who hold me from time to time when tears are in my eyes and I don't have a clue why.

It's quite a thing to walk through an empty house so full of these half-lives.

I wonder if Bronze will come up from below. Will they all

break before his reality? Will he dispel my ghosts? Excommunicate them with a wave of his hand? A great wise man of action come to deliver me from a haunted land.

Will he kiss me then?

I imagine he does.

I imagine after a brief light kiss, he raises a finger to my lips and traces them, as if he were wondering what god would make them feel as they do, as if he were wondering if they were real. And I feel his firm skin pressing against the delicate nerves there, firing delight and confusion to so suddenly be released from their long chastity. He's looking me in the eyes. He doesn't smile and neither do I. We don't contort our faces to hide our souls.

Men with their muses. With their goddesses singing through them like sound echoing in empty vessels. Is this it? Is this what it's like?

Bronze, you're so quiet now. I hear nothing beneath the floorboards. Have you left? Are you on your own in the streets? Sleeping quietly? Are you coming up my stairs this very minute? With your lips and your fingers and your eyes and unsmiling mouth and stark naked soul? Are you coming up now?

When?

When will you be on my stairs with your fist and your echoing knock against my threshold? I won't turn you away this time. It was all a mistake. Maybe everything before you was a mistake. A rehearsal.

I'm not sure I'll be so eager to live with my ghosts now. You are here. Almost.

I think I am out of words. And really, I'm not sure I go in for muses. Either being one or possessing one or possessed of one.

Bronze. Just come hold me while I sing. That is all I require. The tune will wobble and my voice is weak ... but I can sing—in my own voice. No one will hear and the music is out of fashion. But still ... I can sing.

I can sing of the time when I lived so desperately alone and I imagined I heard you beneath the floors.

Printed in the USA
CPSIA information can be obtained
at www.ICGtesting.com
CBHW030448070524
8002CB00004B/28